HARD PRESSED

What Reviewers Say About Aurora Rey's Work

You Again

"*You Again* is a wonderful, feel good, low angst read with beautiful and intelligent characters that will melt your heart, and an enchanting second-chance love story."—*Rainbow Reflections*

Twice Shy

"[A] tender, foodie romance about a pair of middle aged lesbians who find partners in each other and rediscover themselves along the way. ...Rey's cute, occasionally steamy, romance reminds readers of the giddy intensity falling in love brings at any age, even as the characters negotiate the particular complexities of dating in midlife—meeting the children, dealing with exes, and revealing emotional scars. This queer love story is as sweet and light as one of Bake My Day's famous cream puffs."—*Publishers Weekly*

"This book is all the reasons why I love Aurora Rey's writing. It's delicious with a good helping of sexy. It was a nice change to read a book where the women were not in their late 20s-30s..."—*Les Rêveur*

The Last Place You Look

"This book is the perfect book to kick your feet up, relax with a glass of wine and enjoy. I'm a big Aurora Rey fan because her deliciously engaging books feature strong women who fall for sweet butch women. It's a winning recipe."—*Les Rêveur*

"The romance is satisfying and full-bodied, with each character learning how to achieve her own goals and still be part of a couple. A heartwarming story of two lovers learning to move past their fears and commit to a shared future."—*Kirkus Reviews*

"[A] sex-positive, body-positive love story. With its warm atmosphere and sweet characters, *The Last Place You Look* is a fluffy LGBTQ+ romance about finding a second chance at love where you least expect it."—*Foreword Reviews*

"If you enjoy stories that portray two gorgeous women who slowly fall in love in the quirkiest way ever coupled with nosy and well-meaning neighbors and family members, then this is definitely the story for you!"—*Lesbian Review*

Ice on Wheels—*Novella in* Hot Ice

"I liked how Brooke was so attracted to Riley despite the massive grudge she had. No matter how nice or charming Riley was, Brooke was dead set on hating her. A cute enemies to lovers story."—*Bookvark*

The Inn at Netherfield Green

"I really enjoyed this book but that's not surprising because it came from the pen of Aurora Rey. This is the kind of book you read while sitting by a warm fire with a Rosemary Gin and snuggly blanket." —*Les Rêveur*

"[Aurora Rey] constantly delivers a well-written romance that has just the right blend of humour, engaging characters, chemistry and romance."—*C-Spot Reviews*

Lead Counsel—*Novella in* The Boss of Her

"*Lead Counsel* by Aurora Rey is a short and sweet second chance romance. Not only was this story paced well and a delight to sink into, but there's A++ good swearing in it and has lines like this that made me all swoony because of how beautifully they're crafted."—*Lesbian Review*

Recipe for Love

"*Recipe for Love* by Aurora Rey is a gorgeous romance that's sure to delight any of the foodies out there. Be sure to keep snacks on hand when you're reading it, though, because this book will make you want to nibble on something!"—*Lesbian Review*

Autumn's Light—*Lambda Literary Award Finalist*

"Aurora Rey is by far one of my favourite authors. She writes books that just get me. …Her winning formula is Butch women who fall for strong femmes. I just love it. Another triumph from the pen of Aurora Rey. 5 stars."—*Les Rêveur*

"This is a beautiful romance. I loved the flow of the story, loved the characters including the secondary ones, and especially loved the setting of Provincetown, Massachusetts."—*Rainbow Reflections*

"[*Autumn's Light*] was another fun addition to a great series."—Danielle Kimerer, Librarian (Nevins Memorial Library, Massachusetts)

"Aurora Rey has shown a mastery of evoking setting and this is especially evident in her Cape End romances set in Provincetown. I have loved this entire series…"—*Kitty Kat's Book Review Blog*

Spring's Wake

"[A] feel-good romance that would make a perfect beach read. The Provincetown B&B setting is richly painted, feeling both indulgent and cozy."—*RT Book Reviews*

"*Spring's Wake* has shot to number one in my age-gap romance favorites shelf."—*Les Rêveur*

"*Spring's Wake* by Aurora Rey is charming. This is the third story in Aurora Rey's Cape End romance series and every book gets better. Her stories are never the same twice and yet each one has a uniquely *her* flavour. The character work is strong and I find it exciting to see what she comes up with next."—*Lesbian Review*

Summer's Cove

"As expected in a small-town romance, *Summer's Cove* evokes a sunny, light-hearted atmosphere that matches its beach setting. ...Emerson's shy pursuit of Darcy is sure to endear readers to her, though some may be put off during the moments Darcy winds tightly to the point of rigidity. Darcy desires romance yet is unwilling to disrupt her son's life to have it, and you feel for Emerson when she endeavors to show how there's room in her heart for a family."—*RT Book Reviews*

"I really liked this novel. The obstacles seemed realistic and conflicts hinged on differing worldviews and experiences, not simple misunderstandings. All the adults acted like grown ups and talked things out for the most part, even when they didn't handle everything perfect. ...This book has a nice balance of sweet and believable as well as having some pretty hot love scenes. The whole thing was very satisfying and fun. Five stars."—*The Lesbrary*

Crescent City Confidential—*Lambda Literary Award Finalist*

"This book blew my socks off... [*Crescent City Confidential*] ticks all the boxes I've started to expect from Aurora Rey. It is written very well and the characters are extremely well developed; I felt like I was getting to know new friends and my excitement grew with every finished chapter."—*Les Rêveur*

"*Crescent City Confidential* pulled me into the wonderful sights, sounds and smells of New Orleans. I was totally captivated by the city and the story of mystery writer Sam and her growing love for the place and for a certain lady. ...It was slow burning but romantic and sexy too. A mystery thrown into the mix really piqued my interest."
—*Kitty Kat's Book Review Blog*

"*Crescent City Confidential* is a sweet romance with a hint of thriller thrown in for good measure."—*Lesbian Review*

Built to Last

"Rey's frothy contemporary romance brings two women together to restore an ancient farmhouse in Ithaca, N.Y. ...[T]he women totally click in bed, as well as when they're poring over paint chips, and readers will enjoy finding out whether love conquers all."—*Publishers Weekly*

"*Built to Last* by Aurora Rey is a contemporary lesbian romance novel and a very sweet summer read. I love, love, love the way Ms Rey writes bedroom scenes and I'm not talking about how she describes the furniture."—*Lesbian Review*

Winter's Harbor

"This is the story of Lia and Alex and the beautifully romantic and sexy tale of a winter in Provincetown, a seaside holiday haven. A collection of interesting characters, well-fleshed out, as well as a gorgeous setting make for a great read."—*Inked Rainbow Reads*

"One of my all time favourite Lesbian romance novels and probably the most reread book on my Kindle. ...Absolutely love this debut novel by Aurora Rey and couldn't put the book down from the moment the main protagonists meet. *Winter's Harbor* was written beautifully and it was full of heart. Unequivocally 5 stars."—*Les Rêveur*

Visit us at www.boldstrokesbooks.com

By the Author

Cape End Romances:
Winter's Harbor
Summer's Cove
Spring's Wake
Autumn's Light

Built to Last
Crescent City Confidential
Lead Counsel (Novella in The Boss of Her)
Recipe for Love: A Farm-to-Table Romance
The Inn at Netherfield Green
Ice on Wheels (Novella in Hot Ice)
The Last Place You Look
Twice Shy
You Again
Follow Her Lead
(Novella in Opposites Attract)
Greener Pastures
Hard Pressed

Written with Jaime Clevenger
A Convenient Arrangement
Love, Accidentally

HARD PRESSED

by

Aurora Rey

2022

HARD PRESSED

ISBN 13: 978-1-63679-210-1

THIS TRADE PAPERBACK ORIGINAL IS PUBLISHED BY
BOLD STROKES BOOKS, INC.
P.O. BOX 249
VALLEY FALLS, NY 12185

FIRST EDITION: OCTOBER 2022

CREDITS
EDITORS: ASHLEY TILLMAN AND CINDY CRESAP
PRODUCTION DESIGN: SUSAN RAMUNDO
COVER DESIGN BY JEANINE HENNING

Acknowledgments

While test-driving titles for *Greener Pastures*, I became enamored with the phrase "hard pressed." It was a little too racy, though, especially for a book that didn't have cider-making at its core. It proved too good to pass up, though, so I gave Rowan a business partner who could have her own adventures with a rival cider maker, and *Hard Pressed* was born. It also gave me a great excuse to spend more time at Eve's Cidery, a truly phenomenal cidery here in upstate New York. Autumn and Ezra care so deeply about what they do, and their cider is top-notch. I can't recommend them highly enough.

This was a fun book to write and I'm grateful to Sandy, Rad, and the BSB team for supporting it. Ashley and Cindy, you make me snort-laugh—I mean a better writer—with every book. Special thanks to Jaime for the always excellent feedback and to Maria Pena and KD Williamson for the insightful sensitivity reads.

And maybe most importantly, thank you to everyone who reads these stories of mine. I'm so grateful you go on these adventures with me. Thank you from the bottom of my heart.

Dedication

For everyone who grows, tends, harvests, and crafts

Chapter One

Mira scanned the agenda in front of her. Confident she'd covered all the bases, she pushed her chair back from the small conference table and stood. "Thanks, everyone. Let's have a good week."

Others followed suit and her staff scattered to their respective desks and offices. Everyone except Talise, her director of marketing and communications. "Do you have a minute?"

Her gaze flicked to the clock on the wall. "Ten."

"Perfect." Talise tapped a few keys on her laptop. "Have we started planning for Cider Week yet?"

The ten-day stretch in October served to highlight the ciders and cider makers of upstate New York. It was one of their biggest weeks of the year, at least in terms of public events. And she'd chaired the planning of it for the last three years. "Cider Association is my next meeting, actually, so if you want to circle back this afternoon, we can brainstorm."

Talise smiled. "Running the show again?"

She lifted a shoulder. "I mean, if you want something done right…"

"Do it yourself? Or were you going to say 'put a woman in charge'?"

"Same difference, no?" She didn't love that cider, like wine, remained a male dominated field. A white one at that. But she'd carved out her place and had no trouble holding her own. She'd only been the COO of Pomme d'Or officially for a few months, but she'd been doing the job for close to five years.

"Touché." Talise closed her laptop and stood. "Where's the meeting?"

She let herself sigh. "It's virtual."

Talise's lip curled.

"I know. Frederick has decided at least every other meeting should be virtual so the smaller and farther flung cideries can participate more easily."

"It's not a terrible idea." Talise's expression made it clear she was being generous.

"It isn't." Even if she preferred face-to-face and made a point of attending regardless of location, not everyone had that luxury. And the Cider Association served all producers, not just the established ones.

"I'll put myself on your calendar for later today or tomorrow." Talise typed, probably a note to herself, before looking up.

"Let's fold it in with our brainstorm for the reparations initiative. I'm hoping I can get everyone on board with selecting Acres of Equity as the featured nonprofit for the gala."

"I like." Talise nodded as she typed now. She'd been the one to pitch the organization to Mira. Because unlike Mira, who grew up in California wine country, Talise was local. She hadn't grown up on the Onondaga Nation, but her parents had, and the issue of native lands was close to her heart.

"Well, cross your fingers there's not a coup at the board meeting." Not that she was genuinely worried. People liked to talk about doing things their way but rarely wanted to show up with time and energy to make it happen. Especially something that didn't directly contribute to their bottom line. That counted as small thinking in her book, but their loss meant her gain.

"If there is, can I come watch?"

"Ha ha."

Talise tossed her glossy black hair and straightened her shoulders. "I'm kidding, mostly because I think people like what happens when you're in charge."

Mira indulged in a smirk. "Mostly."

Talise headed to her office and Mira returned to hers, where she chipped away at her inbox until it was time for the meeting. At exactly two minutes to twelve, she logged on, testing her camera to ensure a flattering angle and innocuous backdrop. Frederick had already signed on as host and within a minute, names populated the participants box and her screen filled with a checkerboard of faces. Most she knew, casually if not well.

Frederick started with introductions, having members introduce themselves and the cider they represented. It took up the first ten minutes or so of every meeting, but she appreciated putting names with faces—and with cideries—especially the people she'd never met in person. They'd just finished when an unfamiliar face joined, slotting into the bottom right of her screen next to Steve from Seneca Hill Cider.

The woman had short brown hair and a killer smile, not that Mira was in the business of noticing such things. She seemed to be standing in the middle of her production area. And she was soaking wet.

Frederick paused his efforts to approve last meeting's minutes. "Dylan. Welcome."

Dylan. Dylan. Why did that name sound familiar?

The woman lifted a hand. "Hi, hi. Sorry to be late. I got caught up in a tussle with one of my fermentation tanks and lost track of time."

Most of the group chuckled. Mira pressed her lips together in a way that could be amusement even if it was really in lieu of rolling her eyes.

"We were just doing introductions," Frederick said affably.

"Aha. Sorry to have missed that, though I've met most of you and read up on the rest. Dylan Miller, Forbidden Fruit Cider."

Dylan offered a winning smile that earned her smiles and waves from most of the boxes. Mira joined in, even as her mind connected dots. She'd not met Dylan, but she'd heard of her. Breaking rules and attracting attention seemed to be her primary style, at least when it came to making cider. Perhaps it was a more pervasive personality trait.

"Good to have you." Frederick gave a decisive nod. "Now, where were we?"

They returned to approving minutes and the more mundane parts of the agenda. Mira half listened and, since no one could tell one way or the other, kept her gaze trained on Dylan. Dylan darted off-screen and returned with a towel that she proceeded to rub over her head, turning her soggy appearance into more of a sexy disheveled look.

Well, not sexy, sexy. Sexy in that stereotypical white butch way. Like ads for cologne sexy or androgynous swimwear sexy. Not sexy to her. Obviously.

She cleared her throat and grumbled, as irritated with herself for going there as with Dylan for showing up to a meeting in such an unprofessional way.

"Mira?"

Shit. She wasn't on mute. "I'm sorry. My connection must have cut out. What was the question?"

Frederick smiled. "No question. I thought you had a comment on the budget report."

She forced a smile. "Oh, no. No comment."

She clicked herself to mute and tried to refocus her attention. But the second she finished straightening her shoulders and tucking a piece of hair behind her ear, her gaze wandered back to that bottom square. No Dylan, just a shot of stainless-steel tanks. Where the hell had she gone?

She'd no sooner posed the question to herself when Dylan reappeared. She'd finger combed her hair and changed her shirt and, despite what Mira had argued to herself a moment before, looked sexy as hell. Mira shook her head. She needed to get a grip. And maybe get out more.

"Our main topic today is to begin planning for Cider Week. The dates are set, and I know many of you are already planning your in-house events. The gala date is set as well, and we've secured the Statler Hotel in Ithaca. Now we just need to plan it."

Everyone chuckled. Mira waited a beat before unmuting herself. "I'd be happy to chair again."

A couple of thank yous gave way to Don Farrell's booming baritone. "What if we centered some of our smaller producers this year? Let them take the lead?"

Since no one could see her hands, Mira flipped her middle finger. She hadn't been able to decipher if he was racist, sexist, or both, but he made no pretenses about disliking her. Or maybe he merely disliked what she stood for—a successful and well-established brand in the cider industry.

Frederick, ever the diplomat, nodded. "A great idea, but we must be mindful of the limited staffs and resources many of our smaller-scale members are working with."

"What about co-chairs?" Don said, making her wonder if he'd been plotting this all along. Which, of course, made her wonder about his motives. Not a coup, exactly. Just a pain in her ass.

Several heads nodded.

"Appointing co-chairs might be a win for everyone involved." Frederick continued to nod, clearly warming to the idea. "Mira, what say you?"

Mira smiled, even as memories of group projects from grad school flashed in her mind. The kind where she did all the work but had the added stress of trying to get others to pull their weight, and then pretending they had during the group presentation. "I'm happy to step back if someone else wants to take the lead."

She wasn't, but she'd be damned if she came off as the control freak—or worse, diva—who refused to release her grip on being in charge.

Frederick lifted a hand. "Now, now. We wouldn't want you to step back entirely. You've helped put Cider Week on the map."

Damn right she had. "You're very kind. Thank you."

Don didn't miss a beat. "What about our colleague from Forbidden Fruit? She's mentioned a desire to put herself and her brand more in the public eye."

Mira narrowed her gaze, as though that might give her a better view into Don's mind and whatever ulterior motives he had going on. Did he know something about Dylan she didn't? Was he trying to undermine her or throw Dylan under the bus? Maybe both?

"Dylan?" Frederick's eyes shifted slightly, ostensibly looking at Dylan's square on his screen.

Dylan offered an easy smile and Mira wondered how many women she'd talked into bed with little more. "I'm honored and would love to play a bigger role. But I'm sure everything would go more smoothly if I had a charismatic and experienced co-chair at my side."

Seriously? She had about as much use for casual flirtation as she did consummate unprofessionalism. But since she imagined a dozen gazes shifting from Dylan to her, she reined in the death stare and smiled. "Then I guess it's settled."

❖

Dylan strode into the tasting room, where'd she'd left Rowan stocking shelves for the weekend rush. She found Rowan, not exactly where she'd left her, but not much farther along either. "Are you still doing that?"

Rowan shrugged, unfazed by anything the question might imply. "Audrey came out to ask me about the bottle order."

"Ah. So, you spent the last hour making out."

"No, we only spent a few minutes making out. Then she made me do math."

Dylan laughed because she believed it. Audrey and Rowan were still in the hot for each other phase of couplehood, but CPA Audrey was all about keeping things professional at work. "My condolences."

Rowan bowed her head. "Thank you. I'm happy to report that we're going to buy twice as many at a time but pay twenty percent less. We should only have to climb over cases of empties for a month or two."

Rowan was kidding, but barely. They'd reconfigured their space to make better use of what little storage they had as production grew and were once again pushing the limits of their building's square footage. "For twenty percent savings, I'll store them in my garage."

"That's what I said." Rowan laughed. "How was your meeting?"

"Guess who's co-chairing the organizing for this year's Finger Lakes Cider Week?"

Rowan angled her head. "If it's not you, this is a dumb way to tell a story."

"Not true. It could be a half dozen people that you know and would want to hear about."

That got her a bland look.

"But your first guess is right. It is me." Exactly how it happened remained a bit of a blur, but she wasn't about to complain.

"Nice." Rowan abandoned the half-empty crate in front of her and crossed the room. She clapped Dylan on the shoulder. "You're very prestigious, very fancy."

"Are you going to ask who my co-chair is?"

Rowan straightened her shoulders. "Hey, Dylan. Who's your co-chair?"

"Mira Lavigne."

Rowan closed one eye. "Remind me who that is again?"

"Heiress apparent of Pomme d'Or." Mira's parents—a fifth generation wine maker and the only female Black Master Sommelier in the world—had started Pomme and basically kickstarted the New York cider boom.

"Oh." Rowan let the word drag. "Am I remembering correctly that you have the hots for her?"

"I do not have the hots for her." She'd admired Mira but mostly from a distance. Curvy, flawless medium brown complexion, and with that sort of feminine elegance that seemed intrinsic to growing up with money—not her type but definitely the stuff of fantasies.

"But you think she's hot."

"She's gorgeous, but that's not the point." It might be fun to make it the point, to imagine mussing up the almost stringently put together Mira, but she had other more pressing matters. At least for the moment.

"There's a point?"

Dylan let out an exasperated huff, more on principle than taking offense at the teasing. "The point is her marketing department is bigger than our whole staff."

Rowan made a face. "Is that a good thing?"

"It means we're swimming with the big fish."

"And that's a good thing." Rowan's pained delivery didn't come out as a question but made her sentiments clear.

"We aren't going to become big fish. That's not our goal. But swimming with them? Abso-fucking-lutely. The visibility that comes with that is a big deal."

Rowan nodded, appropriately cowed. "You're right, you're right."

She didn't try to hide her grin. "I love it when you say that."

"Shut up." Rowan returned to the stack of boxes but didn't resume unpacking them.

She folded her arms and didn't budge. "Not until you say, 'Good job, Dylan.'"

"Good job, Dylan."

She shook her head. "It hurts my feelings when you roll your eyes as you say that."

Rowan shrugged. "Then next time tell me not to roll my eyes."

"It's a good thing I know you love me deep down."

Rowan batted her eyes instead of rolling them. "I really do."

"Ditto." And she thanked the universe every day for allowing their paths to cross in the mass of undergrads finding their way on the sprawling campus that was Cornell University.

Rowan picked up a bottle of the previous year's extra dry perry. "I have to finish stocking the shelves so my boss doesn't yell at me, but tell me all about it while I work."

This time it was Dylan's turn to roll her eyes. Not that she was truly irritated. Or that Rowan even remotely considered her the boss. But goading each other was standard business practice and had been since Forbidden Fruit was little more than the pipe dream of a couple of restless college students. "Well, Mira volunteered to chair again. But then Don Farrell suggested including a co-chair from one of the smaller cideries."

Rowan frowned. "Wait. Isn't he the blowhard from, oh, what's the place?"

"Serpent Cider." Not bad cider, but not particularly good either.

"Yeah. That's the place." Rowan made a face, clearly sharing the opinion.

"He is the blowhard from there. I thought he hated women, but he's the one who nominated me." A fact that she'd almost missed during her frantic attempt to dry off and change mid-meeting.

"Huh." Rowan's frown became a scowl.

"I know. Maybe he's just socially awkward." She was all about giving people the benefit of the doubt. And not having enemies.

Rowan shook her head. "That's not the same thing and you know it."

"Maybe he's a general jerk and not a misogynist?" He'd been rude to her, but not like he was to Mira on a regular basis at association meetings. Maybe he disliked Mira. Or what she symbolized. "Classist? Or more racist than sexist maybe? Ugh."

"All possible. Just watch your back. I'm not saying he has nefarious motives, but he might not have the best of intentions either."

Well, fuck. That hadn't occurred to her. She'd been so busy soaking up the recognition—the support of her peers as much as Don's nomination—she hadn't stopped to analyze it.

Rowan, as if sensing her doubts, set the pair of bottles on the shelf and brought both hands to Dylan's shoulders. "Hey, I didn't mean to rain on your parade. It's an honor no matter how you got there. And it will be great for visibility, especially since we're going to be able to host an event this year."

They'd already discussed that, now that the tasting room was up and running. Having a say in planning the week would give her the leverage to schedule themselves when and how they wanted. And being visible at the gala would be free publicity right in their backyard. "Right."

"And if you get to hang out with a woman you have the hots for in the meantime, total bonus."

"I don't have the hots for her." She could, but she didn't. One, because it would be unprofessional. Two, because she got a little bit of an ice queen vibe from Mira and that wasn't her jam. Three, because the whole point of co-chairing was to bring Forbidden Fruit to the next level, not chase tail. It might not have always been the case, but at this point in her life, she was mature enough to know the difference and keep her eye on the prize.

Chapter Two

M ira donned the protective coveralls she wore when she visited the production floor, wiggling the shapeless fabric over the swell of her hips. She tucked her curls into a mesh hairnet and checked her reflection in the window overlooking the area. To make sure it was secure, not to see how silly she looked. She already knew how silly she looked.

Luis held the door, as was his custom, and he bowed with a flourish. "After you, mademoiselle."

He was French—and seventy—so she gave him a pass.

Once in the production area, he took the lead, walking her through the rows of fermentation tanks. "This is the Late Summer Harvest. Good blend this year. Nicely sharp, but with soft edges. Like you."

Despite the thirty years he'd spent in the US, he still pronounced "this" as "zis." Much like his displays of chivalry and tendency to liken cider to women, it didn't grate on her the way it might coming from someone younger or American. It helped that he was brilliant at crafting cider. On top of that, he respected her, and her role at the company, without hesitation. And had since before her father officially handed over the reins.

"When will it be ready for bottling?" she asked.

"Very soon. We will do the second fermentation in the bottles and let it age another few months."

She nodded. Her parents had made the decision to exclusively produce champagne-style ciders when they started Pomme d'Or.

They'd leveraged the reputation of Vallée d'Or and traditional winemaking craftsmanship and created one of the most recognized cider brands in the country. She'd spent the entirety of her career learning the business and helping it grow. And when she'd finally been put in charge so her parents could stay in California full-time for their retirement, she hadn't changed a thing.

As her father so often said, don't mess with perfection.

They proceeded to the intake area. With apple season still a few months away, the presses sat quiet. At this time of year, they focused on juice pressed and preserved the previous fall, trucked in from all over New England. "How has the supply been?"

Luis flipped a hand back and forth. "Mostly good. The variety helps. And the barrels, they make even the so-so shine."

"Speaking of, shall we visit the cellar?"

"Mademoiselle, I thought you would never ask."

On their way back through, they passed Eric, a French guy in his twenties Luis had brought over as an apprentice, hosing out one of the tanks. He lifted a hand, offering a good morning as they passed. Mira returned the greeting, even as her mind flashed elsewhere.

Well, not elsewhere. It flashed right to the image of Dylan on her computer screen—wet, disheveled, and sexy. She'd been cleaning tanks, hadn't she? Or something similar. A tussle, she'd said.

It made her wonder about Dylan's operation. How big it was, how many staff she had. She'd heard of Forbidden Fruit, but mostly because she made a point of knowing all the ciders coming out of the region. Good, if a bit all over the place. Like they valued creativity over consistency. Nothing wrong with that, it just wasn't her style. Nor was it, at least in her opinion, the best way to stay in business.

"Mademoiselle?"

She turned to find Luis regarding her with curiosity. "Yes?"

"Is everything okay? You seem, ah, distracted."

She waved him away, annoyed with herself and with Dylan for invading her thoughts uninvited. "Yes, yes."

Luis held the door once again and they headed downstairs. The cavernous space held row after row of oak barrels, just like a wine cellar. Here, they were stacked four high and twenty across. The aroma got her every time and today was no exception. Like autumn and an old library had a baby, with apples providing base notes more than top. She closed her eyes for a moment, breathed deeply, and smiled.

"It's not like anything else, is it?" Luis asked.

"It really isn't."

"You should come down here more often. It's good for the soul. Like oxygen, but better."

She'd heard that before. "You sound like my father."

"He's a smart man."

They walked one of the rows, and she trailed her fingers along the curve of a few of the barrels. "Indeed he is."

It had been somewhat unheard of at the time, but her father had experimented with aging cider in oak before its final fermentation in the bottle. He always joked that it was part inspiration—he was a winemaker at heart—and part having more used barrels than he knew what to do with. After a great deal of trial and error, he settled on a high tannin cider in chardonnay barrels, creating a cider that managed to be both full-bodied and soft, much like the rich, almost buttery wine that had been aged before it. It became Pomme's signature label and had been their best-selling blend for the past decade.

Did Dylan barrel age her ciders?

Even as the question—its very existence in her mind—irritated her, she wanted to know the answer. Wanted to understand who Dylan was and what made her tick. If for no other reason than they'd be working together, and it would make her life easier. And that was reason enough.

She pulled her attention back to the work at hand. Luis had siphoned off a few samples for inspection. They took turns holding each vial to the light, searching for that soft gold Lake Sunset was known for. She joined Luis in tasting but left the commentary and blending decisions to him. He was the expert after all. And despite years of doing it, and knowing a good bottle from a bad, she lacked the intuition to know exactly how to turn the individual notes into the harmony of the finished product.

Fortunately, she didn't need to. She left Luis to his alchemy and shed her coveralls and hairnet, returning to the world where she was an expert. The realm of logistics and communications, pulling together the people and the words and the numbers that kept everything running the way it should.

Back in her office, Mira settled at her desk and went to work on her inbox. Once she had it wrangled to her satisfaction, she turned to the next task at hand: planning Cider Week. She sighed.

She'd need to pull Dylan in, obviously. But for the past few years, she'd kicked off planning with a luncheon at Pomme, inviting representatives from all the cideries that planned to participate, not just those on the association board. Surely, Dylan wouldn't complain about that. It was a great networking opportunity in addition to providing a group brainstorm where she and everyone else could get a handle on the types of events folks were planning. And once they had that, she and Dylan could tackle filling in the gaps and, of course, the gala.

Had Dylan even attended the gala before? Mira had no recollection of seeing her, but that didn't mean she hadn't been there. No bother. If Dylan was clueless, she'd probably be more inclined to hand over control. And co-chairs or not, that would be fine by her.

❖

Rowan angled her head. "Wait. Aren't you supposed to be planning things together?"

"I mean, yes. But this was planning a meeting to plan. I'm not going to get my boxers in a bunch over that. Besides, she's hosting and serving lunch." Dylan shrugged. She actually had gotten her boxers in a bunch when the email from Mira came through. But she'd followed up with an offer to help and Mira gave her every assurance she'd had the lunch tentatively planned in anticipation of chairing again. Dylan wasn't exactly mollified, but she knew enough about people like Mira to pick her battles.

"Ah." Rowan nodded but didn't look convinced.

"You think she's steamrolling me."

Rowan lifted both hands. "No, no. No one steamrolls you. But I think she might try."

She did have the distinct feeling Mira was used to doing things her way. And despite her smile and the acquiescence of her words, she wasn't confident Mira wanted a co-chair at all. Her email hadn't been dismissive, but it had felt rather definitive. "Maybe. I'll just have to win her over with my unflappable charm."

"Unflappable charm, huh?"

"Well, we can't all fall in love with the accountant next door and live happily ever after."

Rowan made a simpering face. "Ha ha. You're just jealous."

"Damn right I am." While she didn't begrudge Rowan and Audrey their bliss, she'd started to wonder if she'd ever manage to find her own. Not that she was in a rush to settle down. It was simply that seeing happily ever after in action put it in the forefront of her mind. "More envious, though. I don't want to steal yours. I want my own. Eventually."

Rowan's features softened. "You'll find it."

Dylan shook her head. "Uh-uh. Don't make that face. You make me feel pathetic when you do that."

Rowan stuck out her chest and jutted her chin. "You'll get your piece of the love pie, yo."

"Okay. No bro speak. That's even worse. You can't even pretend to pull it off."

"I know." Rowan shrugged, clearly not offended. "I did it to remind you there are worse things than my sensitivity and emotional intelligence."

"Right, right." In truth, she didn't mind Rowan's sensitivity. It kept her honest.

"So, when is this lunch?"

"Next week. And I'm supposed to bring what we're thinking in terms of our own events." Which wouldn't be much of a lift since they'd pretty much agreed to do discounted flights and guided tastings all week, along with live music and an orchard walk on Friday.

"Because your co-chair told you to?" Rowan smirked.

"You're an asshole." Though, that had been her initial reaction, too.

"Sorry, sorry. I really am excited for you. And for us. It's going to be so awesome to have our own events."

"And to have our name in front of so many people who've never heard of us." That was the point of all of this. To expand their reach and pick up customers beyond their regulars and the handful of wine stores that carried them.

Rowan bumped her shoulder. "Despite my teasing, I hope you know I'm proud of you."

"And by proud, you mean grateful I'm willing to be the public face of the company so you don't have to."

Rowan grinned. "That, too."

She'd gotten herself into trouble a few times—being too brash or too opinionated—but the overall arrangement suited them both. "I'm going to get back to work now. You going to stick around and help or go baby your trees?"

Rowan made a show of being torn.

"Go. I don't need you anyway." Or maybe more accurately, she could do with some time, just the cider and her.

"It's going to rain tomorrow. I'll be all yours."

They'd already agreed to bottle one of the micro batches of sparkling perry, one made from wild pears foraged from the Finger Lakes National Forest. She lifted her chin. "Yeah, you will."

Rowan headed out, and Dylan gathered her tools. She took them to the corner that held the small rack of bourbon barrels she'd bought the year before. It was their first batch to be aged this way and she'd been hankering to give it a taste.

After popping the cork stopper, she inserted her pipette and siphoned off a few mils. She held it to the light, smiling over the deep golden color, then stuck her nose into the snifter. Hints of caramel and vanilla pushed to the front, making her think of apple crumble.

She took a sip, letting the liquid play across her tongue and the roof of her mouth. It had a long way to go, but she already knew it would be fantastic. And unlike anything they'd done before, even things they'd aged in oak. She returned the stopper to the barrel and repeated the process with two others, making sure they were all moving in the same direction.

She let her mind wander to other ways she could play with the technique. Aging the pommeau perhaps, or the ice cider. The sweetness of those would certainly take to the flavors and aromas the barrels offered. Only, instead of lending sweetness the way aging mellowed whiskey, the bourbon-soaked wood would impart subtlety and depth. Maybe even a smokiness.

Could she have enough blended and aged to do a cordial flight for Cider Week? Probably not, at least not if she wanted everything at its peak. That was okay. This year would be the first of many and they already had a solid slate of ideas. Holding back a few would give them room to expand and people a reason to come back.

It made her wonder what Mira had planned. After doing a tasting at Pomme a few years prior, she hadn't been back. Not because the cider was bad, but because Pomme was what she considered a one-trick pony. Impeccable ciders, but not much in the way of innovation. Not a bad thing, just not her style.

Just like Mira wasn't her style. Despite the teasing from Rowan, she didn't go for the pristine or the polished. Not when it came to cider and definitely not when it came to women. And Mira was both, no question. She would appreciate, but that would be the end of it.

Chapter Three

Dylan pulled into the parking lot at Pomme d'Or and, for the second time that week, thought back to her only other visit. It had been when she and Rowan were trying to get Forbidden Fruit off the ground, and they'd done tastings at every cidery in a hundred-mile radius. At the time, Pomme stood out for its formality—the aesthetic and experience closer to that of an upscale winery. But of course, its proprietors had started out as wine makers, California ones at that.

Funny, she'd forgotten a lot of those details until that moment, sitting in her truck and looking up at the ornate stone and glass facade. It all came flooding back now. Polite staff who'd been trained well but lacked the passion that came with being involved in the process. Proprietors nowhere to be seen.

Had Mira been in charge then? Or were her parents still at the helm? Clearly, the big decisions had been made by them. Pomme had been around for thirty years, with the tasting room open almost since the beginning. They'd played a huge role in elevating New York cider from an afterthought to a vibrant industry with its own identity and culture. It all seemed ironic now, given their status as the behemoth of the Finger Lakes. Not big-box store generic but staid, corporate.

Like the current COO.

Dylan let out a sigh. Mira had been occupying her thoughts more than she cared to admit—to herself or to Rowan, who'd continued to do her fair share of nudging and teasing about them working together. Normally, she'd kick back and enjoy. Engage in some flirty banter, indulge fantasies that could make an afternoon of disinfecting equipment decidedly more pleasant. Mira had her on edge, though.

The haughtiness, maybe. Or knowing that Mira's reputation, or at least Pomme's, had the potential to rub off on her.

It hit her then. Being connected to Mira raised the stakes. While she might relish her spot on the board as far as business was concerned, pleasure was a different animal. When it came to that arena, she made a point of keeping things easy. And based on what she'd seen so far, easy and Mira didn't even belong in the same sentence.

The rap of knuckles against her window just about sent Dylan out of her skin. When she looked to see who'd done it, Steve from Seneca Hill Cider offered a sheepish smile. Dylan shook her head and got out of the truck.

"Sorry about that. I swear I didn't mean to scare you."

She laughed. "Don't you know it's dangerous to sneak up on a cider maker while they're daydreaming?"

Steve shrugged. "Yeah, I just didn't realize you were daydreaming."

She didn't have any business daydreaming. Despite where her mind had gone, she was at Pomme for a business meeting. "I can see how the glass might have obstructed your view of my vacant stare."

That got her a chuckle. "Something good, I hope."

Was it? Edginess notwithstanding, there were far less pleasant things to think about than Mira. "Hard to say."

"Story of my life, friend. Story of my life."

They made their way inside and were greeted by a twenty-something dressed all in black. "Are you here for the luncheon?"

Steve snorted, saving her the trouble. "We are."

The greeter showed them into a private room, where one long table had been set for two dozen. White tablecloths, stemware, and if she wasn't mistaken, apple blossoms in a row of short square vases down the middle. She let out a low whistle before she could stop herself. Luncheon indeed.

"Mira does know how to impress," Steve said.

She supposed there was something to be said for that. There was money to be made from weddings and corporate events and the like. She and Rowan had hosted their first wedding the month before, though it had been a casual affair with rustic decorations and a food truck. "Is she trying to impress us?"

Steve offered a casual shrug. "I think impressing people is second nature to her."

A flip comment, but one that landed with a thud. Before she could process or respond, several members of the board trickled in. Greetings tumbled into small talk and despite every intention of seeking Mira out, the next thing she knew, she was seated at the table with a perfectly plated salad in front of her. Salad plates were cleared, and the main course was served: herb roasted chicken with summer vegetables and this crisp potato galette she could have easily demolished twice over.

When the berry cheesecake appeared and waitstaff made the rounds with coffee, Mira stood from her seat at the head of the table and cleared her throat. "Thank you all for coming today. I know it's not as efficient as a virtual meeting, but I love the camaraderie of a shared meal. We don't get together like this often and I appreciate your indulging me."

Dylan lifted her glass. "If you're serving that potato thing again, I'll show up every week."

That got Dylan a laugh from the group, though Mira's seemed a little forced. "I'll be sure to pass your compliments to the chef. Now, since you didn't all take time out of your day merely for a free lunch—"

"I mean, some of us did." She didn't make a point of being a cutup, but there it was. She couldn't seem to help it.

Mira didn't scold her, but she looked every bit the part of the buttoned-up schoolteacher forced to keep her cool in front of the class clown. It shouldn't give Dylan satisfaction, but it did. "In that case, I'll say, in addition to lunch, we do have some business to take care of, so I thought we could get started."

Everyone chuckled. Don, who'd taken the seat at her left, nudged her with his elbow. "Aren't you supposed to be part of this?"

Before she could come up with an answer that didn't make her look like an idiot, Mira looked her way. "Dylan, care to join me?"

It was hard to say what would have been worse: being left out entirely or her current plight of being included and having no idea what was going on. Of course, her current plight had the added awkwardness of standing next to the impeccably dressed Mira in a Forbidden Fruit T-shirt and a pair of work pants. "Uh, sure."

"I confess Dylan and I haven't had the time to meet yet, but I promise we'll get together with your ideas and put together a schedule and program that will be better than ever. Isn't that right, Dylan?"

Dylan, who'd joined Mira at the head of the table but couldn't even pretend to look like she belonged there, nodded. "Absolutely."

Mira nodded at a woman who'd slipped into the back of the room. Seconds later, the lights dimmed, and a screen came down behind Mira. "I've taken the liberty of plotting the events you've submitted via the survey and laid them out in the schedule. That way we can see what might be missing and devote most of our time to discussing the gala."

Using one of those wireless clickers, Mira marched through a series of slides outlining the schedule so far. Dylan nodded and tried to look like she'd known that was the agenda at least, all the while saying a prayer of thanks she'd submitted her plans ahead of time. Since almost all the participating cideries had a representative at the table, folks talked among themselves and cleared up a couple of overlaps that ran the risk of competing for customers.

When the conversation shifted to the gala and setting a theme, Mira launched into a presentation about using the gala to highlight sustainable agriculture programs. Particularly, she wanted to promote those aimed at supporting communities of color and Indigenous communities, whose ancestral lands comprised most of the land used by both the cider and wine industries of the region. The entire pitch showed meticulous research, and Mira delivered it with genuine passion. By the end, she had the whole room applauding. And the only fault Dylan could find was not having a clue about it beforehand.

After half an hour of questions and comments—complete with Dylan standing around not saying much of anything—the meeting broke up. A smattering of smaller conversations ensued. Dylan hovered, wondering whether she should say anything to Mira about their seemingly discrepant definitions of the word co-chair. But—no surprise—Mira beat her to it.

"Is there a problem?"

The mere phrasing of the question had a snarky comeback threatening to leap from the tip of her tongue. But making an enemy of Mira could wreak all sorts of havoc on her professionally and make the next few months particularly uncomfortable. Plus, she'd already paid the price for being brash and getting on someone's bad side. She owed it to Rowan—and to the business and to herself—to take the high road. "Not at all. I love your ideas."

Mira managed to look smug and a little suspicious at the same time. "Thank you."

"I'm sorry I wasn't part of the initial planning, but I'm looking forward to being more involved."

Not passive-aggressive technically, but a spark of challenge flashed in Mira's ebony eyes before calm, cool, and collected settled over her features. "Absolutely."

❖

Mira kept a smile fixed firmly on her face, offering nods and waves as her fellow cider makers made their way to their cars and drove off. Dylan, of course, was the last to pull away. When she was certain no one could catch a backward glance of her in a rearview mirror, she let the scowl take over and headed back inside.

When she got to the office, she swung the main door a little too hard, causing it to strain against the stop. Margo looked up, startled by the noise.

"Are you all right?" Talise emerged from her office, a look of concern clouding her features.

"I'm fine."

Margo's eyes widened and she made a point of returning her attention to the screen in front of her.

Talise folded her arms. "Let me rephrase. What's wrong?"

"Nothing." She stalked to her office, then turned. "I'm annoyed about the Cider Week thing."

"Are you and that Dylan woman butting heads already?"

Were they? It wasn't like they'd argued. They hadn't really interacted one-on-one even. Save Dylan's comment about looking forward to being involved—enthusiastic but quite possibly passive aggressive. Oh, and the compliments about lunch that clearly had more to do with being the center of attention than appreciating the food. "I just don't like her."

"Ah." Talise nodded knowingly.

Now irritated with herself as much as Dylan, Mira went to her desk and dropped into her chair. Talise, of course, followed. Mira busied herself logging into her computer and picking up a file from her inbox. Talise merely waited.

"I put in all this work to get the ball rolling for Cider Week and all she has to say is she's ready and willing to help. Like she's offended I didn't include her."

Talise angled her head. "Why didn't you include her?"

"Because the luncheon was already planned."

Talise blinked. Waited.

"And because she would have either crashed around with her own ideas or taken credit for mine." It wasn't personal. More her general feelings on trying to get anything done by committee.

"Ouch. Tough crowd."

She was a tough crowd, especially when it came to things she cared about. "It wasn't like she reached out to start planning and I ignored her."

"Yeah, but you knew you were going to get started immediately. She probably didn't."

"Whatever. When she emailed me about the luncheon, I was nice about it."

"Were you nice or were you professional to the point of being curt?"

Mira rolled her eyes, not wanting to consider the possibility that she'd been a jerk about the whole thing. "I told her it was all set and there'd be plenty of things she could help with."

"Mira's little minion."

Since she'd already rolled her eyes, Mira let out a sniff. "She has that arrogant vibe of a cider bro, you know? I'd bet a hundred bucks she uses the word maverick to describe herself."

Talise snickered and didn't even pretend to cover it up.

"It's even more annoying because she's a woman. Like, I expect it from dudes, but I want to think better of the women in this industry."

"Mm-hmm. Mm-hmm."

Despite the agreement in Talise's words and nods, questions lurked. Mira could tell. And she had a feeling they were questions she wouldn't like. "What?"

Talise closed the door and took her time settling into the chair opposite Mira's desk. "Is she attractive?"

"What does that have to do with anything?" If Talise wanted to play that game, she wasn't above playing dumb.

"Just curious." Talise was absolutely not just curious.

She shrugged. "Pretty tall, white, masc of center. Kind of an L.L.Bean butch vibe."

"So, your type."

She should have known Talise would go there. They'd been friends since grad school. Working together for the last decade had only strengthened that friendship. "On looks alone, maybe, though I'd argue I have plenty of types. But please see comment above re maverick."

"Oh, I get it now."

"Get what?" Just like she didn't want the questions before, she didn't want the answer now.

"You're annoyed because she's hot."

Not many people in her life could get away with that sort of line. Just because Talise happened to be one of those people didn't mean Mira had to agree. "I'm annoyed because she's annoying. And because I have to work with her."

Talise lifted a hand. "I'm not saying she isn't annoying. She might very well be. But you haven't actually worked with her yet. The bee in your bonnet is because she's possibly those things and she's hot. If she wasn't hot, you'd break out your impeccable poise and get on with it."

"I am getting on with it. I'm simply indulging in a moment of not liking it. Her hotness is irrelevant." It was, right? She wasn't the sort of woman who would treat people differently—better or worse— because of how they looked. And she definitely wasn't the sort of woman who'd be affected by someone's looks.

"Can I come to the next meeting?" Talise smirked.

"No." Because whatever she might say, Dylan was hot. If Talise knew the extent of it, her teasing would be relentless.

"Fine. I'll go internet stalk her."

Mira huffed even as she filed away the prospect of doing some internet stalking of her own. "Don't be a child."

"Okay, boss. Whatever you say." Talise stood. "As fun as it is to give you a hard time, I'm going to go do some actual work now."

"That is what we're paying you for." The insult was delivered without real feeling and to Talise's back. Talise didn't bother with a comeback. When she'd disappeared completely, Mira returned her attention to her computer. But instead of trolling the internet for random details she might find about Dylan, she drafted an email instead.

Hi Dylan,

I wanted to apologize if you felt left out today. I tend to dive into projects, and I'm used to doing them solo. We should get together to discuss next steps and I want to hear your ideas. What if I came to you next time? I've never visited Forbidden Fruit and I'd love to see what you're doing there. I can do any day but Tuesdays, so let me know what would work for you. I'm looking forward to working together.

Warmly,

Mira Lavigne

She read the message, nodded her approval, and hit send. There. She'd done her due diligence. Now the ball was in Dylan's court. Whatever Dylan decided to do with it, she'd deal. She'd certainly dealt with a lot worse. And either way, Dylan's hotness had—would have—nothing to do with it.

Chapter Four

Dylan handed Rowan her phone and tapped her foot impatiently while Rowan read the email from Mira. Rowan made a tutting sound and handed the phone back. "So, she did steamroll you."

Dylan stuck her phone in her pocket and folded her arms. "Steamrolled implies I was somewhere in the vicinity of the process."

Rowan cringed. "That bad?"

Objectively, the meeting had been fine. No one seemed bothered by how much Mira had taken the lead. They were probably used to it. And, truth be told, Mira's ideas for the gala were fantastic. It was standing there like a prop while Mira put on her show that stuck in her craw. "Pretty bad."

"But she's apologizing, right? Trying to make nice?"

"I mean, on the surface."

Rowan shook her head. "You think she's trying to placate you."

It had crossed her mind. Maybe intentionally, maybe not. Either way, she had a difficult time imagining Mira yielding any meaningful amount of control. She shrugged. "It wouldn't be the first time."

Rowan's eyes narrowed. "It wouldn't?"

"Not with Mira, I mean." She waved a hand. "In general."

"Ah. You do tend to take people—and their words—at face value."

Dylan jutted her chin. Why was it so difficult for people to mean what they said and say what they meant? "You say that like it's a character flaw."

"Not a flaw at all. But people are complicated."

Now who was placating? "Women are complicated, you mean."

That got her a laugh. Rowan smiled. "Well, for our intents and purposes, they're the more relevant demographic."

She let out a snort. Not indignation, exactly.

"She's probably used to holding her own because that's the only way to be taken seriously. And sometimes the best way to get your way is to let people think your idea was theirs."

The cider world had decent female representation, but it was still a boys' club. The whole beverage industry was. Carving out space—much less visible space—had proven as much of an art as making cider itself. An art she'd struggled with often and epically failed at on more than one occasion. Mira might have the impressive pedigree, but she was still a woman of color. It bummed her out that Mira didn't see her as an immediate ally. "She didn't even give me the chance to be on her side from the beginning."

Rowan lifted a shoulder. "Sometimes habits become second nature."

"And sometimes they're an indication of one's true nature."

"You think it's the latter?"

The words bossy, control freak, and ice queen had crossed her mind, but she'd done her best to reserve judgment. It was her turn to shrug.

"So, what are you going to do?"

Seeing as she was unlikely to impress Mira with their shoestring operation, she didn't have a lot of choices. "I'm going to be charming and pick my battles."

Rowan pressed her lips together.

"You disagree?"

"Oh, no. You're charming as fuck when you choose to be. I'm thinking about all the times doing exactly that has gotten you what you wanted."

It had. In her personal life, sure. But also in getting Forbidden Fruit into stores and restaurants, in convincing food trucks to take a chance on Friday nights at a cidery whose tasting room had no track record. Most of the time, she'd been right, and everyone wound up happy with the results.

There was no reason dealing with Mira needed to be any different. Unless Mira turned out to be one of those women stubborn merely on principle. That's where she got herself into trouble. When it came to finessing stubborn people who were stuck in their ways for no good reason, her impatience flared, and she inevitably ended up crossing a line without even realizing it.

"You should decide ahead of time what you want."

"Huh?" Her mind had run off in the direction of how satisfying it could be to kiss a stubborn woman. Not where her thoughts needed to be and not at all where Rowan was going.

"I said you should decide what you want. Like, how much say do you really want to have? How involved do you want to be? Don't take things on to prove a point then not have the bandwidth to follow through."

An annoying but fair question. She didn't know how Mira spent most of her days, but she seemed to have more staff at her immediate disposal than the entire payroll of Forbidden Fruit. Dylan had ideas, but really, she wanted to garner visibility for Forbidden Fruit. Trying to win Mira over might be satisfying, but it wasn't the point. Neither was spending half her time planning an event that might boost business but didn't get cider pressed, blended, or bottled. "Are you implying I might get carried away?"

"I'm not implying anything. I'm saying it flat-out."

She laughed. She and Rowan had been through a lot in the fifteen years they'd been friends. Going into business together had multiplied that tenfold. "Noted."

"Besides, if you're not careful, you might end up like me." Rowan offered a playful shrug.

"What's that supposed to mean?"

"You know." This time Rowan wagged her eyebrows with about as much subtlety as her mother asking about her latest girlfriend.

"I don't." She usually did, but in this instance, she really didn't.

"Madly in love with the woman who starts off thinking you're nothing but trouble."

The reference to Rowan's own love life should have made her laugh. Watching her relationship with Audrey unfold, nearly implode on a couple of occasions, and turn into a mushy happily ever after had been the high point of the last year or so. But the implication—even joking—that she might be on a similar path had her stopping her tracks. "No way, man. No. Way."

"Mm-hmm."

"I'm serious." She rolled her shoulders a few times and tipped her head back and forth in an attempt to literally shake off the idea. "Now get out of here so I can work."

Rowan picked up her hat and strode to the side door but turned back before opening it. "You let me know when you schedule that visit. I can't wait to meet her."

❖

Mira arrived at Forbidden Fruit a little after one and entered through the tasting room. No customers yet, but it looked like they'd just opened for the day. The space had the look of a recent remodel—clean and bright but made cozy with natural wood and quirky apple-themed accents that worked with the warehouse vibe it had going.

Dylan, who seemed to be waiting for her, greeted her with a smile. She wore gray pants and a button-down this time, making Mira wonder if she had dressed for the meeting. She'd opted for a more casual skirt and blouse than her usual work attire, not wanting to feel starchy and overdressed. The combination—or perhaps juxtaposition—left her with thoughts about meeting in the middle. Made her wonder whether Dylan might think the same.

"Welcome to our neck of the woods." Dylan spread her arms before extending a hand.

"You've got a great space here." More casual than Pomme, and without a restaurant attached, but it offered a nice setting for both tasting and shopping. And large metal-and-glass, garage-style doors opened onto a large patio and lawn area dotted with picnic tables and fire pits.

"Thank you. It was a long time coming."

She couldn't relate to that part, but it left her ruminating on how she'd have outfitted Pomme if the decision had been hers. "Looks like it was worth the wait."

"This is pretty much all there is to see of our retail side, but I thought you might like a tour of the production area." Dylan's smile had that charming, permanently at ease quality that didn't quite manage to make her relax.

"Sure." Mira realized the enthusiasm in her voice didn't match Dylan's, so she cleared her throat. It was one thing to be reserved, quite another to be rude. "That would be fantastic."

"I'll resist a running commentary about how size doesn't matter, but I feel it's only fair to tell you I'm thinking it."

She couldn't help but soften at the good-natured self-deprecation and the implied compliment about her own operation. "Then I'll say, for the record, that it's what you do with it that matters."

"I love it when a beautiful woman says that to me."

Only then did the innuendo of her words catch up with her. Along with a few choice images she absolutely didn't need taking up space in her mind. She cleared her throat again, grateful Dylan couldn't see the flush that warmed her cheeks.

"Apologies." Dylan lifted a hand. "I didn't mean to sound forward."

Any appreciation of the apology melted into the embarrassment of knowing Dylan sensed her discomfort. Even if Dylan didn't ascribe that discomfort correctly, it felt like a moment of weakness. And she didn't show weakness. "You're fine. Lead the way."

Dylan opened her mouth but seemed to think better of whatever she was on the verge of saying. Instead, she angled her head. "This way."

She followed Dylan through a set of swinging doors. Not two steps in, they stood sandwiched between two rows of fermentation tanks. Smaller than the thousand-gallon tanks at Pomme, but substantial. Though they didn't have lines attached or much room to maneuver. "You make full use of your space."

"You should see us shuffling them around with the pallet jack."

Mira glanced down and, sure enough, each tank sat on a wooden pallet. "You move them?"

"Believe it or not, that's more efficient and cost-effective than running fixed lines from the press and to the bottler."

"It makes sense. I've just never seen this setup. It's quite genius, really." And made her wonder if it was Dylan's brainchild or common practice with smaller producers.

"Genius, huh? I should warn you flattery will get you everywhere."

She'd meant it as a professional nod, but Dylan's response gave her pause. Was Dylan flirting with her? Or was that how people like Dylan interacted? "I'll be sure to remember that when I want something."

Dylan gave her a curious look that, for the life of her, she couldn't decipher. "Noted."

She'd meant it in a lighthearted way, but maybe her attempts to be casual and easy were coming off as anything but. The possibility bugged her. Handling people was as innate to her as breathing. "Anyway, I'm impressed."

They looped the space. Everything—from the grinder and presses to the bottler and boxes of corks—were crammed into the one room. Efficient, creative, and undoubtedly Dylan's domain. It gave her a pang of something akin to longing. Not that she wanted what Dylan had, but it made her think about what it would be like to do more than a weekly visit to the production floor. Or to build something from the ground up.

"Should we get down to business?" Dylan gave her an expectant look.

"Yes, of course." She followed Dylan back to the tasting room, wondering how distracted she'd looked and kicking herself for being awkward.

"I can't offer you the kind of spread you put out last week, but I'd love to pour you a glass. And we have cheese and charcuterie type snacks."

Since trying each other's products was professional courtesy as much as anything else, she smiled. "I'm fine food-wise, but I'd love a cider."

"Preference? Would you like a menu? A flight?"

"A glass is fine but surprise me."

Dylan gestured to a high-top table and headed to the bar. The guy behind it looked not a day over eighteen, but he and Dylan seemed to have rapport that went beyond seasonal college student help. When was the last time she'd exchanged anything more than pleasantries with the tasting room staff?

A minute later, Dylan joined her at the table with a pair of glasses. "We just rolled out our wild foraged perry. But I have our Ellis Bitter, too, in case you're a cider purist."

She was a purist, but admitting it seemed unnecessarily snobbish in the moment, so she accepted the perry and took a sip. Like cider but not. Pear forward, for sure, but the finishing notes held vanilla and the essence of leather. The mouthfeel managed to be substantial and supple at the same time. "This is lovely."

"Why do I get the feeling that's a concession as much as a compliment?"

She tried for a conciliatory smile. "I admit I don't drink a lot of perry."

"Well, I'm glad you took a chance."

Dylan didn't comment further, though Mira got the distinct impression she had opinions. "Shall we talk about the gala?"

"Absolutely. One sec." Dylan stood.

While she pulled her laptop from her bag and set it up, Dylan snagged a leather-bound journal from behind the bar. It felt symbolic of how different they were—how differently they approached life—but she kept the observation to herself. Just like she kept it to herself that Dylan pulling an exquisite fountain pen from the pocket of her work pants was downright disarming.

"Okay, I know we need to talk logistics, but I want to hear more about this ag program. I'm not familiar with it."

She gave the elevator pitch—one she'd practiced in anticipation of conversations just like this. Dylan seemed interested, but also like it was all new to her. Not the idea of reparations, exactly, but that it might have anything to do with her or her work.

"Did you grow up around here?" Mira asked.

Dylan lifted a shoulder. "Buffalo. Well, a suburb of Buffalo. I admit it was rather blue collar, and very white."

"Ah." Like so many things about the ways people experienced privilege and race, it surprised her and it didn't.

"I mean, we learned about the Haudenosaunee and stuff. I'm not entirely clueless."

Mira lifted a hand, not wanting to put Dylan on the defensive. "I didn't say you were."

"And I've heard of reparations. Just not with cider, if that makes sense. Wasn't cider brought by the colonizers?"

She appreciated that Dylan knew at least that much and seemed genuinely curious about the rest. "It's more about the land. Most of the land we grow apples on—wild or cultivated—is land stolen from Indigenous people. On top of that, BIPOC people make up less than two percent of the agricultural producers in New York."

Dylan looked sheepish. "I'm totally on board. I didn't understand the whole context of where you were coming from is all."

She sighed. That was the problem. Not only was she carrying the mantle of this work, she had to educate people about why it mattered. Which she didn't mind doing, but it made it feel like twice the work sometimes. "I get it."

"What if we did a cider collection to raise money on top of the gala?"

The abrupt shift caught her off guard. "A collection?"

Dylan nodded, her serious expression giving way to excitement. "Yeah. Like, we get several producers to contribute one cider. Maybe a small batch or special run or something. They donate them or do it at cost or whatever, and we put it together as an exclusive package. The proceeds go to the ag project."

She'd been toying with the idea of a small run or a unique label at Pomme to do just that. A collaboration hadn't occurred to her. "Do you think other producers would go for it?"

Dylan shrugged. "I would. In a heartbeat."

"Even if it meant producing however many bottles at no profit?"

"It would be free publicity, though. For those of us without marketing departments, there's value in it. Plus the whole good cause thing."

She nodded, letting the idea percolate. "Okay, I see that."

"I've thought about trying to do something along those lines with other cideries but haven't managed to come up with an angle that would entice people to buy it. A good cause, a perfect holiday gift. It's a twofer. And we could set a number so folks would know what they were signing up for."

"Limited edition, which also makes it feel exclusive. Look at you, thinking like a marketer."

Dylan laughed. "I have my moments."

Excitement bubbled up, making her forget her plan to work with Dylan grudgingly. "What if we did a three-bottle set and a six? Different price points, but it would also allow producers to participate at different levels too, based on capacity."

"Look at you, thinking like the little guy." Dylan lifted her chin.

A backhanded compliment, but since she'd essentially dished out the same, she took it. "Should we put a call out and gauge interest?"

Dylan tipped her head back and forth. "That seems fair, especially if it's something that's going to get promotion during Cider Week."

Mira nodded, wheels turning. Logistics and calculations, figuring out how to manage distribution. Talise could develop the marketing campaign. She'd get to flex her creative muscles and do it for a cause she cared about. "I can draft an email."

Dylan tipped her head again but left it angled. "Or I could."

She could tell it was a poke as much as an offer, but Dylan managed to be playful about it—teasing but not mean. She folded her arms. "I was only offering."

"Were you?" Dylan mimicked the gesture but for the life of her, she'd swear it was flirting more than a jab.

"I was. I happen to spend most of my day at a computer."

Dylan made a face. "My condolences."

"It's a choice I made freely. And I'm very good at what I do." More bravado than the situation warranted, but again, they seemed to be in banter territory, and she was shooting from the hip.

"I have no doubt." Dylan's smile was more of a smirk. "Since the cause behind it is your idea, it probably makes sense. You should get the credit."

"I don't need the credit." The deflection was reflexive more than accurate, but Dylan didn't need to know that.

"No?"

The question made her laugh even as it got her hackles up. "Do you enjoy giving me a hard time or is that sort of thing habit for you?"

"Yes." Dylan didn't hesitate but laughed, too. "I'm cool with you sending the email, but seriously, what else can I do?"

Because she didn't want to break the rapport they seemed to have going, she ignored the dig. Instead, she ran through the list of tasks in her mind, searching for one she was willing to share. "We need to select the menu for the gala. You could do that, or we could do it together."

"Together sounds fun."

What was that gleam in Dylan's eye all about? "Okay, why don't you reach out to them and get a couple of options and you can email me. Or text. I can text if that's easier."

"Well, it will be quicker."

"Got it. Text." They had each other's numbers; she didn't know why she was being weird about it.

"Next week okay for you?" Dylan smiled again and the gleam remained.

"It's great." Mira swallowed, annoyed that she noticed. "I suppose I should let you get back to work."

"Eh?" Dylan shrugged, then laughed. "Thanks for coming out my way."

"Happy to. Thank you for the tour. And the cider." She stood. "I'll see you soon."

Dylan grinned full on now. "It's a date."

Her mind tripped, then raced. Not entirely trusting herself to say something articulate, she merely nodded and gathered her things. But of course Dylan lingered and walked her to the door. Outside, she filled her lungs with fresh air and shook off whatever that weird sensation had been. "Have a good week."

"You, too. Take care."

Since Dylan seemed in no hurry to go back inside, she booked it to her car. Fortunately, a group of six arrived and were heading into the tasting room. Dylan greeted them and escorted them inside.

Finally alone, she blew out a breath and let her shoulders slump. By all accounts, the meeting had gone well. They'd gotten along. They'd divided some tasks. They'd even agreed on some things. So why did she feel so out of sorts? And why, of all things, was that flirty look in Dylan's eyes front and center in her brain?

Chapter Five

For the second time in as many weeks, Dylan ironed the shirt she put on for work. It might be a personal record for her. She got to work on boxing up the wild crab they'd finished labeling the day before. She'd planned to leave it for the intern, Jamal, but decided she'd do well to stick with a task that couldn't leave her filthy by lunchtime. She'd just finished the last case when Rowan walked into the production room. She gave Dylan the once-over and let out a suggestive whistle.

Dylan rolled her eyes. "Really with that?"

Rowan shrugged. "You're the one who came to work looking like a hot date waiting to happen."

"I mean, I kind of have a date." It wasn't a date by any stretch of the imagination but joking that it was somehow felt preferable to admitting she wanted to impress Mira. Well, not impress. Hold her own. Look like she belonged at a business lunch at the Statler.

Rowan wagged her eyebrows like a cartoon character. "Hubba-hubba."

"You're ridiculous."

"It only seems fair given how much flak you gave me over Audrey."

She had given Rowan a lot of flak about Audrey. But Rowan had been attracted to, then half in love with, then all the way in love with Audrey. "This is different. I'm not going to fall for Mira. Or even hook up with her."

"Neither was I, friend. Neither was I."

"I'm looking to make a good impression and stay on her good side." She straightened. "For the good of the company, I might add."

"Right, right. Just like I wanted to be on Audrey's good side so she'd be our accountant and not sabotage our arrangement with Ernestine."

Oof. She'd walked right into that one. The fact of the matter was, as different as the situations were, they had some parallels. Only she didn't have a thing for Mira the way Rowan had with Audrey. Sure, she thought Mira was gorgeous, but that was more of an objective reality. And for all she knew, Mira was straight. At the very least, Mira was clearly uninterested. So, yeah. Totally different. "Not the same."

"If you say so."

"I do. And I've got to go or I'm going to be late for my date."

"Go, go. We can't have that." Rowan shrugged again, this time more resigned. "But for the record, you're the one calling your business lunch a date."

She had, but she'd been deflecting her own discomfort. Mira's beauty wasn't what had her on edge. Mira had money and class written all over her—impeccable clothes, salon-level hair and makeup, the whole nine yards. Which said nothing of the way she commanded a room and made it seem effortless. Even if she turned out not to be a complete snob, that sort of thing was in her DNA. Dylan might dance around the edges of that with a willing partner, but it made her squirrely. It wasn't her world, and she didn't want it to be. "I'll call you later. Don't break anything while I'm gone."

Rowan's grumbled comeback about who was more likely to break things made her laugh and helped her relax. Since it was a perfect day for a drive, she cranked the radio and rapped along to classic Snoop Dogg, thinking maybe Rowan had a point about spending as many days as possible out in the sunshine. Feeling nostalgic as she rolled into town, she took the long way around campus, crossing the one-lane bridge over the gorge and thinking about the handful of times she'd gone skinny-dipping in the waters below.

Had Mira gone skinny dipping in her younger days? It was hard to imagine her doing so now, but perhaps she'd been a little wilder, a little more carefree at some point. She'd done that quite a bit lately—wondering about the sides of Mira she'd yet to see. Like Mira was a puzzle she wanted to solve, or maybe more accurately, like Mira had a shell around her that Dylan wanted to crack.

Not that it was any of her business. She was merely curious. And maybe, just a little, loved a challenge.

Even with the detour, she'd given herself an extra window of time and arrived early. It gave her a small surge of satisfaction to arrive ahead of Mira. But when Mira strolled up exactly one minute before the agreed upon time, it left Dylan to consider if she'd done so on purpose. Of course, that took a back seat to appreciating Mira herself, looking flat-out stunning in a form-fitting dress with vibrant yellow flowers. Her hair, which had been styled straight their last two meetings, was now a halo of bouncy curls that perfectly matched the vibrancy of her attire.

She stepped forward and did her best not to stare. "Hi."

Dylan might have been going for professional in her own choice of attire, but the once-over Mira gave her was anything but. "I hope you haven't been waiting long."

The formality of the comment warred with Mira's body language, leaving Dylan unsure how to play things. "Only a couple of minutes."

"Oh, good. Shall we?"

"By all means." Dylan held the door out of habit more than any conscious attempt at chivalry, and Mira breezed through like she was accustomed to such things.

"Do you know if we go to the restaurant or somewhere else?"

She'd spent plenty of time in this building but had no clue how the front of house operated. "I don't."

Just like when Dylan held the door, Mira didn't hesitate. Her gaze swept the room and, after landing on the concierge desk, she walked right over. A warm smile, a pleasant greeting, and then, "We're here for a consultation with the head of catering. Would you point us in the right direction?"

It wasn't like she couldn't have handled such a simple task, but the aplomb with which Mira moved through spaces left Dylan slightly in awe. Had she been raised with it? Or did it come with being the kind of beautiful, feminine-presenting woman that garnered attention without trying? Whatever it was, it reminded Dylan she had neither the breeding nor the bearing to make that sort of confidence come naturally. Not that she lacked confidence—ego even—in other arenas. But this, this was different.

After some pointing and navigating, they found themselves in a small room adjacent to the main ballroom where the gala would take place. The head of catering turned out to be a middle-aged woman named Helen who made no pretenses about flirting with Dylan—big smile, a pat on the arm, the whole deal. Mira looked the slightest bit irritated by it all, but that might have been wishful thinking on Dylan's part.

Helen got them situated with a folder of menus and pricing sheets and reviewed the basics of an event like theirs. "I've got some samples for y'all to try, then we can sit down and hammer out exactly what you want."

Dylan didn't have to fake her own big smile. Helen's wink and her South Carolina drawl did all the heavy lifting. "That sounds fantastic."

Helen disappeared and a server appeared with place settings and water glasses, reminding her of both her stint at the Statler in college and the years of waiting tables at her family's restaurant as a teenager. When he'd gone too, leaving Dylan and Mira momentarily alone, Mira gave her a slightly amused, slightly exasperated look. "Are you a consummate flirt or is this a special occasion?"

Dylan answered with a shrug and a smile. She hadn't been looking to show off, but it somehow felt like she and Mira were back on equal footing. Perhaps confidence really came down to that—knowing when and how to leverage one's strengths.

❖

When the food came out, Mira's mind went to work, silently making the selections she'd convince Dylan of one way or the other. Helen returned with descriptions and explanations of what would work as part of a station setup versus a passed hors d'oeuvre. When she was done, she made little circles with her hands. "I'm going to leave you with these. Feel free to make notes on the menu. I'll come back in a few and we can regroup."

Helen's attention remained mostly fixed on Dylan, but Mira jumped in anyway. "Thank you so much."

Dylan nodded. "Yes. Thanks."

Helen retreated to the kitchen and Mira studied the plates in front of them, debating whether to start with the tomato jam bruschetta or the crispy Brussels sprouts. But when she turned to ask Dylan what she wanted to try first, Mira found her shaking her head. "What's wrong?"

Dylan chuckled. "Nothing."

"You don't have to try anything you don't want. You won't hurt anyone's feelings."

"It's not that," Dylan said.

"Then what is it?" She wouldn't have pegged Dylan for being a picky eater, but what did she know?

"I just had flashbacks of waiting tables here in college."

"You went to Cornell?"

Dylan folded her arms but didn't stop smiling. "You don't need to sound so surprised."

"I'm not surprised, I'm…"

"Surprised." Dylan reached across the table and speared one of the Brussels sprouts with her fork.

Well, yes. Though she didn't want to admit it. "I didn't get the business school vibe from you."

"And what makes you think I went to business school?"

She'd walked right into that one. "I stand corrected. So, what did you study?"

"I started out in hotel management."

Mira smirked. "I think that counts as business."

"Fair point. My parents own a restaurant but didn't want me to feel trapped in that. But I didn't know much else. I figured if I knew the restaurant side and learned the hotel side, I'd be able to land a decent job." Dylan lifted a hand. "Career. My parents very much wanted me to have a career."

It made her wonder what kind of restaurant. And if Dylan's reference to growing up in a blue-collar neighborhood was accurate or exaggeration. And how Dylan got to cider making. And, maybe just a little, how her parents felt about it. Since most of those questions strayed into personal territory, she settled on, "So, what happened?"

"I met Rowan and we started hanging out with ag school kids. I dabbled in the viticulture program and food science before putting together an interdisciplinary major while we noodled around making cider in our apartment."

"And your parents were okay with that?" Hers might have been supportive of a different path than the family business, but they certainly wouldn't have tolerated dabbling and mind changing.

Dylan shrugged. "They wanted me to be happy. And there are enough wineries and cideries in New York that they figured I'd make out okay."

"Huh."

"My mom even mentioned Pomme as a company that probably had good opportunities and would keep me close to home." Dylan laughed then. "Though I'm pretty sure if I'd come to work for you, we'd both have regretted it."

She figured they were around the same age, but she'd done her MBA right after her bachelor's. It was strange to imagine the possibility of Dylan establishing a career at Pomme before she'd even arrived. The thought left her rattled, so she turned her attention back to the food. Helen had arranged an impressive selection: a sampling of what a cheese and charcuterie station would hold, warm hors d'oeuvres that could be passed, a plate of mini desserts. Some of it wouldn't work for their event, but it was all delicious.

"Are you really into the food, or are you thinking about how glad you are not to have me playing mad scientist in your production room?"

She didn't relish being transparent, but the question made her smile. "Yes."

"Probably for the best. I'm sure you would have fired me by now. But, damn, I'd have had some fun with all that gorgeous equipment. Not to mention the financial resources."

Mira almost went for a mini corn dog but thought better of it. They weren't hosting the county fair. "You know that's not how it works, right?"

As if drawn to the plate of fried things by the power of suggestion, Dylan snagged one of the corn dogs and chased it with a fried pickle. "Those are fantastic, for the record. And it's not how what works?"

"Pomme. Being bigger doesn't mean we have money to throw around on wild ideas or experimentation that might not go anywhere."

Dylan raised a brow, incredulous.

"Our staff and overhead are very much on track with our revenue." It sounded stiff and corporate even to her, but it was true. Not to mention too late to take it back.

Dylan tipped her head. "Okay. But I bet you could experiment more than you do."

She imagined the hundreds, if not thousands, of conversations she'd had with Luis through the years. He made passing comments about shaking things up, trying new techniques. He never pushed for them though. She wondered for the first time if that was because he was content or because her father had quashed his ideas enough times to lock them safely in the realm of daydreams. "My father has a saying. Why mess with perfection?"

"Humble."

She snickered before she could stop herself, but her need to defend kicked in almost immediately. "It's more that he took risks when he was younger. Like branching out into cider in the first place. He's built a company he's proud of and he's happy with how things are."

"And you? Are you happy with how things are?"

She'd expected a quip perhaps, something along the lines of standing still being the same as moving backward. The gentleness of the question—the intimacy of it—caught her off guard. "Of course I am."

"Okay." Dylan's hands came up in a show of concession. Her face had that "I don't want to start a fight" look more than an "I believe you" look.

"I get that you're all about forging new paths and making your mark. I'm not like that. My job is to shepherd a successful company and protect the livelihoods of the people who work for me. That makes me happy." Though, even as she said it, the reality left her a little hollow.

"Totally fair." Dylan nodded and her expression sobered.

"Maybe we should focus on the food." That's what they were there for. Not to probe each other's deepest longings.

"That I can do." Dylan grinned and went for a pork belly slider that looked amazing but also like a trip to the dry cleaner just waiting to happen.

They worked their way through the plates, commenting and taking notes. It surprised her how similar their tastes were, even if their opinions on what should be served at the gala didn't remotely mesh. After arguing about the corndogs for longer than was reasonable, Mira huffed out a breath. She tried for a calming one as the muscles in her jaw tightened. "I think we should keep it simple, elegant, and classy."

Dylan angled her head. "Because that's what cider is?"

"Exactly." It was nice that Dylan could concede the point. Maybe they'd end up on the same page after all.

"That's what your cider is." Dylan punctuated the statement with a finger jab on the table.

"So, you're saying yours isn't those things?"

It had felt like a clear gotcha point for her, but Dylan sat back in her chair and pressed her palms into the table's edge. "Some of it is. Some of it is casual and easy. Some is brash and bold. Some is funky and weird."

She sniffed. Why anyone would aspire to funky and weird was beyond her. And yet even as her hackles rose, she couldn't deny that Dylan had a point. Not just about her cider but lots of ciders. The gala—and Cider Week as a whole—was supposed to showcase everyone. God, she hated being wrong. "Fine."

"Fine?"

It was entirely possible Dylan understood and simply wanted her to give in more concretely. She loathed that and respected it at the same time. "You're right."

Dylan had the grace to keep her smile in check. Not entirely but not full-on smug. Something told her Dylan could rock a smug grin like nobody's business. The only time she tolerated those was after someone gave her a spectacular orgasm. And since there was no way in hell that would ever happen with Dylan, it boded well that she was able to keep her relish to herself.

"So, we're going to do it my way?" Dylan asked.

"What if we compromised? Since we're going with the stations concept, we can get away with things that technically don't go together."

Dylan raised a brow, but then she grinned. "Like us?"

Dylan's delivery was playful, the statement unequivocally true. So, why did it leave her disappointed? Because she was being an idiot, that's why. Dylan had her all riled up for no good reason. She gave a decisive nod, as much to convince herself as Dylan. "Like us."

Chapter Six

A fter negotiating the final menu compromises and going over tentative numbers, Helen handed them over to the beverage manager to discuss the unique setup they'd need in lieu of a traditional cash bar. "Austin will take good care of you," Helen said with a parting wink directed unabashedly at Dylan.

He strode in a moment later, iPad in one hand and a cluster of stemware in the other. He set the glasses down deftly and took the seat next to Mira. "Ladies, fantastic to meet you."

Mira shook the hand he extended. "Thanks for meeting with us."

Dylan did the same, though her smile seemed forced. Probably didn't appreciate being referred to as a lady.

Austin flashed a pristinely white, almost too perfect smile. "Of course. We want to make sure all your needs are taken care of."

She wasn't a fan of the smarm, but it came with the territory. Dylan ran a hand up the back of her neck and made a point of looking away, either not used to it or not concerned with being subtle. Mira took that as her cue to take the lead. "I'm sure you will."

Austin, who'd already angled himself toward Mira, shifted his full attention to her. "So, I understand you'll be serving cider exclusively and plan to provide cases yourselves."

"For alcohol, yes. We'd like your standard soda and water package for the non-alcoholic options."

"Gotcha." Austin tapped at the screen of his tablet.

Dylan cleared her throat, as though remembering she wanted to be part of the conversation. "All of the participating cideries will be contributing. We're hoping to set up a drop-off window instead of a single delivery."

"Of course." Despite responding to Dylan, Austin's eyes didn't leave Mira. "And I have here you want to do a flat charge and three-ounce pours."

She could sense Dylan's irritation, but there was no point in making things awkward. "Yes. We want to encourage sampling, but not over-sampling."

"Moderation is good, at least in some things." Austin gave her an appreciative look.

Dylan pointed to the stemware Austin had set on the table. "Do we need to pick a single glass?"

Austin spared Dylan a look this time but shrugged. "I imagined you would, but we can handle whatever you throw our way."

Dylan looked to her this time. "I'd go champagne flute for sparklings, but I think a standard wine glass works better for stills."

Mira wasn't a big fan of stills, so she sometimes forgot about them. "That's a good point."

"Done." Austin typed more things into his tablet.

"What else do you need from us?" Mira asked.

"Your number, maybe?" Austin gave her a knowing look, waited a beat, then laughed. "Kidding. I think we're all set. But you have to promise to reach out if you need anything from me."

She ignored the come-on dressed up like a joke but kept a smile on her face. "Oh, we will."

"Excellent. You ladies have a good day." He offered her a lingering smile and Dylan a dismissive nod.

When he'd gone, Dylan made a gagging gesture. Mira shrugged. "I know."

"I can't believe you put up with that." Dylan shook her head and shuddered.

"Trust me, it's easier that way." Straight guys might be a handful, but straight guys with bruised egos could be flat-out trouble.

Dylan didn't look convinced. "If you say so."

"I do. Besides, we can't all have the luxury of being hit on by the Helens of the world."

Dylan shook her head. "Not the same thing. The Helens are harmless."

"Well, I do my best to handle the Austins so they're harmless, too." There'd been a few times when it hadn't worked, but she mostly got what she needed and got away unscathed.

She was spared further argument by Helen's return. Dylan seemed to relax under her attentions, which diffused any lingering tension. Mira asked if they could get a peek at the ballroom. "It's easier to finalize the event layout when you have the shape and scale of the space in your mind and not just on paper," she said.

Dylan, once again at ease, nodded affably. "Oh, I'm learning all about how to organize a reception. My sister is getting married this fall and because I own an event space, I've been roped into reception planning."

"That's sweet of you." It was, even if she had a hard time imagining Dylan as a wedding planner.

"Nothing like what you pull off at Pomme, but we've done a couple of weddings at the cidery. Enough that I know where to put things in the room to get a good flow." Dylan's hand came up in a stop signal. "I drew the line at centerpieces though."

She smiled because it was funny, but also because it tracked so closely with the direction of her thoughts. "It's good to know your limits."

They toured the ballroom and haggled only a little about the location of the stage and the mix of regular and high-top tables. In the end, Dylan deferred to her. "You've done this before," she said.

For all the things Dylan had opinions about, it surprised her Dylan would play that card now. She couldn't decide whether to welcome it or be suspicious of it. "I have."

"You know how the program part of the night goes. I attended two years ago, but my memory is fuzzy."

"Ah." A perfectly logical explanation, but it didn't jibe with the obstinate nature she'd ascribed to Dylan.

"Why do you look so surprised?

Did she admit having such a set idea of Dylan's personality?

"You think I'm a blowhard."

"No." She wouldn't use that word. At least not to Dylan's face.

"You're lying."

"Okay, maybe I did at first. But I'm getting to know you and you're much nicer than that." She cringed at perhaps the worst attempt at a compliment ever.

Dylan laughed. "It's okay. I thought you were corporate and uptight."

Not the first time someone used that word to describe her. "And now?"

"I'm getting to know you and you're much nicer than that."

It was her turn to laugh. Only it came out as a decidedly ungraceful snort. "I deserved that."

Dylan shrugged. "I think it's progress."

Indeed it was. Helen rejoined them and took notes on the decisions they'd made. They walked out into the summer sunshine together and Mira found herself surprisingly sad to see the meeting end. "I'll have my marketing manager work on some promo for the reparations package in addition to the general Cider Week stuff. Other than going over that, I think we're probably where we need to be."

"Sounds good."

She couldn't tell if it had to do with Dylan's smile or maybe some residual desire to smooth things over after the whole blowhard thing. Or maybe it was something else entirely. But she wanted to see Dylan again, and not at the next Cider Association meeting. "Would you like to do lunch again?"

"Sure." Dylan hesitated just enough to send Mira backpedaling.

"We don't have to. A phone call is fine. Or Zoom." Backpedaling and feeling foolish.

"No, it's not that. I like meeting in person. Midday can be a challenge is all, especially if we're doing any kind of production."

Oh. She mentally kicked herself for not thinking about how different Dylan's workday would be. "I certainly don't want to get in the way of production."

"How would you feel about dinner?"

Not a date invitation, but it felt like one. Way more than Dylan's passing comment when scheduling this lunch. It made her feel less foolish and more self-conscious at the same time. "Um."

"I mean, I suppose we could do breakfast, but dinner seems like more fun."

Mira swallowed the flutter of excitement she had no business feeling. "Dinner would work."

"Excellent. Thanks for being flexible."

She nodded, the wind falling from her sails. They were discussing professional courtesy not a romantic evening. "Of course."

"Shall we meet in the middle?"

"What about Seneca Hill Cider House?" The casual atmosphere and likelihood they'd see people they both knew was exactly the vibe she needed to set. The vibe she should have been thinking about in the first place.

Dylan grinned. "I'll never say no to that."

There. That put them back on solid, even footing. "Name the day. Well, after next week at least. My parents will be in town."

"Oh, nice."

It would be nice. Mostly. Even if her father would critique any decisions that hadn't been his and her mother would give him disapproving looks but not get in the middle. "It's their annual pilgrimage to check on the state of things."

Dylan angled her head and her eyes softened. "You or the business?"

She lifted her shoulders and let them fall. "Both."

"I see." Dylan's expression held understanding.

"Pomme is still their baby in a way." As much as she was, if not more.

"Did they open it together?"

An innocent question and one she got often enough. Since she and Dylan were barely in friendly territory, she decided to stick with her stock answer. "They did. My father was running the winery in California and my mother had just become a Master Sommelier and wanted to take a sabbatical."

Dylan nodded with that look of wonder most people had when she explained what her parents did.

"They came to New York, planning to get in on the Finger Lakes wine market before it took off, and decided cider had more potential for growth and would expand their footprint in the industry in a different way."

"Yeah." More nodding. More wonder.

"Anyway. I'm in charge, but it's still their company." A fact she didn't resent, but also one she didn't forget.

"That makes sense. And kind of cool that it's a family affair."

She couldn't tell if Dylan meant that or was merely being nice, but it didn't really matter one way or the other. "We'll talk shop, but we'll have a good visit, too."

"Well, that'll be nice, I'm sure." Dylan's tone said a lot more than her words.

"It will." And even if parts of it weren't, Dylan certainly didn't need to know that.

"So, how about the week after next? You can take the week off to enjoy family time, then we'll get back to planning. I could do any day."

How much she'd manage to enjoy family time remained up for debate, but the prospect of seeing Dylan again gave her a small surge of excitement. A fact she'd no doubt dissect later but let herself enjoy for now. "Tuesday?"

"Perfect. Where did you park?"

She angled her head toward the Hoy Road garage. "You?"

"Down toward College Town so I could snag bagels while I'm here."

It occurred to her she had no idea where Dylan lived. It also occurred to her that where Dylan lived was none of her business. "Are they really good bagels?"

"Yes, but also a carryover from going to school here. Rowan and I snag a dozen for each of us whenever we're close by."

"I've been known to sneak a loaf of sourdough into my carry-on when I visit California."

Dylan grinned in a way that brought out creases at the corners of her hazel eyes. "Careful or I might ask you to bring me one, too."

It was casual banter, the kind friends or even acquaintances might have. But she couldn't stop herself from thinking about her next trip to the West Coast and wondering if she and Dylan would be seeing much of each other by then. Wondering but maybe hoping—and a little wanting—too.

❖

After picking up bagels—and more tubs of parsley garlic cream cheese than the bagels probably warranted—Dylan ran a few errands. She got back to the cidery as the food truck pulled in. She went over to say hello before heading inside to make sure they were ready for the rush that would begin a little after five.

She found Rowan stacking the wooden boards that held the glasses for cider flights and Clarissa, their recently hired bartender, arranging glassware. Audrey was there, too, tidying the laminated menus and dry erase markers customers would use to make tasting selections. "Well, look who decided to join us," Rowan said.

"Be nice to me or I'll keep all the bagels to myself."

Rowan stopped what she was doing. "Rosemary salt?"

"And parsley garlic cream cheese." She lifted the bag she'd brought in to stash in the cooler until closing time.

"In that case, welcome back. You're right on time." Rowan offered a cheesy, eager smile.

"Pretty Bird is here and firing up the fryers. The band should be here any minute. What else needs to be done?" Dylan asked.

"Not a thing, thanks to these two." Rowan tipped her head at Audrey, then Clarissa. "Just get ready to pour."

"Music to my ears." She headed to the cooler in the back and stashed her loot, then washed up and claimed her spot behind the bar as the first of the happy hour crowd trickled in.

An hour later, she handed a cider flight to a waiting customer and wiped up a couple of droplets that had spilled. It was the first time since five they didn't have clusters of people at the bar waiting to be served. She let out a sigh, equal parts fatigue and happiness. "Good crowd tonight."

"I think it might be our biggest so far," Rowan said.

They'd started Fridays at Forbidden Fruit with the grand opening of the tasting room. The idea had been to offer a happy hour vibe and live music during the summer months, when customers could spill onto the stretch of lawn and soak up the scenery as much as the cider. Tonight was week four and they'd managed to book both a popular local band and pretty much everyone's favorite fried chicken food truck. "Yeah, I think we might need to talk about bringing in some extra help."

At that exact moment, Audrey skirted around the end of the bar with an armload of flight boards holding empty glasses. "What was that about extra help?"

Rowan took them from her and planted a noisy kiss on her cheek. "We think it's time to hire some."

Audrey swiped the back of her hand across her brow. "I approve this plan."

"I do, too." Clarissa, the one full-time staff person they'd managed to hire so far, looked up from restocking the cooler under the bar.

Rowan smiled. "Well, I guess it's settled."

"Yeah. We gotta keep these two happy." Dylan tipped her head in Audrey's direction. "And maybe stop using our CFO as a bartender."

Rowan started loading the glassware into a rack for their brand-new dishwasher. "There is that."

Audrey planted her hands on her hips. "For the record, I like being a bartender. It uses a different part of my brain."

Rowan's arm slid around Audrey's waist and gave it a squeeze. "You're not getting bored with us, are you?"

Audrey beamed at Rowan. "Never."

"Good." Rowan pulled Audrey closer and kissed her. Like, really kissed her.

She wasn't usually one for the mushy or the romantic, but the two of them were pretty damn adorable. Still. "Okay, now. That's enough."

Rowan and Audrey parted, but they took their sweet time about it. Again, she didn't really mind.

Since pretty much everyone was outside, all but two of the stools at the bar sat empty. Audrey perched on one of them. "Now that we have more than thirty seconds to catch our breath, how did the meeting with Miss Fancypants go?"

Before she could entertain a reply, Rowan stuck out both hands. "Oh, my God. I completely forgot to ask."

"It's all right. We've been busy since I walked in the door."

Rowan shook her head. "Sure, but I've been dying to know. Did you flirt, or did you fight?"

"Rowan." Audrey shot Rowan an admonishing look.

Dylan tipped her head at Audrey. "Thank you."

Audrey whipped her head back around, sending her ponytail swinging. "Of course. But, like, also answer please."

She rolled her eyes on principle. "Neither."

"Well, that's disappointing," Audrey said.

Rowan lifted a finger. "Hold up. What does that mean?"

Technically, she could argue they'd done both. But she'd been so adamant about keeping things above board, she didn't want to lead with that. "We chatted, picked the food for the gala. It was all very professional and friendly."

"I'm eavesdropping just enough to call bullshit," Clarissa said from her position at the other end of the bar.

"How did I get so outnumbered?" Dylan asked.

Rowan clapped a hand on her shoulder. "When you signed up to organize an event you've only been to once, got yourself saddled with a gorgeous powerhouse of a woman who doesn't like you as your co-chair, and became the easiest thing ever to poke fun at."

It was fair. Fair by their standards, at least. "Fine. We fought a little, flirted a little, and managed to compromise a little. I think we might manage to get along after all."

"Was that so hard?" Rowan stuck her hands out again, this time in a gesture of vindication.

"Wait, wait, wait." Audrey tapped a finger on the bar. "Define 'get along after all.'"

Before she could think of a clever answer—or decide whether to confess making dinner plans with Mira—a pair of women came in from the patio, each holding a board of four empty tasting glasses. Audrey popped up to collect them, and Dylan pounced on the diversion. "Can we get you two anything else?"

"Actually, I'm going to have a glass of the Rustic," the brunette said.

"And I'd like the Baldwin," her friend added.

Dylan got to work pouring glasses even though Clarissa could have easily handled it. Rowan finished loading the dishwasher and set it to run. Alone with her thoughts, at least for the moment, she wondered if Mira's friends were also giving her a hard time about their working together. She couldn't picture it, if for no other reason than it was difficult to imagine Mira being easy and loose enough to be on the giving or the receiving end of that sort of teasing. But what did she know, really? Mira might be a completely different person around her friends.

Did it matter? Or maybe more accurately, did she care? The answer was yes, whether she liked it or not. She wanted to get to know the other sides of Mira. Because if Mira had a playful, easy side, she absolutely wanted to see it. And if she didn't, it might help tamp down the raging attraction she still didn't want to admit but could no longer deny.

CHAPTER SEVEN

Mira abandoned the half-written email and allowed her gaze to wander to the view outside her office window. With Dylan's idea for the reparations package, she felt even more enthusiastic about pitching Acres of Equity as the beneficiary of this year's Cider Week Gala. And with both Pomme and Forbidden Fruit already on board, even a couple of others would make the venture worthwhile, both in terms of fundraising and visibility.

Spearheading Pomme's leadership in the project would be one of the first big initiatives she implemented since taking the helm officially. And even though it wouldn't directly contribute to the bottom line, it was something she could be proud of. Something her parents would be proud of.

Thinking about her parents sent her mind back to her lunch with Dylan and Dylan's teasing about her wanting credit for things. But also to how open and easy Dylan's parents seemed about whatever she decided to do with her life. Well, maybe not whatever. But simply wanting her to have a career—ostensibly one that proved successful but mostly one that made her happy and kept her close to home.

Her parents hadn't pressured her to go into the family business. If she'd discovered a different passion, she had no doubt they would have been supportive. Assuming, of course, it was professionally sound and something she could do successfully. Success was a big deal in her family. She didn't have to be the best at everything she did, but she had to land somewhere in the vicinity.

She'd always thrived under that level of expectation, that pressure. But had it held her back from doing other things? Even trying other things? Things that might excite her or feed her soul, but that she might not be very good at.

She suddenly had this vision of her childhood dance classes. She'd thrived in the structured precision of ballet, but modern and even jazz had left her feeling awkward and exposed. So much feeling, so much expression. She shuddered but promptly laughed at herself. Some things, it seemed, never changed.

"Are you staring into space?" Talise, who rarely bothered with a hello, stood in the doorway and smirked.

"Huh? What? No."

Talise came the rest of the way into the office and folded her arms. "Let me rephrase. You were staring into space. What's up?"

"Planning my parents' visit." Not a lie.

"Oh. Okay. So, not your date with a certain small batch cider maker."

She frowned. "It wasn't a date."

As she so often did—particularly when Mira was being stubborn about something—Talise sat, folded her hands, and rested them on the desk. "Figure of speech, baby cakes. The fact that you're splitting hairs says more than what I may or may not have chosen to call it."

The irony, of course, was that she'd spent all sorts of time thinking about Dylan in ways that had nothing to do with cider technique or event planning or family dynamics. This just didn't happen to be one of those times. "I'm being petulant because you caught me daydreaming."

"About…" Talise made a slow, sweeping gesture with her hand in lieu of finishing the sentence.

"About Dylan, but not in the ways you're insinuating."

Talise shrugged. "More of a concession than I was expecting."

"Good, because that's all you're going to get."

That got her a forlorn sigh.

"I know the turnaround would be tight, but do you think we could get a rosé cider to bottle by Cider Week? Small batch, I mean. Like a limited edition run, or a test case."

Talise looked over one shoulder, then the other, before pointing to herself. "You're asking me that question?"

Talise knew even less about the nuances of crafting cider than she did. But she wanted an opinion—any opinion—before broaching the subject with Luis. Or with her parents. "I mean, like, theoretically."

"Again, not your girl. At least on the production side. Could we name it, label it, and promote the hell out of it? Absolutely."

She didn't actually doubt that part, but it was nice to have the sentiment reinforced by her marketing director. "I'm going to talk to Luis. If he doesn't shoo me out of the production room and ban me from it permanently, I'll let you know."

"Hasn't he been hankering to try new things since before either of us started working here?"

"I'm pretty sure he's been hankering since before we were born."

Talise shook her head. "I mean this with both the respect and affection that he's due, but your father can be such a stick in the mud."

She laughed because she agreed, and because Talise was the only person at the company who knew she also felt that way sometimes. Still, the need to caveat won out. "He just used up all his bold thinking in his younger days."

Talise laughed this time. "Yes, yes. Yves Lavigne changed the industry."

"Perfected it, even." Mira smirked, a mixture of amusement and resignation.

"And why mess with perfection?"

The fact that Talise could finish the sentence said loads. Yves always said he ran his business like his employees were family. It was a point of pride for him and a trait she wasn't sure she'd ever be able to replicate. But now, for the first time, it occurred to her that the opposite was true as well. He ran his family like a business. A knot of sadness caught her right between the ribs.

"Hey, you okay? I was teasing. I didn't mean to cross a line."

Mira cleared her throat and smiled. "No, no. My mind drifted in a different direction is all."

Talise narrowed her eyes, clearly unconvinced.

"It's actually really nice to have a kindred spirit on that front. I love the business my parents built, and I love that they trust me enough to put me in charge of part of it. But..." She fumbled for the right words.

"But it doesn't give you a lot of room to make your mark."

Was that it? She'd never thought that sort of thing mattered to her. It was the stuff of big egos and people without a legacy to inherit. In other words, not her. But what if it was? What if she wanted more than the approval of her parents and the knowledge of a job well done? Once again, her thoughts turned to Dylan. She had no desire to mimic Dylan's brash, stand out for the sake of standing out approach to things. But maybe there was something to be said about forging one's own path, and for doing things with passion and not merely precision. "Did you ever take dance lessons as a kid?"

"Dance lessons?"

"Like ballet or tap." She'd continued ballet into high school but given it up in favor of things she could do better and that would look good on her college applications.

Talise laughed. "Yeah, no. My dad poured all his longing for a son into my extracurriculars. Lacrosse, volleyball, basketball. The whole nine yards."

She had a vision of a teenage Talise, all limbs, wielding the ball with confidence. "I bet you were fun to watch on the basketball court."

"I was terrible."

"Really?" She'd never excelled at real sports. Her brain knew what to do, but her body didn't always get the memo.

"My coach told my father I was too stubborn and independent."

Mira bit her lip to keep herself from laughing. "I really do love you."

"It's because we're so much alike." Talise winked. "Why are you thinking about dance lessons?"

Somehow, the jumble of thoughts and memories and questions coalesced. "I'm thinking of starting them again."

"Oh, wow. That's cool." Talise's eyes lit up with what seemed to be more enthusiasm than surprise.

"I mean, I'm pretty sure they do classes for adults. It might be a fun way to mix up working out." She went to the gym for convenience more than anything else. Pilates kicked her ass in all the right ways, but it didn't offer much in the way of inspiration.

Talise nodded her approval. "I am one hundred percent behind this plan."

She pursed her lips. "Enough to join me?"

Talise narrowed her eyes. "Hard no on ballet or tap, but I'd be willing to try belly, African, or hip-hop. Oh, or burlesque."

Mira's inner prude clutched her pearls. She swallowed. "Burlesque?"

Talise lifted a shoulder. "That's what I'm offering. Take it or leave it."

"I'll see what's out there and get back to you." Even as the idea terrified her, it thrilled her.

"I'll look forward to it."

Talise left and Mira turned back to her computer and pulled up a browser. She typed in some key words and closed her eyes as the results loaded. Dance lessons might not be the answer to her problems, but they couldn't hurt. And, if nothing else, she now had something to do with her lunch break besides stare out the window and think about Dylan.

❖

"Dear God, what is that smell?" Rowan came into the production room, neckline of her T-shirt pulled up to cover her nose.

Dylan let out a grumble. "Well, it was supposed to be the Spigold."

Rowan lowered the fabric from her face, but immediately cringed and pulled it back up. "Did you murder it on purpose, or did it die of natural causes?"

She chuckled despite her frustration. "Oh, it was all natural."

"It reminds me of when we accidentally left that mostly empty bin of apples for like four months and everything rotted."

The pungent aroma accosting her senses now did bear a striking resemblance to that pool of moldy goo. "At least this time will be easier to clean up?"

Rowan tipped her head in a way that acknowledged that small win. "What happened?"

"The yeast must have died off."

"Ah."

"Yeah." She put a lot of stock in wild yeast strains. The fermentation progressed differently than when they used commercial yeast and the taste was a whole different ballgame. And, if she was being honest, there was an ego factor. Doing that delicate dance with Mother Nature, getting the results she wanted with nothing more than her knowledge and finesse. Mostly, she pulled it off. Every now and then, Mother Nature knocked her on her ass.

"How bad is it?" Rowan climbed the ladder Dylan had abandoned and peered into the tank. Her body contorted when her gag reflex kicked in and she hurried back down.

Her disappointment didn't wane, but Rowan's reaction managed to distract her from it. She shrugged. "Pretty bad."

Rowan lowered her shirt again, winced, but left it down. "You seriously never get to critique the fish slurry again."

"That's not the same thing. You make that vile concoction on purpose."

"Yes, but my concoction makes for a better harvest. That"—she gestured to the tank—"is eighty gallons of pure waste."

Distraction vanished. Disappointment, joined by anger, took center stage. Shame lurked in the wings. "I'm sorry."

Rowan took one look at her face and her features softened. She clasped Dylan's shoulder. "Hey. I was yanking your chain. This shit happens. Just like sometimes we lose half a crop before the fruit even sets. You don't blame me when June drop happens."

The comparison should have made her feel better, but it didn't. "Don't you get tired of being a shoestring operation? Wouldn't it be nice if a disappointing harvest or a single bad batch of cider didn't cut into the bottom line and make us wonder what the fuck we're even doing?"

Rowan's face morphed from an expression of empathy to one of concern. "Do you wonder what the fuck we're even doing?"

She sighed. She rolled her eyes. "No."

"Well, clearly you are, at least a little. Or you wouldn't have asked." Rowan put her other hand on Dylan's other shoulder and gave both a squeeze. "What's going on? Talk to me."

Usually, Rowan's ability to channel the wise and willing counselor made her do one of two things: talk it out or laugh it off. Today, she was in the mood for neither. "I need to deal with this."

"We'll deal with it." Rowan put the emphasis on we. "Then we'll talk."

"And maybe tell Audrey not to bother coming in today." Her epic fail didn't need any more of an audience than it already had.

Rowan nodded in agreement. "I left her at home so she could take a call from a client up in Seneca Falls. I'll send her a text and—"

"For the love of all that is good and holy, what is going on in here?"

The comedic perfection of Audrey's entrance, paired with the contortion of her face, broke the tension. Dylan offered an innocent shrug. "What? You don't like it?"

Audrey continued to look pained. "Is it supposed to smell like that?"

She shook her head. "No, no it is not."

Rowan stepped forward. "It happens sometimes when the yeast that's meant to do the fermenting dies and mold takes over."

Audrey's nose wrinkled in disgust. "Oh."

Rowan lifted a shoulder in a casual shrug. "It's a risk of wild fermentation but one we're willing to take. It means we have to suffer the consequences on occasion."

Leave it to Rowan to come to her defense even when it wasn't technically needed. The reminder—that they were in this together, that they made the big decisions about how to do things jointly, that they celebrated or struggled as a team—lifted her spirits. She spread her arms wide. "Welcome to consequences."

Audrey looked suspicious at best.

"I was going to text you and suggest you work at home today," Rowan said.

Audrey nodded slowly. "Yeah."

Rowan kissed Audrey's cheek. "I'm going to help Dylan here. Why don't you take the laptop and maybe the three of us could have lunch at the house today?"

Audrey's nod quickened. "Absolutely. I'll make something fun and treat us all."

Dylan folded her arms, almost amused at the unspoken tag team thing they had going. "No one died, you know. You don't have to coddle me."

Rowan bowed her head in exaggerated reverence. "A cider died, Dylan."

She let out a snort laugh before she could stop it. "Fair enough. Thank you both for making me feel less shitty about that."

Rowan smiled. "It's what we do, right?"

It was. "Yeah."

"And it's a small consolation, but I'll figure out the best way to write it off," Audrey said.

Audrey's encouraging tone did as much to buoy her as the words and gave her an overwhelming rush of gratitude that Audrey had come into their lives. She might be Rowan's soul mate, but she was good for both of them, and for Forbidden Fruit. "I'm sure you will."

Rowan gave a decisive nod. "Okay. It's settled then. Audrey, you do your thing. We're going to get this tank drained and cleaned."

Audrey tipped her head toward the rolling door that constituted their shipping and receiving area. "And maybe air the place out."

Rowan laughed and Dylan did, too. And it wasn't even forced. It was fine. It would be fine. They'd weathered bigger storms—literally on a few occasions—and suffered bigger losses. Things might still be tight, but they were less of a shoestring operation than they once were. "That, too."

Audrey smiled but narrowed her eyes. "You're okay, right? I mean, I know it sucks, but...?"

It struck her that Audrey directed the question at her, not Rowan and her collectively. She'd really become a part of the team—and Dylan's friend—as much as Rowan's girlfriend. "But it will be okay. And I'm okay."

"Good. I'm going to grab what I need and get out of here before I pass out." Audrey offered a parting wave and hightailed it to the small office in the back corner of the building.

Rowan planted her hands on her hips. "Okay. What first? What do you need? How can I help?"

It wasn't so much that Rowan didn't know what to do when a batch of cider turned and needed to be pitched. She deferred because she knew it would give Dylan at least a hint of feeling in control. Dylan didn't consider herself a control freak by any means, but it made a difference in moments like these.

She pointed to the door Audrey had indicated a moment before. Rowan went to open it and Dylan grabbed the set of hoses they reserved for cleaning, as opposed to the ones that moved good cider across tanks and barrels. Then they got to work. It struck her how quickly two pairs of hands could empty, scrub, and sanitize a tank. It would make her feel better if it didn't also reflect how quickly thousands of dollars of cider could disappear down the drain.

At least it hadn't been bottled yet. Their second year in operation, she had a batch fail during the bottle fermentation. Talk about devastating. To her ego and to any hope they had of breaking even that year. They'd come a long way since then.

It made her wonder about a place like Pomme. After thirty years in production, did they still have wins and losses, highs and lows? Did Mira?

She knew for a fact they didn't wild ferment, so this particular debacle wouldn't happen. But did Mira ever take chances? Or, rather, did she let people within the company take chances? Pomme cider might be the industry standard in a lot of ways, but she couldn't remember the last time a truly new or unique product came off their line. Was that Mira's decision or was she simply at the helm, holding the course set by her father over the last three decades?

"You're not stewing, are you?"

Rowan's question cut through the haze of her wandering mind. "Just wondering if large scale operators like Pomme ever endure this sort of calamity."

"Like Pomme or like its beautiful but prickly COO?"

Leave it to Rowan to cut right to the chase. "Kind of one and the same."

"Eh? I'd say one is strictly professional."

"And the other?" She knew where this was going.

Rowan shrugged. "Less so."

She'd be lying if she said Mira hadn't invaded her thoughts with increasing frequency over the last couple of weeks. Especially after her visit to Forbidden Fruit and their lunch of sparring that ended in mutually agreeable compromise. Not to mention the dinner plans that weren't really necessary for gala planning.

Dylan shook her head. She might find Mira intoxicatingly beautiful. And she might wonder about how Mira ran her business. But physical attraction and professional curiosity didn't add up to anything more than that.

Chapter Eight

As had become their tradition, Mira picked her parents up at the airport and brought them to their preferred hotel. After helping them with the luggage, she left them to get settled and freshen up for dinner. Down in the lobby, she opened her laptop to deal with some of the email that had piled up over the course of the afternoon not spent at her desk.

The flash of a text notification caught her attention and she picked up her phone. Seeing Dylan's name on the screen made her heart beat a little faster even before she opened the message. It shouldn't, but whatever.

Do you ever have epic fails? Then, *Professionally, I mean.*

She pursed her lips one way, then the other. *Um.*

Not that I'm uninterested in your personal life, but I'm not sure we've crossed that line yet.

The honesty made her smile, as did the awkward, toothy grimace emoji. She considered sharing the hip-hop heels class she'd managed to talk Talise into, or the adult ballet she'd signed up for solo. She hadn't failed—yet—but she had a heavy dose of nerves that she'd sailed past rusty and would make a complete fool of herself.

If you have to think hard about it, I think the answer is no.

She blew out a breath. She was thinking hard, but not for the reasons Dylan probably thought. The malaise that had contributed to seeking out the dance classes in the first place swirled in her mind. *I haven't. But I haven't taken a lot of risks either.*

While she waited for Dylan to respond, she tried to conjure the big decisions she'd made in her career thus far. Did the rosé idea she'd barely formulated count? Definitely not in its current burgeoning state. Other than shifting more into social media marketing and a line of eco-friendly packaging that made a couple of their varieties more picnic-friendly, there hadn't been many. And even those were more tweaks than true changes to the business model.

Blessing or curse? Dylan asked.

The question could have been a dig, but even with the flatness of the medium, it read as sincere. *Yes.*

Dylan sent back the laughing emoji.

When Dylan didn't immediately elaborate, or hint at the why behind her question, Mira asked, *Are you probing my weaknesses, or did you have a fail?*

As much as she wanted to know the answer, the elevator dinged, and her parents emerged. She tucked both her phone and her laptop away and stood. "Ready?"

"Famished." Dad patted his belly.

Her mother shook her head but smiled. "More like reasonably hungry given the rather opulent brunch we had during our layover, but yes, ready."

She drove them to Roux, her current favorite place in Rochester. It boasted modern takes on creole fare and a wine list on par with restaurants in much bigger cities. They spent the first part of the meal catching up—Dad's acceptance that he needed to be on high blood pressure medicine and Mom's latest crop of mentees from the wine program at the community college. When conversation turned to her, she realized she had less going on in her personal life than they did. Yes, they were essentially retired, but still. She made a joke about it, but her mother tutted and shook her head.

"You work too hard," Mom said.

She smiled at the memory of family vacations that had as much to do with wine and cider research as relaxing and family time. "I'm pretty sure I come by it naturally."

"Work doesn't feel like work when you love what you do," Dad said without missing a beat.

Much like her father's opinion on perfection, the comment had almost mantra-like status. She embraced it, even if she didn't aspire to workaholic status. She lifted her glass. "I'll drink to that."

"But you're young and you're not trying to get a business off the ground. You should take time to rest. To play," Mom said.

Mira reached across the table and grabbed her mother's hand. "Who are you and what have you done with my mother?"

That got her a laugh. "I'm just saying that balance is good. Retirement is teaching me to relax. I don't want you to be in your sixties before you figure it out."

Dad waved a hand and tsked his disapproval. Mira grasped for something to say that would make her seem like a remotely well-rounded human being. "Oh. I'm starting dance classes next week. Talise and I are doing them together."

"Oh, how exciting." Mom clapped her hands together. "What kind?"

"Well, hip-hop because that's what I could talk Talise into, but I signed up for ballet, too."

Her mother's features softened. "You loved ballet."

Her parents might not have been the warm and fuzzy kind, but they never missed a recital. She'd loved that as much as the fancy costumes and performing on stage. "I did. I'm a little nervous to jump back in after so many years, but I'm looking forward to the challenge."

That seemed to resonate with her father, even if the rest of it didn't. "A little challenge is good for a body. It keeps the mind sharp."

Mom shook her head but continued to smile. "But more importantly, it will be something you do for you."

"It'll count as exercise and a hobby," Mira said. Even though saying it like that made it sound more like a business decision than something she was doing for fun.

She thought her mother might comment on that, but she seemed to be mulling it over, perhaps wondering whether to read more into it. She was spared further questions by the arrival of their entrees. Not ninety seconds in, Dad made his move. "And how are things at Pomme?"

"Really, Yves?" Mom needled him on principle, but they both expected it.

"What?" He shrugged, all innocence. "It's not like we wouldn't get around to it soon enough."

"Yes. Tomorrow. When we're spending the whole day there. Tonight is for family. I don't even know if our daughter is dating anyone." Mom turned to her with an expectant look, like it would be particularly helpful if she could whip out a new significant other to prove her point.

"Well…" She wanted to help, if for no other reason than it made her sad to think she was more comfortable talking about work than her love life. Unfortunately, the face that appeared front and center in her mind belonged to Dylan.

While the fact of it irritated her, between the meeting at Forbidden Fruit and their lunch at the Statler, she'd spent more time with Dylan than anyone else outside of work. And there was the matter of that dinner invitation. Not essential to the Cider Week planning by any means, but not technically a date. Even if she kind of wanted it to be.

"Yes?" Mom's eager look made her regret the dangling lead.

"No, no one at the moment. I've been really busy co-chairing Cider Week."

Mom looked slightly deflated, and Dad swirled his chardonnay. "Co-chair? Isn't that a demotion?" he asked.

Her father meant well, but he couldn't get out of his own way sometimes. She lifted her chin. "Actually, it's been really nice to share the responsibilities. And I've been paired up with the owner of one of the smaller, newer cideries. It's been great to get her perspective."

Mom clearly liked the sound of that. "That seems like a win-win. What have you learned?"

Leave it to her mother to slip into teacher mode. Better than is-she-single-and-your-type mode. "I'm thinking we might experiment with some smaller batch runs. Single varietals, maybe a rosé. That sort of thing."

Mom raised a brow and Dad frowned. "That's quite a leap while you're still getting your footing," he said.

There was no derision in his tone, but she bristled nonetheless. "My formal title might be less than a year old, but I've been doing the job for close to five."

"What's the appeal? What's the angle?" Mom asked. Although Pomme was her company, too, she never had the same possessiveness that her father did. Which came in handy.

"Craft cider is booming right now, especially in New York. I think we should try for a share of that market."

Dad's frown became a full scowl. "Are we losing market share?"

She hadn't planned on broaching the idea and didn't have the data she'd normally compile to back up her argument. Of course, this was barely an idea to begin with. More of a kernel. A seed she'd let Dylan plant. And now she was running with it and barely knew what she was talking about.

"Mira." Her father's scowl remained fixed.

"Sorry." She cleared her throat. "Our sales are steady, with slow growth. But they're not expanding at the same rate as cider consumption as a whole."

Dad folded his arms, in full business mode now. "How far off pace are we?"

"I don't have the exact numbers, but of course I'd run them. Give you a fully fleshed out proposal." Because even though she was COO, they still called the shots. The big ones at least.

"Is this something you want to do? Or something you believe the company should do?" Mom, more perceptive and also less stubborn, regarded her with curiosity.

Mira straightened her shoulders. For something she'd pitched on the fly, she was weirdly all in. "Both."

Mom seemed to like that answer. Dad narrowed his eyes. "Has Luis been needling you?"

"No. I don't think we're making the most of his talent, but I think he's made peace with the role of staying the course." She, apparently, had not.

Dad grumbled and Mom gave an affectionate smile.

"I'm not making a formal proposal, but I think we need to consider it if we want to stay current, stay relevant."

More grumbling from Dad. This time, Mom let out an exasperated sigh. "Yves, isn't that why we opened Pomme in the first place?"

Dad's concession was reluctant, but a concession. It made her realize how rarely that happened. Or maybe more accurately, how rarely she pushed for her own ideas. That truth remained with her for the rest of the meal and the drive back to their hotel. By the time she got home, her body was tired, but her mind hummed with possibility.

Gloria rubbed her legs, seeming to sense Mira's energy and deciding that meant it was time to play. She indulged them both, sitting on the floor cross-legged with Gloria's favorite feather on a stick. Did Dylan have a cat? Something told her Dylan was a dog person. Maybe she lived out in the country and had chickens and goats.

She shook her head. Silly thing to wonder. It didn't stop her from wondering, of course. Fortunately, tabbies didn't read minds and she could keep her wondering to herself.

She got ready for bed, but took her laptop with her, thinking she could do some research that would allow her to throw a more formal presentation together in the morning. While it loaded, she snagged her phone and realized she'd missed a slew of texts from Dylan.

Such a fail. I lost an entire batch of cider.

That was followed by an explanation, a caveat about the size of the batch, a joke about Schadenfreude, and wishes for a good evening. She felt bad having left the conversation hanging. After a brief internal debate about how late was too late to text someone who technically still fell into acquaintance-slash-business-associate territory, she drafted and sent a series of replies.

She certainly didn't expect Dylan to text back. Nor did she expect the small surge of delight when Dylan did. And when Dylan asked about the time with her parents.

She answered. Dylan replied with emojis, commentary, and even more questions. About work and family and completely random things that no one else asked her. *What's your favorite part of your job? Do you have siblings? What do you do for fun?*

She talked about seeing the new packaging she'd designed on a store shelf for the first time, the pros and cons of being an only child, and her foray back into dance classes. Dylan confessed there was a photo of her wearing a tutu somewhere in the deep recesses of her parents' basement. When she flipped the questions back on Dylan, Dylan told her all about her family's restaurant, her sister's eagerness to take over, and the bridal shower that would be consuming most of her upcoming weekend.

The next thing she knew, an hour had gone by and all she'd managed to do was chat with Dylan. It was silly really. Strangely easy. So unlike her. And, she realized, fun.

❖

Dylan avoided bridal showers as a matter of course, but this one was different. One, because it was her sister. Other than Rowan, there was no one on the planet she felt closer to. Two, because it was her sister and if she didn't, their mother would have her head. So she got up extra early on Saturday morning and made the drive to Buffalo instead of the cidery.

She arrived just in time for Mom to send her on a run for more ice but managed to get back before guests showed up. After proper hellos with her parents, she beelined for the backyard in search of the happy couple. Jason, having worked an overnight at the fire station, was still en route, but she found Emily arranging lawn chairs so guests didn't have to stay crammed inside.

When Emily spotted her, she bounded over with the energy of a little kid. "You're here."

She opened her arms and they had the kind of hug that warmed her from the inside. "Of course I'm here. I wouldn't pass up the chance to watch you squirm awkwardly at being the center of attention."

Emily swatted her arm. "I resemble that remark. So, what's new in the land of applohol?"

The word, which Emily had invented when she was fourteen and learned Dylan had started dabbling in cider, had stuck. And because Emily stood by it—even as a thirty-year-old woman—she smiled. "Another day, another bottle."

"Sure, sure."

"And you, my most favorite bride-to-be?"

Emily rolled her eyes at the description. "Don't say that. It makes me feel high maintenance."

Her sister was anything but. "No, no. You're thinking bridezilla."

"Ugh." Another eye roll. "Could you not?"

"You're nothing like a bridezilla. And I adore you. You know that, right?"

That got her an elbow to the ribs but then a hug. Emily let go and let out a sigh. "I miss you."

"I miss you, too, jerk face." Much like applohol, the childhood insult had stuck. Only now she meant it as a term of endearment.

"Butthead." Just like Emily's nickname for her.

"You know you and Jason can come visit me, too. I have a spare room and I'd let you sleep in the same bed, even before the wedding."

Emily cackled. She and Jason had been living together for the better part of a year. "We might take you up on it. No disrespect to Mom, but she's driving me up a tree."

Their mother took wedding planning very seriously. "That bad?"

"We spent three hours with the florist. Three. Hours. Other than a bouquet, I don't even care if we have flowers."

Dylan laughed. "Better you than me."

"Speaking of, I see you didn't even bring someone with you to this shindig. You are no help."

"It's not my fault I got dumped." She should have thought of Brianna, who she'd dated for several months and who she'd anticipated bringing to both this—her mother's brilliant idea for a Jack and Jill shower—and the wedding. But the face that appeared in her mind belonged to Mira.

Emily narrowed her eyes. "I'm pretty sure it's kind of your fault."

It kind of was. Brianna had been ready to move in together and she hadn't. In part because she'd only lived with one girlfriend prior to that, and it had ended very badly. But also because in her heart of hearts, she'd known Brianna wasn't the one. It seemed fairer to both of them to own that before taking things to the next level. "Yeah."

"Anyone new on the horizon?"

Had Mira not already been on her mind, she would have popped in then. "No."

"Ooh, quick denial. Methinks there must be more to the story."

She was spared an insincere denial by the arrival of one of Emily's high school friends and her husband. Dylan took the reprieve and hightailed inside to the corner of the kitchen that had been set up with drinks. She'd no sooner popped the cap on a bottle of summer ale than her mother slid in next to her.

"No date?" Mom asked, as casually as she might have commented on the weather.

"You know Brianna and I broke up."

Mom didn't miss a beat. "But that was in January, and this is July."

"And I've been kind of busy." Stupid busy, really. Though she always managed to make time for dating when there was a woman she wanted to date.

Mom wagged a finger. "Don't talk to me about busy."

It was a fair point. Her mother had helped run the restaurant, raised four kids, and gone back to school to finish her degree—all at the same time. "Fine. I've been distracted. I'm co-chairing Finger Lakes Cider Week this year. It's an amazing opportunity to boost our signal statewide."

Maternal pride trumped maternal meddling. "That's wonderful, honey."

"You'll never guess who my co-chair is."

"I'm sure I won't."

"The COO of Pomme d'Or. You know, the place you said I could get a job if Forbidden Fruit tanked after a year."

Mom beamed. "Look at you, running with the big dogs."

Pride had been the right lever to pull. Dylan spent the next ten minutes fielding questions about her role and how much visibility she'd get, along with what she and Rowan were planning for their in-house events. That got her safely to the gifts and games part of the shower. It all felt a bit het for her tastes, but better than the alternative of a girls-only fiasco and having women she barely knew dress each other—or her—in toilet paper wedding gowns.

She used the flurry of activity to catch up with her baby brother, Scott. Though with ten years as a firefighter under his belt, she could hardly call him a baby. "Did Mom give you a hard time about getting a girlfriend?" he asked.

She chuckled. "Obviously. You?"

"Well, I've been seeing someone for a couple of months, so it was more the 'why didn't you bring her?'"

"Why didn't you?"

Scott tipped his head toward the living room, where most of the guests were engaged in a rowdy rendition of what sounded like the newlywed game. "Have you met our family?"

She grimaced before grinning. "We're not all bad."

"Not bad at all." He shook his head. "Just, you know, a lot."

She couldn't argue. And even though they were talking about bringing girlfriends home, it made her wonder how Mira would get along with her relatives. Probably a little too loud, a little too blue collar, for her tastes. Especially given what she'd learned about Mira's parents. Money, yes, but also West Coast sophisticated. Dylan's middle class suburban roots couldn't hold a candle to that. Not that she wanted what Mira had. Even if it came with a nice financial cushion to fall back on.

"What about you? Seeing anyone?"

The question made her realize how silly it was to be thinking about Mira at all. "Not at the moment."

"Thank God for Emily, right?"

In addition to getting married first, Emily lived, breathed, and loved the restaurant. Even though their parents had never put any kind of formal pressure on their kids to take over, Emily wanting to made it easier for her and Scott to do their own thing. Middle kid or not, Emily held the title of golden child. Dylan clinked her beer bottle to Scott's. "I couldn't have said it better myself."

The rest of the party passed in a blur. She stuck around long enough to help clean up and convince her mother that she needed to work the following day and really shouldn't stay over. After the full round of good-byes, Emily offered to walk her out.

Since Dylan had parked on the street, they stood at the end of the driveway, like they had on countless mornings waiting for the school bus. Emily squeezed her tight. "Just to confirm we're not done with that conversation. You've got the hots for someone. I can tell and I want to know everything."

She squeezed Emily back. "I promise there's nothing to tell."

"I'll be the judge of that. I'm going to check with Jason and text you a couple of options for a visit. Probably before school starts and we lose the summer help."

"Name the day." Her conversation with Scott flashed through her mind. She gave Emily a light punch on the arm. "I'm really happy for you."

Emily jabbed a finger right in her chest. "I love it when you get all mushy, but it doesn't mean you're off the hook."

"I'm never off the hook with you and I wouldn't have it any other way. Love you, jerk face." She gave Emily another hug and headed for her truck before she got really mushy.

Emily called after her, "Love you, too, butthead. See you soon."

Emily went inside and Dylan sat for a moment before pulling away. She had this weird desire to text Mira, to check in and make sure the business part of the visit with her parents had gone okay. But even though they'd crossed the line into chatting about things not directly related to Cider Week, she hesitated. Were they friends now? They didn't feel like enemies, but friends was maybe a stretch. Especially since they seemed to be rocking that persistent, low-grade hum of energy that might be residual animosity, but could just as easily stem from sexual tension.

Was that a thing? She thought so, even if she didn't have much experience with it. She tended to go for easy relationships, and nothing about Mira felt easy. Save, perhaps, that nagging notion that it would be all too easy to kiss her.

CHAPTER NINE

Mira closed down her computer a little before five, gathering her things and stopping into Talise's office on her way out. "Do you need anything before I go?"

Talise's head swiveled from her computer, and she gave Mira an appraising stare. "Are you leaving at five o'clock like a normal human?"

"You say that like I work all hours. I'm usually out of here by six."

"Mm-hmm. With your laptop. Do you have your laptop?"

She patted the oversize Kate Spade bag slung over her shoulder. "As a matter of fact, I do."

Talise frowned. "That's too bad."

"I have dinner plans, though." The second she said it, she knew the moment of I-have-a-life smugness wouldn't be worth the teasing that ensued.

"Do tell."

"It's just a meeting with Dylan to do some Cider Week planning, but it's better than a salad with my computer at home."

"Just a meeting with Dylan." Talise's voice lilted with insinuation.

"Stop. What are we, in high school?"

"Nah. If I'm going there, I'm going all the way there. Middle school for the win." Talise hummed the k-i-s-s-i-n-g song.

"I'm leaving now." Because she wanted to be on time. Also because she'd given more than a passing thought to kissing Dylan and Talise absolutely did not need to know that.

"Okay, but if you do kiss, you have to tell me."

"Good night, Talise."

"Good night, baby cakes."

Mira offered a wave and headed down the back stairs, darting to her car between the drops that had begun to fall from the monochromatic gray sky. After situating herself and queuing up her favorite women in business podcast, she started the drive down to Seneca Hill.

Between the rain and the fact that it was a Tuesday, the parking lot at the Cider House was nearly empty. Not that she'd complain. While crowds were good for business, she appreciated the vibe of a quiet restaurant. It was a short dash to the door, but she ducked under an umbrella anyway, not wanting to look like a drowned rat. In general. Obviously. Not because she was meeting Dylan.

Inside, Dylan was already waiting. She managed to look cool, collected, and perfectly casual. Also, dry. It shouldn't put her on edge. But as she shook her dripping umbrella and decided against shoving it into her bag, a wave of self-consciousness swept over her. She patted her hair for errant curls and resisted the urge to smooth her dress.

"Hi." Dylan's greeting was as easy as her posture.

"Hi." She straightened her shoulders and tried not to look as fidgety as she felt. "I hope you haven't been waiting long."

"Only a few minutes. I have a habit of running early."

Not a trait she would have ascribed to Dylan before they started spending time together. "I'll have to remember that. You have me feeling late."

"You're right on time."

It could have been a come-on and she found herself a little disappointed that it wasn't. "Thanks."

"Looks like it's really coming down now."

"Yes, I seem to have timed my arrival at exactly the wrong moment."

Dylan looked her up and down. "It's probably not professional to say you can pull off the damp and frazzled look, is it?"

It most definitely was not. It was about as unprofessional as the way her pulse ticked up at Dylan's slow, appreciative assessment of her. "Well, since being either of those things isn't very professional to begin with, I'll let it slide."

"Oh, good." Dylan smiled. "I like to think we've moved into friendly territory anyway."

Had they? She wouldn't have used that word, but it fit. Even if attracted but in denial about it felt slightly more accurate.

The hostess appeared and saved her having to come up with a suitable reply. A moment later, she sat across from Dylan at a cozy corner table overlooking the lake. She remained partial to the view from Pomme, of course, but this one was nothing to sneeze at, even with the low clouds and haze of rain.

She ordered a glass of cider, more out of habit than anything else. She liked staying on top of what other producers were putting out. When Dylan did as well, she couldn't help but wonder if Dylan's motivations were the same.

"So, how was your time with the parents?"

Her thoughts shifted from the menu in front of her to the conversation over dinner the first night of their visit. The one where she'd gone on and on about innovation and taking chances. The one that felt like Dylan had crept into her subconscious and was doing the talking more than she was. "It was good."

Dylan's eyes narrowed briefly. "Okay, not feeling the small talk. That's cool. I was thinking of trying the cast iron mac and cheese. But I'm totally up for sharing if you're into that."

"Sorry. I didn't mean to be short."

Dylan lifted both hands. "No need to explain. Family dynamics can be weird. Or maybe you're uber private. Feel free to ask me all about my sister's bridal shower if you want to change the subject."

Was she overly private? She wasn't a share everything type, sure, but she considered herself good enough at conversation that she could deflect gracefully. "I'd love to hear about the shower, but it's fine. I'm fine. It was a nice visit. And we discussed some ideas for new products and marketing campaigns."

Dylan nodded slowly, like she wanted to ask more but couldn't decide if she should.

"I've been thinking about a new product line, and we were discussing options." Which sounded better than saying she impulsively pitched something she'd never really considered in a moment of professional—or was it personal?—claustrophobia.

"Oh, like what?"

She could play the trade secret card. Or admit her plans were half-baked at best. But for some reason, she didn't want to. Plus the fact that she'd been the one to bring it up. "I think Pomme should get into the small batch game, play with single varietals and micro regions."

"You do?"

The surprise in Dylan's voice held more enthusiasm than her father's had. But instead of making her feel better, it made her wonder what the hell she'd been thinking. "I'm not sure it's the right fit for our brand, but it's a trend we've been ignoring."

Dylan's expression registered somewhere between a cringe and scowl.

"What?"

"I'd rather not think about something I pour my heart and soul into as a trend."

She resisted the urge to roll her eyes. "It's not a bad word. It's a statement of fact. And it's why both of us are in business."

Dylan ran a hand over the back of her neck and told herself to relax. Mira wasn't trying to insult her. She merely had a very different relationship to cider. Hell, she had a completely different worldview. Seeing things differently didn't mean they had to be at odds about them. "You're right."

Mira smirked. "Why do I get the feeling you don't say that very often?"

She mimicked the face. "Okay, pot."

Mira pressed her lips together, but then broke into a genuine smile. "Takes one to know one?"

She hadn't thought she and Mira had a whole lot in common, but stubborn seemed to be a shared trait. In her book, there were worse things. "All right. So, you basically want to be more like me. I could give you some pointers."

"My guy has been crafting cider since before you knew what an apple was."

As much as Dylan liked to push the envelope, she didn't thumb her nose at the wisdom and expertise of the generation that came before her. She wouldn't be where she was without their dedication and willingness to take risks. "Touché."

"Honestly, he's always after us to try something new."

"Us?"

"I'm COO, but my parents still have executive control. They trust me, but mostly to keep the ship afloat and the course steady."

"Ah." Sounded dreadful to her, even if it came with deep pockets and space to play. Hell, especially in that case.

"Not to be egotistical or anything, but it's what I'm good at."

"I have no doubt." She didn't, either. In a perfect world, she'd have Mira handling the logistics so she could focus all her attention on what she really cared about—making cider. Well, not Mira exactly. Someone like her. Like Audrey, but with responsibilities for marketing and distribution and stuff beyond keeping the books.

"Anyway. I think we might dabble. I'm trying to decide if we could pull off something new for the reparations package."

She didn't know whether to be impressed or incredulous. "As in, starting it now?"

"I know, I know. It's rushing it."

Rushing it wasn't the half of it. Where did Mira think she was going to find single varietal juice at this point in the year? Which said nothing of the volatile aromas and flavonoids that would be lost along the way. Not that it was any of her business. "If you're even considering it, you must have some damn impressive suppliers."

Mira smiled. "I do, but I know what you mean. Maybe a unique blend more than a single varietal at this time of year. Have you ever done a rosé?"

If it felt like a setup, Dylan brushed it aside. "As a matter of fact, I have."

Mira's eyes lit up with genuine enthusiasm. "You have?"

"Well, technically, *am* not *have*. Present tense. My first batch is scheduled for disgorging and corking next week." A project that had been in the making since Rowan planted their first Dolgo and Geneva Crab trees in the orchard adjacent to the cidery. They'd wanted to play with the color the vibrant red flesh brought to the party in addition to the bright acidity.

"Did you grow the apples yourself? Are they as gorgeous as the pictures I've seen?"

It was one thing to know something Mira didn't know, especially about the nuances of making cider. It was another thing entirely to have something Mira didn't. Something she wanted. "Rowan deserves the credit for growing, but yes. We planted a few dozen trees, hoping to eventually yield enough fruit for a true rosé. Last fall was the first time we harvested enough to make that happen."

Mira nodded slowly, enthusiasm giving way to something more calculating. "You're not putting it in the reparations package, are you?"

She wasn't, but the idea of Mira throwing together an entirely new cider in three months bugged her, so her instinct was to let Mira squirm. "Afraid of a little friendly competition?"

Something in Mira's eyes shifted. Whether she was offended by the insinuation or considered the very idea of competition ludicrous, Dylan couldn't tell. She opened her mouth and closed it before saying, "No, that's not what I meant."

Irritation or not, Dylan's good nature kicked in. "I was kidding."

It vanished as quickly as it appeared, but Dylan caught the flash of self-consciousness. "Right. Of course." Mira's chin lifted. "I just don't want the package to feel redundant."

"We wouldn't want that." Any lingering annoyance faded. In its place, a somewhat unexpected delight in throwing Mira ever so slightly off her game. "Don't worry. I'm going with our Ellis Bitter I think. It was a small harvest last year, so a limited run. I think it will help nudge our small but passionate club subscribers to order the package."

Mira frowned. "Hmm."

"What?"

"I guess I figured you'd go with one of your more popular ciders. Leverage the exposure to potentially new customers."

Dylan lifted a shoulder, no longer sure if they were teasing each other or having a serious business conversation. "Oh, I think it will do that, too. But the point of the reparations project is to raise money, right?"

Mira sighed. "Yes. And to raise awareness of the causes we're going to support."

"So, what's the problem?" Because even though she couldn't see it, Mira definitely had one.

Mira straightened her shoulders and did this little hair toss that, under other circumstances, would be sexy as hell. Even under these circumstances, it was pretty damn sexy. "No problem."

Dylan didn't believe her, but their server chose that exact moment to check in. Of course, they'd been so busy talking, neither of them had decided what to order. Mira begged another couple of minutes, and they focused their attention on the menus. Dylan looked up to find Mira staring at her. "Now what?"

This time Mira smirked. Again, sexy, even if she shouldn't be noticing. "So, you're getting the mac and cheese?"

It came with chorizo, charred poblano peppers, and the promise of heartburn before the night was through. "I might regret it later, but yes."

"Regret?"

"When I hit thirty, my ability to eat whatever I want whenever I want, without consequences, disappeared. I'm told it's quite common, but I'm bitter and, on occasion, in denial."

Mira laughed. Rich and sexy and carefree—it made Dylan imagine what it must be like to spend time with Mira completely out of work mode. "I think we have that in common."

"The tendency toward heartburn or the bitterness about it?"

"Yes."

Okay, see? This easy, fun side of Mira was nice. She knew better than to say so but made a mental note to try to get Mira in this mood before they had to do serious work or make big decisions. "So, I'm guessing you're the kind of woman who makes more sensible decisions."

"Actually," Mira tipped her head, "I was wondering if you might consider sharing."

Pretty much the furthest thing from her mind in that moment was going sharesies. Sure, they'd done that at the Statler, but it hadn't been a choice. Doing it on purpose was the sort of thing you did with close friends. Or on a date. "I could be persuaded. What are you offering?"

Mira made a show of running her finger up and down the menu. "My default would be the beet and goat cheese salad. Getting some greens to balance all that richness. But something tells me you're anti salad."

"What makes you think that?"

Mira's eyes narrowed before she offered a friendly shrug. "You have a bit of a bro vibe."

Mira didn't make it sound like an insult, but Dylan got the distinct feeling it was. "I'm not a bro. I am, however, allergic to beets, so I'd go for the spinach with strawberries and bleu cheese."

Mira bit her lip as she smiled. "I'm open to that. And I stand corrected."

If they'd been on a date, Dylan would have delightfully picked up each and every signal Mira dropped. Since they weren't, she told herself to simply relax and enjoy the ride. Easier said than done. "Then it sounds like we're decided."

They jumped into business first, reviewing the updated draft schedule of the week and Mira's suggestions for the run of show for the gala. Dylan shared her progress on the reparations project, including the participants so far, package options, and price points. Satisfied she'd gotten the project off the ground, she readily handed over responsibility for the marketing materials to the person who had a dedicated marketing expert.

But even with all the decisions and details they ironed out, personal anecdotes and genuine curiosity about each other seemed to weave their way seamlessly into the conversation. Mira asked about the shower, and about her family more generally. She seemed fascinated by the idea of growing up in a restaurant, of the years spent washing dishes and waiting tables.

"Is that why you gave up dance?" Mira asked, clearly teasing her.

"Oh, no. My mother would have been thrilled to have me stick it out." She whipped out her phone and pulled up the screenshot of the photo she'd gone out of her way to find. It was even better than she remembered—full leotard and tutu, lopsided pigtails, ratty sneakers, and look of pure disdain. "But even she had to admit it wasn't a look or an art form I could pull off."

Mira looked at the picture and let out a snort of laughter before covering it with a cough and apologizing.

"I think I'd be offended if you didn't laugh." She tucked her phone back in her pocket.

Mira chuckled. "Did she make you suffer for long?"

"Fortunately, no. My sister embraced it, at least when she was little, and I got to do little league instead."

"That seems much more up your alley."

"For sure. I love that you're getting back to it, though. I confess I throw most of my energy into the cidery and have let things like hobbies languish."

Mira let out a sigh. "I'm familiar with the affliction."

For all the telling herself it was a professional meeting, Dylan couldn't help feeling like it was a particularly enjoyable first date. Or second. Maybe third? Whatever the number, definitely a date.

When the check came, Mira snagged it, claiming the write-off and promising Dylan could get the next one. Any inkling she might have to argue took a back seat to thinking how much she'd like there to be a next one. Outside, the rain had stopped, leaving the evening decidedly cooler. A nearly full moon poked through the dissipating clouds. It gave her a sense of the air being alive, something she associated with the promise and potential of seasons changing, even if it happened to be the middle of summer. "Nice night."

Mira smiled. "It is. It'll make for a pleasant drive home."

The practicality of the comment made her wonder if Mira gave any thought to the energy of air after a storm. If she ever drove with the windows down to soak it all in. "For sure."

"And since I'm going home to myself, I can put the windows down and not worry about my hair turning into a bird's nest."

Dylan chuckled at getting such a delightful answer to the question she hadn't voiced aloud.

"You laugh now. You should see my hair after."

A wind-tossed Mira would be beyond sexy. But like so many of her thoughts this evening, it leapt out of business and right over friendly territory, so she kept it to herself. "I think it's a reasonable price to pay on a night like this."

Mira nodded but didn't speak. They walked slowly, stopping between their respective vehicles as though by design. Mira looked at Dylan. "Thanks for meeting me. This was nice."

Had they been on a real date, the comment would have registered tepid at best. Yet it strangely made what was ostensibly a business dinner feel a hell of a lot like a date. "It was. Thanks for doing dinner instead of lunch."

Mira glanced at her feet before returning her gaze to Dylan's face. "Of course."

Business dinner or not, every cell in Dylan's body read the moment as ripe for a kiss. She knew better but damn. She extended her hands and sort of opened her arms. "Would it be awkward to hug?"

Mira somehow looked relieved and disappointed at the same time. "Not at all."

She expected the embrace to be brief if not awkward, but it was neither. Mira lingered long enough to leave her wondering if maybe she should have gone for a kiss after all. And when Mira did pull back, she didn't go all the way, creating a proximity that Dylan could only describe as electric.

"Miss, you forgot your umbrella." Their server's voice, the crunch of his shoes on gravel as he crossed the parking lot toward them, broke the moment.

Dylan shifted back immediately, but somehow a fraction of a second slower than Mira.

"Oh, thank you so much," Mira said.

"Not a problem. Glad I caught you. Have a good night."

The server returned to the restaurant as quickly as he'd emerged. Mira's gaze followed him, and she seemed almost reluctant to look at Dylan. "So, I'll be in touch?"

Not a dismissal but so totally a dismissal. "Sounds good."

"Okay. Take care, then. Safe drive home."

Dylan nodded, but Mira was already retreating to her car and didn't see. "You, too."

By the time Dylan got in her truck, Mira's BMW was pulling out of the parking lot. She started her engine and sat, wondering if she'd imagined the whole thing. No, her mind didn't play those kinds of tricks on her. Fleeting or not, they'd had a moment. The brief contact left her skin tingling and the rest of her even more revved up than before.

Whether or not Mira felt the same was a mystery. And whether the hug solidified a friendly vibe or drew even more attention to the unspoken chemistry between them remained to be seen.

Chapter Ten

Mira brushed a fingertip over her lips and closed her eyes. Just like in her car the night before—and in the shower after she got home and even after she'd gotten into bed—she imagined Dylan's mouth on hers.

She wasn't usually one to relive a kiss. To be fair, she could count the number of truly memorable kisses in her life on one hand. Still. She didn't daydream, even about those. Maybe she could embrace this as a healthy departure. Letting her imagination take center stage and seeing what sparks ensued. Which was all well and good, but with one glaring problem.

She and Dylan hadn't kissed. They'd hugged. Like friends. Only not like friends at all.

She sighed. Would Dylan have kissed her if they hadn't been interrupted? Would she have kissed Dylan? On the drive home, she told herself it was better they hadn't. Her body had disagreed, but she wasn't in the habit of letting her body run the show. And now, in the light of day, she wasn't sure. Because even though it wouldn't have been the mature or professional thing to do, the longing to see what it would be like hadn't left.

And with that longing? A gnawing sense that in her rush to be rational and responsible in all things, she'd made decisions and settled for things that weren't all that satisfying. In her love life. In her professional life. Even her hobbies. Pretty much in all aspects of her life, she played it safe. But at what cost?

"You know, if I keep catching you daydreaming, I might have to tell your supervisor." Talise strode into her office and took a seat without further greeting or invitation.

"I'll have you know I was questioning my life choices, not daydreaming."

She'd meant to be funny, but Talise frowned. "Oh."

"Not in a dramatic, midlife crisis sort of way."

Talise pointed at her, making little circles with her finger. "You're way too young for a midlife crisis. Don't even use that phrase."

"Fine. I'm not in crisis is the point I was trying to make. Midlife is just semantics."

Talise shook her head. "Saying midlife is never just semantics."

She'd never balked at getting older, but Talise practically had a meltdown when she'd turned thirty. And even though they were both still south of thirty-five, Talise had already begun to lament the prospect of forty. "Age doesn't determine anything you don't want it to."

Talise let out a humph. "Says the woman who has her life entirely figured out."

It was her turn to frown. She'd never been the sort to brag about having her shit together, but she'd felt that way pretty much since college. Career, industry, company—all laid out before her in a tidy path. Sure, she wanted to fall in love and probably get married, but since she didn't have that burning desire to have children, it never felt like a rush. Now? Now a kiss that hadn't even happened had her questioning everything. "I'm pretty sure I don't."

"Well, yes. Because you're not an arrogant asshole. You're open to new things and personal growth and all that." Talise raised her arm and made a large, circular sweeping motion with her hand.

"I appreciate you saying that." Even if it felt glaringly untrue. Impulsive new product lines notwithstanding.

"So, who pissed you off?"

"What? No one. I'm not pissed off." An argument weakened by the snippiness in her voice and the frown line she could literally feel between her eyebrows.

"You don't question your life choices because you're in a good mood. Something set you off." Talise got up to close the door and sat once again "You're not required to share that sort of thing with your employees, but you should probably clue in your best friend."

Talise managed to look utterly sincere and smugly satisfied at the same time. Mira might not like it, but she respected it. "Spending all this time with Dylan has me feeling like a worker bee, buzzing around and tending the hive. Getting the job done. But to what end?"

"Yikes."

"I know. I'm being dramatic. I'm thirty-three years old and I've only been officially in charge for a few months. I need time to settle in. On top of that, taking over a successful company is way more of an accomplishment than trying to turn things into the Mira show."

Talise nodded. "Aha. You pissed yourself off."

Had she? Sort of. At the very least, she was getting on her own nerves. About work and about Dylan.

"Worse, really, than someone else doing it. Because you don't even get the satisfaction of your own righteous indignation," Talise said.

She laughed. Talise was one of the smartest and most straightforward people she knew. And she was right. "Yeah."

"Is this when I ask you about spending so much time with Dylan?"

She could say she wasn't, but she'd just said she was. Similarly, she could say she needed to, but Talise knew perfectly well that she didn't. "I didn't want to like her, but I think I do."

"Like her as a fellow cider maker you might learn and get inspiration from? Or like as someone whose pants you'd like to get into?"

"Ha ha."

Talise angled her head back and forth. "Not that those things are mutually exclusive."

"Could you not? It isn't like that." Only it totally was.

Talise didn't even dignify that with a response.

"I mean, finding her attractive does complicate things, but only because it means she pops into my mind more than she should. Which makes me think about the other stuff, too. And it all sucks." Since she was already throwing a tantrum, she folded her arms for good measure.

"Aw, baby cakes. That might be the most honest thing you've ever said to me."

She made a face and let out a whine.

Talise tutted. "I know. Feelings. You're not a fan."

She wasn't a robot. Or, as one woman she dated so crassly put it, an ice queen. She simply valued logic and reason and keeping things simple. Was that really too much to ask? "I don't mind useful feelings."

"You know that's not how feelings work, right?" Talise asked, in a way that felt more genuine than rhetorical. "Or maybe more accurately, feelings are useful but not always in ways you'd like or find convenient."

She did know. She'd minored in psychology and learned more than she'd bargained for about defense mechanisms and coping strategies and the like. Most of the time, it helped her keep perspective, a nice tidy distance between herself and anything that had the potential to get too messy. Why wasn't that working this time?

"You think you're above all that," Talise said.

So, off her game and an open book. Great. "I'm not above it, I simply don't have time for it."

"Wait, does that mean you're shutting down your quarter-life crisis or embracing it?" There was a gleam of humor in Talise's eyes, but curiosity, too.

"I haven't decided yet." Mira let herself pout.

"You know what? I think that counts as a win."

"It does?" It sure as hell didn't feel like one.

"Absolutely. You're being open to the universe. Good things come to those who open themselves to the universe." Talise spread her arms wide.

"Like you do?"

Talise winked. "Don't knock it till you've tried it."

Mira folded her arms. "Are you referring to sleeping with anyone and everyone or something else?"

"Uh-uh." Talise wagged a finger. "You sleep with anyone. I might be poly, but I am squarely in the sleeps with women camp."

They'd had this argument before. Well, not really an argument. More a friendly debate about whether monogamous and bi made for more options or lesbian and poly. The most recent installment happened only a week ago, when Talise shared her plans to go out with a couple looking to open their relationship. The whole conversation had left her feeling like a stick in the mud. Or, at the very least, boring as hell.

"You gonna sleep with Dylan?" Talise asked.

Her ego said maybe, and her body held firm in pretty please territory. Fortunately, her heart abstained in matters like this, so her brain got the deciding vote. "Absolutely not."

❖

Rowan strode into the production room looking perfectly happy and completely relaxed. "Good morning."

Dylan narrowed her eyes. The singsong tone giving Rowan away more than anything else. "You got laid this morning."

Rowan nodded and didn't even pretend not to be smug. "I did."

"I miss those days."

"Speaking of, how was your date last night?"

At this point, it seemed silly to argue it hadn't been a date. Or at least something close to. "Pretty good."

Rowan's shoulders slumped in either disappointment or exasperation. "Seriously? That's all I'm going to get?"

"I don't know. It was nice. Good food, good conversation. We barely argued. And we had a moment at the end."

Rowan looked incredulous. "A moment?

"Yeah. We hugged and it, you know, lingered." She opted not to mention being interrupted.

Incredulous morphed into shocked. "Lingered."

"Yeah, lingered. It went on for a few seconds." A few really fantastic seconds.

"You embraced, you mean. Embracing is more than hugging. Embracing is practically kissing."

She'd spent the entire drive home and the better part of the night thinking about it. But then she'd tucked it neatly into the box of things about Mira that didn't make sense. It was a pretty big box. "There was no kissing."

"Uh, but you could have kissed. You were obviously thinking about a kiss. That's a big deal."

"Small deal at best. As opposed to actually kissing. That," she paused for effect, "is a big deal."

Rowan folded her arms. "I'm pretty sure you said the exact opposite when I almost kissed Audrey."

"That was different."

"How?"

So many ways. Right? "You'd been zinging off each other for weeks. Attraction, feelings, the whole deal. It was pretty damn inevitable by the time you got around to it."

"And you haven't been zinging off Mira?"

Zinging wasn't the half of it. If Rowan had seen them together, no doubt the teasing slash harassing would be off the charts. "Well, she's uptight and I'm not, so if you want to call that zinging."

"You're really not seeing any parallels here?"

Arguing that Audrey hadn't been uptight in the beginning—or that she and Rowan hadn't had a bit of that classic love/hate thing going on—would be disingenuous. Still. Rowan and Audrey were made for each other. Maybe they hadn't been willing to see it at first, but she had.

Oh, God. Was she being Rowan in this scenario? Clueless and stubborn about what was right in front of her? No. Even if she sparked with Mira, she couldn't imagine two people being less suited for each other. And even if she set that part aside and went for a hookup, she'd be left with an endless supply of awkward run-ins at Cider Association meetings and events. Not that she couldn't be friendly after, but she had a feeling Mira didn't operate that way. The whole thing had big mess written all over it.

Rowan punched her lightly on the arm. "I'm dying to know what sort of rabbit holes you're going down right now."

"What makes you think I'm going down rabbit holes?"

Rowan raised a brow.

"Fine. I am."

"Thank you. I don't mind when you argue with me, but that was insulting to my basic powers of observation."

Dylan rolled her eyes.

Rowan grinned. "So? Were you at kissing, dating, sex, or wedding bells?" Rowan might be her best friend, but she could be as annoying as hell sometimes.

"I was thinking about the awkward seeing each other at meetings and functions after it ends badly," Dylan said.

"Oof. When did you become such a cynic?"

"I'm not a cynic." She was simply smart enough to know that indulging her attraction to Mira was bound to bite her in the ass.

"Disagreeable, too." Rowan made a tsking sound and shook her head.

"What did you want, again?"

"Uh, you asked me to help you choose the cider for the reparations package."

Oh, right. She'd been so busy being defensive, she'd forgotten that part. "I was thinking about the Ellis Bitter."

Rowan nodded slowly. "It's a pretty small batch. We were going to put it in the fall cider club boxes, but we don't have to."

"I think it would be a fantastic way to show off what we do," Dylan said.

"And then we could introduce Ernestine's Orchard with the club boxes."

They'd decided to name the inaugural run of rosé after Audrey's aunt, the woman who'd befriended Rowan and bequeathed them the orchard that accounted for more than half their annual harvest. "Exactly."

Rowan sighed. "I wish we'd thought to name a cider after her before she passed away."

"Yeah, but she would have hated it if we'd done it when she was alive."

That got a chuckle. "She would have."

"So, we do it now and hope that from whatever great beyond is currently graced with her presence, she can see it and get a kick out of it."

Rowan let out a sigh and smiled a melancholy smile. "Yeah."

It wasn't like they didn't still talk about Ernestine. Enough anecdotes and quips had permeated the collective consciousness of Forbidden Fruit that she remained a fixture even after passing. Still. They didn't often talk about the deeper stuff. About missing her. Dylan lifted her chin in Rowan's direction. "You okay?"

Rowan took a minute before she answered. "I mean, mostly. It's just...there are things I wish she could see. Like the tasting room or how much Audrey has embraced farm life. Or that Audrey and I ended up together after all."

She felt that way about her grandmother. Beatrice Miller had been a force, running the bar at the family restaurant until her reluctant retirement at the ripe old age of ninety-two. She'd been one of the reasons Dylan started dabbling in cider in the first place. "She knows. Somehow, cosmically or from heaven or someplace I can't even wrap my head around, she knows. And she's really fucking happy for you."

Rowan nodded. "You're right."

"I do love it when you say that," Dylan said.

"Well, I figure it's the least I can do since you're not getting it from any of the other women in your life."

Dylan feigned a haughty expression. "I'll have you know my mother thinks I'm right about almost everything. Except how often I visit."

"That's sad, dude."

She shrugged. "Hey, I take it where I can get it."

Rather than teasing her further, Rowan bumped her shoulder. "Don't we all."

Dylan sighed. She might try to keep relationships simple, but smart, opinionated women were her thing. She couldn't help it and for the most part, she didn't want to. That was the problem, really. Mira was shaping up to be exactly that sort of woman, and Dylan's attraction to her was ramping up by the day. But lingering hug or no, she had the feeling Mira's penchant for propriety and self-control would win out above all else. Which meant she was left to her own devices and a vastly increased likelihood she'd get herself into trouble.

Chapter Eleven

How would you feel about having a shadow for a day?
Dylan had read Mira's text probably a hundred times by now. Along with the ones that followed: one asking if she could spend an afternoon watching and learning how Dylan approached cider making, one offering a marketing consult in exchange, and then several ironing out the details to make both happen. Rowan had teased her; Audrey had raised an eyebrow before giving a knowing smile. It still seemed slightly surreal. And yet it was happening today.

She got to the cidery early, wanting to take care of a few mundane tasks before Mira's arrival. She also wanted to tidy and set up some specific things she thought Mira might appreciate and enjoy—sans audience—only to find Rowan poking around her tool closet. "Aren't you supposed to be out in the field today?"

Rowan emerged, a refractometer in one hand and a tube of pH test strips in the other. "Trying to get rid of me?"

"Yes." She could say that because it was Rowan. And also because she didn't worry about Rowan sticking around just to mess with her. Though maybe she should.

"I'm not sure I should leave you two unchaperoned," Rowan said as she tucked implements into the canvas messenger bag she took with her to the orchards.

"Well, I'm sure I don't want an audience. Besides, you have work to do."

Rowan's eyes gleamed. "I do."

She loved that Rowan could happily spend hours driving around, tromping up random hills and down various dirt roads, just to check on their favorite foraging sites. She didn't mind doing those things as part of the harvest, but the constant vigilance it required to test sugar levels and acidity and determine the exact right time to harvest left her impatient and cranky. Not that she minded doing the exact same thing with the contents of a fermentation tank. Which Rowan, of course, detested. One more reason they were a good team. "Well, you better get on it then."

Rowan did a final check of the contents of her bag and closed it. "I'm getting. You know, you're not very subtle."

"Neither are you. Now scram." She made a shooing gesture with both hands.

Rowan headed to the side door but turned. "Don't do anything I wouldn't do."

Dylan folded her arms. "I've literally walked in on you and Audrey making out in the middle of the production room."

"Exactly." Rowan winked and ducked out without further comment.

She scowled at the door as it swung closed before snarkily mumbling, "Don't do anything I wouldn't do."

The problem was that it didn't take much effort at all to imagine kissing Mira between the fermentation tanks. Or maybe up against the table they used to box up cases for distribution. Hell, she'd imagined kissing Mira enough times that she could picture it in pretty much any setting. But for all that Mira had essentially invited herself over for the day, she had no idea if Mira felt the same.

She was spared further stewing by the sound of tires in the gravel parking lot outside. Since Clarissa was already there to set up for their opening at noon, it had to be Mira. She headed for the main entrance, the one in the tasting room, rather than the side door she and Rowan used to come and go. She flipped the deadbolt and opened it to find Mira, hands on hips, studying the patio and lawn.

"Good morning."

Mira turned with what appeared to Dylan to be a knowing smile. "Good morning. You know, you have a great setup here. I didn't really notice it last time."

"We wanted to expand our capacity without the cost of expanding the building. It has seasonal limits, obviously, but it's helped us become more of a destination than a stop along the way. Especially when we bring in food trucks and live music." Mira hadn't asked, but it was hard not to brag, at least a little.

"You do that?"

"Only on Fridays so far, but we're hoping to expand. You don't?" She hadn't meant it as a jab, but it sort of came out that way.

Mira didn't seem offended. "The restaurant is open, but we do so many weddings, there's not a lot of wiggle room for less formal events."

It made her wonder which brought in more revenue in the long run. Of course, Pomme handled their own catering, so that made a difference. Not that she had a burning desire to get into that game—the catering or the wedding. "Makes sense."

"So, I wanted to start by saying thank you again for having me for the day. I know I basically invited myself."

She had, but Dylan hadn't minded. Partially so she could show off, partially because she wanted Mira to see another side of cider. To see Mira get excited about the cider itself and not just the bottom line. But also, if she was being honest, she simply wanted to spend the day with Mira. "Nerding out about cider is basically my favorite thing to do. No arm twisting required."

Mira's unguarded smile made Dylan's pulse trip. "Well, I'm still grateful."

"So, what would you really like to see and do? You've already had the grand tour."

Mira hesitated, as though choosing her words carefully. "I guess I'd like to learn your approach to small batch cider. How you decide what to run as a single varietal versus a blend, how you ensure the apples you get yield the flavor profile you want."

It was the heart of what she did and, in many ways, what set her and cider makers like her apart from places like Pomme, whose offerings year to year were steady and similar, if not identical. "I think the first step is to accept that quality is the bar, not consistency."

"Say more."

It was her turn to smile. "I'd rather show you."

"Well, then, lead the way."

Rather than repeat the tour from Mira's first visit, she brought Mira directly to the table where she'd staged a blending and sampling area. Bottles and beakers with everything from a quince-apple blend to the pommeau she'd begun to age in bourbon barrels lined the table. "This is everything we have in process and will put out this year, plus a couple of last year's thrown in for comparison."

Mira's eyes went wide. "You didn't have to go to this much trouble."

She bumped Mira's shoulder lightly with her own. Like doing so proved she could be casual and friendly. Whether she was trying to prove that to Mira or to herself, she didn't know. But as nonchalant as the contact should have been, a crackle of energy zapped through her, and casual was the absolute last word she'd use to describe it.

It happened again when their hands brushed reaching for the same bottle. And when Mira grabbed her arm in delight over a perry that accidentally got a third fermentation and turned out all the better for it. "I can't believe you didn't make more of this," Mira said.

Dylan tried and failed to ignore the tingling along her skin. "It was an off year for that batch of trees. We were lucky to harvest the pears we did."

Mira shook her head. "Do you think you'll be able to replicate it this season? If you could scale up production, it would sell like hotcakes."

"We'll try the method again, even if doing it on purpose will be kind of fussy and expensive. It's a wetter summer, though. It'll be a different starting point so who knows what the end result will be."

"It's so much riskier than blending for consistency, but I'm starting to understand the potential for reward." Mira lifted a hand. "Just don't tell my father I said that."

That single comment said so much about the Pomme business model and answered so many questions about how much Yves still pulled the strings. "It's not for everyone, but we think it's worth it."

Mira nodded slowly and Dylan could practically see her wheels turning. "Yeah."

"Speaking of, I thought we'd end with an experimental tasting."

Mira raised a brow. "Experimental tasting?"

"We're about ready to roll out a couple of this year's ciders, but they need a little, you know, quality control."

"Ah."

"Is sampling the goods frowned upon at Pomme?" She meant it in a teasing way, though it wouldn't surprise her if the answer was yes.

"Luis, he's our master cider maker, handles most of that. I'm sure not a batch goes to bottle that he hasn't tried a dozen times." Mira frowned. "Or, rather, a batch of bottles goes out. I know there's a second fermentation in the bottle that makes the cider what it is. He samples that, too."

"I know what you meant." Though the hurried explanation seemed to be a moment of vulnerability Mira hadn't shown so far.

"Okay. Good. I do join him sometimes, but it's more high-level stuff. Picking up on the subtle variations of each year's blend so I can work with my marketing team on the ad copy and communications strategy."

Dylan made a face but couldn't help it.

"You'd do well not to turn your nose up at marketing."

"I don't turn my nose up at it. It just isn't my number one priority. Making cider is."

Mira sighed, clearly unimpressed with the answer, and probably the trace of righteousness that had crept into her tone, too. "Does it make the top ten?"

"I'm going to plead the fifth and ply you with cider."

Mira gave her a once-over. "I won't argue, but I'm not going to forget this conversation. Maybe I'll manage to win you over when you come for that consult."

Most days, she'd rather leave the marketing to their twenty-year-old intern. But the prospect of spending another day with Mira appealed on multiple levels. Even if the tables were turned and Mira got to play the expert. "Deal."

❖

Mira studied the glasses Dylan had poured, relieved neither Talise nor her father could be a fly on the wall. Her father would balk at fraternizing so intimately with the competition. And Talise would tease her mercilessly about none of this having a thing to do with cider, or with competition. Though the thought of competition got her thinking. She moved her finger back and forth over the glasses. "Which of these are you submitting to this year's cider awards?"

Dylan gave her a suspicious look, though her eyes held mirth. "I'm pretty sure I'm not supposed to tell you that."

She folded her arms. "What, exactly, do you think I would do with that information?"

Dylan shrugged, the look on her face suggesting she enjoyed the back and forth as much as Mira did.

"I think you should go with one of the rosés." She pointed to the glasses in question, one the color of apple blossoms and the other reminiscent of raspberries.

"And why is that?"

"Because I decided to roll out a rosé too, and we could go head-to-head." Dylan had been joking about competition when they'd been talking about the reparations package, but a real competition had its appeal. Especially if it involved both of them being out of their comfort zone.

"Um."

Sure, a part of her remained unconvinced a rosé cider would be taken seriously by anyone not in the party bus or bachelorette party crowd. The pink cider boom a few years prior had played out like a white zinfandel redux, at least as far as she was concerned. And while quality blush-hued wines had come out the other side of that fad intact, it had taken a long time. But she'd thrown the gauntlet. She couldn't take it back now. "Chicken."

"I haven't even answered you yet."

Mira smirked. "Yeah, but I can tell you don't want to. You're not so subtle when you're irked."

Dylan offered a smirk of her own. "You mean like you were irked when Don suggested me as your co-chair?"

Her spine straightened of its own accord and her chin lifted. "I don't know what you're talking about."

"Yes you do. You smiled but your jaw was tense enough to crack a walnut. I could see it even on my tiny laptop screen."

She could double down, but it would make her seem petulant more than righteous. So instead she did a little shimmy with her shoulders. "Okay, fine."

"See? That wasn't so hard."

It wasn't. Why was that? As a matter of principle as much as personality, she didn't go for women—or men, for that matter—who poked and prodded her into doing things out of her nature. And yet here she was. Spending the day with Dylan and acting all sorts of not herself.

"So, are you going to help me pick which one?" Dylan asked.

She eyed the glasses again, then Dylan. Maybe it was because Dylan made it feel like a mutual give and take more than a battle for the upper hand. "Are you asking me to?"

"Pomme has won a gold medal more times than not, hasn't it?"

"Not quite." Though it had won more than any other producer in the state since the Cider Association started handing out recognitions.

"You getting modest on me?"

"Absolutely not. I have every intention of beating you." They could both be recognized with gold, but that wasn't the point.

Dylan's slow smile seemed to imply all sorts of things that had nothing to do with a little professional competition. "I'm going to enjoy watching you try."

Given Pomme's track record of wins and Forbidden Fruit's none, it was a bold statement. Exactly the sort of egotistical assertion that would have set her off only a few weeks before. But just like Dylan's smile, it seemed to imply a more personal challenge, one where they both might come out on top.

God, what was she even thinking?

"Now who's the chicken?" Dylan asked.

If she was in her right mind, she'd take a step back and say she'd only been joking. She had no idea if Luis could pull off a rosé cider in time for Cider Week, much less one she'd put up against the best of the best in the state. She could already see the disapproving look from her father.

And yet. She'd already run the idea by Luis. Talise, too. If she didn't start taking chances now, when would she? Going toe-to-toe with Dylan was a bonus. It certainly wasn't the primary motivation, right? Right.

"So, you can dish it, but you can't take it?" Dylan gave her a light elbow to the ribs.

"No, I'm deciding whether you'll take my honest opinion or think I'm trying to fake you out."

Dylan leaned close, closer than the conversation warranted. Closer than Mira's poor hormones could reasonably handle. "Are you trying to fake me out?"

She shook her head, suddenly unable to form words.

With their heads—bodies—this close together, she caught a hint of Dylan's perfume. Or, more likely, cologne. A little citrusy and a lot woodsy, it made her think all sorts of things she had no business thinking.

She braved a look at Dylan's profile, only to have Dylan shift her gaze and catch her staring. But even as embarrassment crept in, desire dominated. She couldn't look away. To be fair, Dylan couldn't either. Or didn't want to. Whatever the reason, it created the kind of energy that feeds on itself, intensifying like a wildfire in the wind.

She bit her lip. Dylan's parted. The stars aligned.

The first brush of Dylan's mouth over hers came softer than she would have expected. Not tentative, exactly. More like an open-ended question, one Dylan left for her to answer.

She could have pulled away. Maybe should have pulled away. But damn, it felt good. And when was the last time she'd done something solely because it felt good?

She angled her body, opening herself in invitation. When Dylan did the same, Mira answered with a kiss that left no doubt of her desire. The kind that all but begged Dylan to sweep the table clear and take her right then and there.

Of course, that wasn't what happened. They weren't in some steamy movie where the characters were all impulse and no consequence. She, at least, was a mature, adult woman. One who lived and breathed with the awareness that her actions had consequences.

Still, the kiss went on and on. She didn't try to stop it. More than that, she participated fully. Did everything in her power to coax Dylan deeper. Dylan's hand came to the back of her neck, her grip confident and firm. Her own fingers scratched lightly at the skin above Dylan's collar.

She lost track of the glasses and bottles in front of them, the production equipment all around. All that remained was the press of Dylan's mouth and the thrumming in her body that felt somewhat familiar and yet altogether new. That and the unsettling realization that she didn't want it to end.

It was Dylan ultimately who pulled away first, though her smile made it seem like a moment of appreciation more than regret. But the pause provided enough time for Mira's senses, her rational mind, to return. To the fact that they'd kissed, but also to the where and the when and the how.

"This is a bad idea, right?" Mira asked. For once, she would have welcomed Dylan's dissent.

Dylan angled her head, neither agreeing nor arguing.

"Yeah. It is." Mira blew out a breath and sat back.

"It was a hell of a kiss though."

"Yeah. It was."

Dylan nodded, though it seemed reluctant. "I get it."

Even though she'd been the one to declare it a bad idea, she wasn't sure she did. Or she did but didn't want to. She wanted it to be in the "we're going to do it anyway" subset of bad ideas. She didn't have a lot of experience on that front, but she finally understood the appeal. If only Dylan would provide the nudge.

"I hope you're not upset," Dylan said.

The look of genuine concern on Dylan's face pulled her back into the realm of rational thought. "I'm not. I hope you aren't either."

Dylan scratched her temple. "This probably isn't what you want to hear, but I'm never going to be upset about kissing a beautiful woman."

It sounded like a line enough to remind Mira of why she was in the business of acting like the sane, rational adult. It was too bad, really. "So, back to colleagues."

Dylan shook her head but smiled. "Back to friends."

"Friends." She gave a decisive nod and stuck out her hand. "Like it never happened?"

Dylan took it, but instead of the good solid shake she expected, Dylan merely held it. "Oh, I wouldn't go that far."

"No?" She didn't know how they'd manage to be in the same room otherwise.

"I don't forget kisses like that." Dylan lifted the index finger of her free hand. "But I respect women's boundaries, so I can behave like it never did if that would make you feel better."

It made her feel foolish, but she didn't see another choice. Not if they were going to work together and manage to avoid getting naked. "I think that would be for the best."

"Okay, then. So, we're agreed?" Dylan asked.

If a shadow of disappointment lurked in Dylan's eyes, she chose to ignore it. Instead, she gave the firm handshake Dylan hadn't. "Agreed."

Chapter Twelve

Rowan laced her fingers together and set them on the small table in the break room—the sort of outward display of calm that left Dylan guessing at her true thoughts. "Did you have sex?"

"No. Jeez. We kissed. That's all." Though she'd sure as hell wanted to do more. Two days later and it remained practically all she could think about. "And then we agreed it was a bad idea."

Rowan let out a sigh. "Yeah."

"What does that mean?" She expected Rowan to concur, even if part of her wanted something else.

"When Audrey and I kissed the first time, we agreed it was a bad idea, too."

Dylan tried to conjure the memory of Rowan and Audrey before they were Rowan and Audrey. "I thought you went from just friends to having sex in one fell swoop."

Rowan shrugged. "We did. We kissed, we agreed it was a bad idea, and then Audrey argued we should sleep together anyway to get it out of our systems."

Audrey was stubborn enough that it didn't surprise Dylan she'd say such a thing. Honestly, it was the sort of thing she'd wished Mira had said in the moment. Even if the ultimate outcome of Audrey and Rowan's hookup should have sobered that idea right out of her. "I see how well that worked out for you."

Rowan's blissful smile would be gross if she and Audrey weren't so genuinely perfect for each other. "I knew it wasn't going to work out like that. I'm just glad Audrey came around to my way of thinking."

The prospect of Mira coming around had Dylan suppressing a snort of laughter. Yes, they'd finessed a handful of compromises, but she was pretty sure Mira kept a chart to make sure they remained perfectly balanced tit for tat.

"So, what are you going to do?" Rowan asked.

"About what?"

Rowan shot her a bland look.

"Play it by ear, I guess. I'm really hoping things don't get stiff and awkward." Like they'd started to when they agreed to be friends and shook on it.

"Get stiff and awkward again, you mean," Rowan said.

Ugh. "Yes. Again. Though I feel compelled to point out she started out way stiffer than me."

Rowan lifted her chin. "You sure you want to brag about that?"

Dylan rolled her eyes. "Oh, my God. You're such a child."

Rowan shrugged, unfazed by the insult. "What do you want to happen?"

"I don't care as long as whatever it is doesn't suck."

That got her a scowl, complete with crossed arms. "I don't feel strongly whether you hook up or not, but for the love of God, please don't say that to Mira."

Dylan huffed. "Come on. I'm not an idiot."

Rowan made a judgy face. "Are you sure?"

She wasn't. Okay, maybe she was. At least a little. An idiot for kissing Mira in the first place, knowing full well Mira would do exactly what she'd done.

But damn if it wasn't one of the best kisses of her life. Weeks of anticipation concentrated into a single, perfect moment. The almost joyful spontaneity of it. Mira's mouth, that managed to be soft and demanding at the same time, melding so perfectly with hers.

It was almost as though all the disagreements, all the clashes, of their initial meetings had fed an underlying sexual tension. And that sexual tension turned into a tinderbox waiting to ignite. It made her think of the flashy reaction between sodium and water her high school chemistry teacher had used to demonstrate volatile compounds. Of course, the volatile compounds analogy had her smiling even as it made her cringe. Would Mira find it funny? Would she say the same?

Maybe it had been sexual tension all along. Her attraction to Mira had been there, albeit veiled. All that trying to convince herself Mira wasn't her type. And she knew without a doubt she wasn't Mira's. Still. A kiss that spectacular could only leave her wanting more.

"Earth to Dylan."

She let out a sigh that came out laced with a growl. "I'm an idiot. But I learn from my mistakes."

Rowan nodded slowly.

"She put the brakes on, and I respect that. I'm not a creeper."

"But you want to have sex with her." Rowan made it a statement, not a question.

Dylan stuck out both hands, not even trying to hide her exasperation. "I mean, have you seen her?"

Rowan smiled. "In fact, I have. She's unquestionably beautiful."

Another sigh, this time wistful. "Unquestionably."

"But you're not one to fall for a pretty face. Not solely a pretty face, I mean."

No, she wasn't. "Mira is so much more than that. She's smart and opinionated and funny and stubborn and most of the time I can't decide if I want to kiss her or argue with her."

Rowan came over and slapped a hand on her shoulder. "Oh, friend. You're a goner."

Dylan took a step back. "I can't be a goner."

"Why not?"

"Because I'm pretty sure I'd be going by myself."

"Ah." Rowan nodded. "Well, at least you know what you're dealing with. And for the record, you're nowhere near the realm of you don't care."

She groaned. "I hate it when you're right."

"I know."

"Can we talk about something else now? Anything else?"

Rowan grinned. "Of course. I think the Tydeman's Early are about ready."

"Yeah?" It was the first of the varieties to ripen in Ernestine's orchard, a harbinger of the frenetic harvest season to come.

"Next week at the latest."

"Nice." She loved the harvest, the pressing that came with it. Even if it meant weeks of backbreaking work to pull in enough fruit for an entire year of production.

"And I'm thinking about asking Audrey to marry me."

Her brain tripped momentarily but made the leap to follow Rowan's conversational swerve. "Dude? For real?"

Rowan's demeanor had remained casual when she dropped her bomb, but now it morphed into something almost giddy. "I know it's kind of fast."

Rowan and Audrey had been together just over a year, though that year had come with enough ups and downs to last a decade. Not the kind that made her worry about their chance at a long and happy future, though. More the kind that made it seem like they'd learned enough about themselves and each other to confidently weather any storms that came their way. "When you know, you know."

Rowan's features softened. "Do you really believe that?"

She did. She'd never experienced it herself, but it sat at the core of who she was. As a cider maker and as a person. "Your gut is smarter than your brain. You have to trust it."

"Is that what you're doing with Mira? Trusting your gut?"

The problem with Mira was her way of putting the area south of Dylan's gut in the driver's seat. All while she remained in the calm, cool, and collected realm of intellect. The combination had disaster written all over it. "I'm going to try, my friend. I'm going to try."

❖

Talise folded her arms and didn't even try to hide her disapproval. "Let me get this straight. Not only did you spend a day dabbling in cider craft, you offered a marketing consult in exchange for it?"

Mira frowned. "Not exactly."

"Oh, good. Because I can think of about a thousand reasons why that's a bad idea. Not to mention the number of people who'd lay into you for either one of those things."

"What is that supposed to mean?" She knew exactly what it meant.

Talise, who knew she knew exactly what it meant, didn't say anything.

"Dylan was only too happy to show off. I'm not going to pass up the opportunity to see what other cider makers are doing. Especially if we're going to expand into something they're already doing well."

"And Luis, who actually knows enough to get something out of that sort of thing, would have turned his nose up at the opportunity to play and talk shop for a day."

"You're implying that I don't know enough to get something out of it, and I'm offended. Besides, it wasn't a 'let's play' kind of day." Though she'd yet to decide what kind of day it had been. Other than confusing, arousing, and sexually frustrating.

Talise smacked her lips. "Oh, I didn't say you didn't get something out of it. I just don't think it had to do with cider."

"I told her I wanted to learn more about the craft side of things and she's enough of a cider nerd that she couldn't say no. Especially after knowing my father pooh-poohed the whole thing." Which she wouldn't normally admit, but it seemed less dangerous than the idea that Dylan was simply happy—eager?—to spend the day with her.

"You didn't tell me you'd started baring your soul to her."

"It was a passing comment, not a therapy session. Why are you picking this apart?" Probably for the same reasons she'd been going out of her way not to.

"Because it doesn't make sense as is. Which leads me to believe there's more to it than you're telling me. Which means you're keeping something from me. I need to figure out whether to be irritated with you or worried about you."

She really valued having a best friend smarter than herself. Even if she had to remind herself of that fact when said friend needled the truth out of her. Though, to be fair, she wouldn't have opened the can of worms in the first place if she hadn't, at least on some level, wanted to be needled. "She kissed me."

Talise might have been expecting something, but she clearly hadn't expected that. Her eyes got huge and her mouth fell open, the look of exaggerated surprise almost comical. "She kissed you?"

"I may have kissed her first. That part is a blur. But it definitely turned mutual. So, really, we kissed." Saying it out loud had the memory of Dylan's mouth on hers springing to life, humming through her muscles and sending a tingling sensation dancing along her skin.

"I knew it." Talise wore smug really well, but still.

"Yes, fine. We both know I'm not good at hiding things from you."

Talise shook her head. "No. I mean, yes, that is true. But I meant I knew you and Dylan were going to hook up."

It became her turn for the wide-eyed gape, on principle if nothing else. "We did not hook up."

"I mean it in the general sense, not the technical one. For the record, I approve. And it makes a lot more sense for all this to be about kissing the competition more than the relative merits or flaws of sharing trade secrets."

In hindsight, both felt like lapses in judgment. Though she honestly couldn't bring herself to regret either. "You think I'm an idiot."

"Not at all. I'm honestly thrilled that you've got something saucy going on. I'd simply prefer to talk about it than around it."

"Fine. We can talk all about it. Over a glass of wine after work." She made circles with her hands to indicate their surroundings. "Not here."

Talise grinned. "Deal."

"Besides, the marketing thing is practically mentoring. Dylan's marketing team consists of a college student intern." That part hadn't even felt like a stretch. Hopefully, Talise agreed.

"Why didn't you say so?" Talise stood. "I'm always happy to coach the next generation of marketing professionals."

She thought about the way Dylan's face lit up when she talked about Jamal, how he'd been placed with them initially to learn cidermaking but had found a passion for marketing instead. She and her partner had kept him on, but worried they weren't providing him with the benefits of an established, structured marketing department and people in it who could teach things beyond simply providing experience. "You're a pain in my ass sometimes, but you're a good egg."

"I know." Talise went to the door but paused and turned. "Is it just Jamal, then, coming for the day?"

It could have been an innocent question, but it so wasn't. "Dylan's coming, too."

"Ah." Talise's smirk said what her words didn't.

"Because Jamal is a college student. He might do a lot of their marketing work, but he's not running the show."

"Mm-hmm."

Mira pursed her lips. "Isn't there something I could antagonize you about for a change of pace? This incessant teasing about Dylan is getting old."

"Is it?" Talise tipped her head. "I'm still enjoying it immensely." "Tell me how your date was."

Talise closed the door she'd been about to walk though and crossed the room to drop into the chair opposite Mira's desk. "It's not polite to gloat."

"That good?" She set her computer to sleep. "I need details."

Talise crossed her legs and stared at the ceiling for a moment. "You know how I always said poly was great, but threesomes were overrated?"

"Yes, it's a deeply rooted belief we share, if for different reasons."

Talise brought her gaze squarely to Mira. "So, I was definitely wrong."

Meaning sank in and she regretted being in the office. "Is that so?"

"That whole triangulation thing?"

She sat forward, more out of amusement than a need for specifics. "Mm-hmm."

Talise licked her lip and quirked a brow. "When the two other vertexes are both pointed at you, it works."

Mira certainly had her share of sexual fantasies. More than a few included receiving the attentions of two lovers at once. But her one foray into that territory had been, well, awkward at best. Talise dabbled in unicorning with couples, meaning she had more—and more varied—experiences, but she'd never been wowed either. "I hope you're going to give me more than that."

"Of course. But like you said, not here." She mimicked Mira's gesture from a moment before.

Mira groaned.

"Hey, what's good for the goose."

She rolled her eyes rather than finish the saying. "Drinks tonight?"

"Absolutely. Between work and class, though. I've got plans after."

It wasn't appropriate—as Talise's supervisor or even for work in general—but she couldn't resist. "Reprising the threesome?"

Talise didn't say anything, but the look on her face was all the answer Mira needed.

"I'm glad one of us is getting laid."

Talise, who'd gone once again to the door, turned. "Sounds like you're primed to rectify that situation."

She didn't wait for a reply, leaving Mira alone with her thoughts. Thoughts that included the smell of Dylan's cologne and the playful intensity in her eyes. Thoughts of Dylan's mouth and what it would be like to have that mouth on hers. What it might be like to have that mouth other places. And maybe, just a little, thoughts about what it might be like, for once in her life, to throw caution to the wind.

Chapter Thirteen

Jamal leaned toward Dylan and sniffed a few times. "Dude, are you wearing cologne?"

She backhanded him lightly on the chest. "Yeah. And I ironed my shirt. Because it's a business meeting."

His expression remained incredulous. "You're trying to impress the chick."

She folded her arms. "We don't call women chicks."

Jamal mimicked the gesture but let his shoulders sag. "You know what I mean."

"I do. Which is why I'm calling your ass out."

"Sorry." He might be twenty, but his pout made him look about fourteen.

"I'll let it slide if you tell me why it matters."

He cleared his throat. "Because we're friends, but I need to practice my professionalism when I'm at work."

She nodded. "And?"

"And because referring to women as chicks is disrespectful. Even if I don't mean it disrespectfully, it plays into misogynist stereotypes."

"Thank you." For a guy barely out of his teens, he was actually pretty good with stuff like that. But she and Rowan had taken it upon themselves to make him a fully-fledged feminist by the time he landed his first real job.

"But seriously, I was yanking your chain more than any disrespect to Ms. Lavigne."

She loved that he used the formal salutation to prove his point. "Is that really the thing to say to your boss?"

He shrugged. "I figure when my boss asks me if I can drive my own car so she can go hang out with Ms. Lavigne after work, I can get away with it."

Jamal might be starting his sophomore year of college, but he had the savvy of someone a decade older. It gave him a leg up as an aspiring marketing executive. It probably gave him a leg up in the romance department as well. "I also have a meeting at Northside Wine. And you're the one who said he needed to get back for a hot date."

"Study date, D. Study date. Accounting is kicking my ass."

It had kicked hers, too. "But this study date is at your girlfriend's, is it not?"

He didn't even bat an eye. "Because my girlfriend is hella smart. Besides, if I've learned anything from you and Rowan, it's that sometimes you can mix business and pleasure."

Hard to argue with the truth. And Jamal didn't even know about the kiss she'd shared with Mira smack dab in the middle of the production area less than a week prior. Or the flirty texts Mira had been sending her despite their agreement to keep things platonic. "I'm not going to tell you not to, but I am going to say proceed with caution. And buyer beware."

That got him laughing. "I feel you. I feel you."

"Good. Now that we have that squared away, are you ready to go?"

"I was born ready, D."

She double-checked the contents of her messenger bag, confirming that both her trusty journal and the Forbidden Fruit laptop were tucked inside. She imagined Jamal would be taking most of the notes, but Audrey had prepared a file of things she might need to reference, and being able to pull them up might make her seem better at all this than she actually was.

She locked up and she and Jamal got on the road in their respective vehicles. She kept an eye on him in her rearview mirror, enjoying the flashes she caught of him grooving to something that would probably make her feel old and uncool. And while she'd told herself she'd spend the drive prepping for the much needed booster shot to their rather anemic marketing strategy, she mostly spent it thinking about kissing Mira.

At Pomme, the same young woman who'd greeted her at the luncheon escorted them into a small conference room with a glossy table, a coffee station set up on the credenza along the back wall, and a wide row of windows overlooking the rolling hills above Seneca Lake. "Ms. Lavigne will be right with you."

"Thanks," Dylan said.

The young woman left. Jamal looked her way and let out a low whistle.

"I know." She might have technically attended an Ivy, but the corporate polish never failed to catch her off guard.

"Imma be professional, but damn."

"Wait till you see—"

Mira and a woman Dylan didn't recognize breezed in, sparing her the regret of finishing the thought, at least out loud.

"I'm so sorry we kept you waiting," Mira said.

Dylan shook the hand Mira extended. Friendly but all business, like the last time. Had Mira thought about that kiss even half as much as she had? Did she want to know the answer to that? She shook off the question, along with the all too vivid memories of Mira's mouth under hers. "We just got here."

"Oh, good." Mira offered a smile, but her attention shifted almost immediately to Jamal. "We haven't met, but I feel like I've heard a lot about you. I'm Mira. This is my director of marketing, Talise Hill."

Talise was taller than Mira, with a lighter complexion and long black hair, but she had the same sort of impeccable feminine style that Dylan could appreciate if not relate to. Dylan might have expected Jamal to fumble at being the focus of two gorgeous women, but he stepped forward and offered a winning smile. "Jamal Goodman. It's a pleasure to meet you, Ms. Lavigne, Ms. Hill."

Mira returned the smile and Dylan reminded herself that a surge of jealousy in this moment would be beyond irrational. "Feel free to use our first names. We're not so formal around here."

For all that Dylan didn't mind the professional banter that came with being the face of Forbidden Fruit, the interaction highlighted how much it was a learned skill for her. Mira and Jamal made it utterly apparent that, for some, it was innate.

Talise didn't wait for any further cue from Mira. "It's great to meet you, Dylan. I've been hearing a lot about you, too." A look passed between Mira and Talise. A fraction of a second, tops, but the moment of exasperation—on Mira's part at least—was unmistakable. Rather than cow Talise, it seemed to spur her on. She not only accepted the handshake but covered both their hands with her free one. It left Dylan wondering if she should go along with it or play the straight man.

"Thank you so much for having us today," Dylan said.

Talise opened her mouth, but Mira cut in. "Cider makers help each other. It's part of the culture, right?"

That was certainly the case when it came to producers her size, or to folks just starting out. This felt different. Not that she'd have called Mira a curmudgeon—even before they'd gotten to know one another—but she wouldn't have put Mira or Pomme in the category of share and share alike. Not that she was about to say so now. "Indeed it is."

Talise took the lead and Jamal asked more than enough questions to keep the conversation going. She did her best to listen and not get caught staring at the Mona Lisa smile Mira seemed to be rocking. Easier said than done, especially when Jamal started asking about audience differentiation in targeted social media campaigns and Talise grilled him about the latest in SEO. She did manage to take a few notes, including one to pay Jamal more than the hourly wage they'd agreed to when his job shadow ended and he joined the payroll as a paid intern.

As their scheduled time came to a close, Jamal asked a few final questions, more about his career path than his work at Forbidden Fruit. She'd encouraged him to do so and hoped Mira and Talise didn't mind. The next thing she knew, he and Talise had their heads together like she and Mira weren't even in the room. A perfect opportunity to allow her focus to shift back to Mira.

"I can't thank you enough for today. I'm sure Forbidden Fruit will benefit, but Jamal will, too. He's a great kid." And deserved more than their tiny operation could legitimately offer him.

"It's nice that you've taken him under your wing. So many teens from rural areas don't get the access to the opportunities, or to the people, who can help them make that leap from classroom to real life."

"Yeah. We brought him in as part of a career exploration program through his high school. At the time, he wanted to learn the cider industry, but now that he's in college, he has his sights set on advertising. Or maybe sales."

Mira smiled. "He's got the personality for it."

Dylan laughed. "For sure. And he already knows more about marketing than Rowan and I put together. That's not saying much but still."

Mira laughed. "Same with Talise. It's good for us to know our strengths, right?"

"For sure."

"Are you sure tonight is still good for you? To get together, I mean?" Mira asked. She continued to smile, but she seemed hesitant, almost like she expected—wanted?—Dylan to back out.

"It's great for me if it still works for you. I'll wrap up my meeting at Northside no later than five. It'll be nice not to drive all the way home and then regret not grabbing dinner somewhere."

That seemed to tip Mira's scales. "It'll be nice to make dinner for more than just me."

The comment made Dylan want to know how often Mira made dinner for other people. Fortunately, Talise and Jamal seemed to wrap up their conversation before she could get herself into trouble by asking. She expected Mira and Talise to leave them to see themselves out, but Mira followed them to the main entrance and Talise tagged along. They launched into requisite final pleasantries. She made a comment to Talise about hoping their paths crossed again soon before saying to Mira, "And I'll see you in a few hours."

A look passed between Mira and Talise. Just like during introductions, a hell of a lot got conveyed without a single word. This time, the exasperation seemed to belong to Mira, while Talise radiated a combination of surprise and delight. She instantly regretted the comment about seeing Mira later, but it hadn't occurred to her that it might be the sort of detail she should keep to herself. Well, not until it was too late.

Since it was too late, she hustled Jamal out to the parking lot and sent him on his way. And since she didn't have much of a cushion to get to her meeting in Rochester, she did the same. Maybe she should have worried about putting Mira in an awkward position or, at the very least, digested the strategies and suggestions Talise had given them over the course of the afternoon. Yet as she drove into the afternoon sun, the only thing occupying her mind was how much she was looking forward to seeing Mira again so soon.

❖

Talise gripped the edge of the conference table with both hands. "You did what, exactly?"

Mira jerked her head in the direction of the conference room door, which stood wide open. "Could you not broadcast our conversation to the entire office?"

"You invited her over? To your house?" Talise's shocked expression didn't change but she switched her voice to an exaggerated stage whisper.

Mira let out a huff, regretting that she hadn't anticipated Dylan's comment and found a way to divert it. "Well, you don't need to sound so scandalized."

"I'm not scandalized. I'm…"

"Scandalized."

Talise tipped her head back and forth. "More flabbergasted. I think it's a fantastic idea, but I thought you'd decided not to go there."

"We're not going anywhere. She has a meeting with a buyer in Rochester and will be done around dinner time. We're having dinner. And working. It's not like I told her to pack a bag."

Talise angled her head and regarded her with genuine curiosity. "You know that's exactly how hookups work, right?"

She'd thought about hooking up with Dylan. She hadn't been able to stop thinking about it since they kissed. But she certainly hadn't said anything of the sort to Dylan. Or to Talise. "Who said anything about a hookup?"

"You did. You implied it at least. You might as well have asked her to Netflix and chill."

"Stop it. That's what teenagers do."

Talise closed one eye. "Adults do, too."

Mortification set in. Mira closed her eyes.

"You're like, the most clueless smart person I've ever met."

Usually, Talise's ribbing over her general lack of coolness didn't bother her. She didn't mind being the mature, sophisticated one—even if it came with the implication of being uptight. This was different, though. This was about Dylan and sex and the very real possibility she'd jumped into the deep end without even realizing it. Or, maybe more accurately, without realizing she'd managed to be obvious about it. "What if she thinks I invited her over for sex?"

"Are you inviting her over for sex?"

Mira dropped her elbow on the table and pinched the bridge of her nose.

"I'm going to take that as a yes."

The satisfaction in Talise's voice had her shoulders straightening. "No. Not a yes."

"A maybe?" Talise was having way too much fun with this.

Mira took a deep breath and let it out slowly. "Maybe. Maybe a maybe."

"Well, that's something at least. I'm glad you're not lying to yourself about it."

"But even if I'm entertaining the possibility, I don't want her to think that's what I'm doing."

Talise's head tipped yet again and her eyes narrowed. "Why not?"

The most obvious answer was that she didn't want it to feel orchestrated or inevitable. There was also the matter of not giving the impression she wanted Dylan more than Dylan wanted her. But both of those answers had a certain wishy-washiness to them. Not to mention an utter lack of confidence, in her own desires as much as Dylan's desire for her. If that kiss was anything to go on, the ship of wanting each other—and making it beyond obvious—had sailed. "I don't know."

Talise bit her lip and nodded slowly. "But I thought you knew everything."

Since there happened to be a stack of folders right in front of her, Mira picked one up and smacked Talise's arm. "Don't be obnoxious."

"I'll stop harassing you on one condition."

She set the folder down. "What's that?"

"I get a full report."

She didn't have a bevy of friends with whom she shared the details of her love life. For the most part, she didn't miss it. Maybe because there wasn't much to share. She dated, obviously, but it usually had to do with mutual interests and the convenience of having built-in dates to the myriad of events and functions that made up her social calendar. If she was lucky, some decent sex got thrown in. Sometimes a man, sometimes a woman. But always the same. Friendly, fun, and no chance of developing into something more.

Dylan threw a wrench in all of that. But why? It wasn't like Dylan had expressed a romantic interest. Not a capital R relationship one, at least. If anything, Dylan seemed almost too willing to take Mira's refusals at face value. It made the borderline desperation of her own desire especially jarring. But what if she'd gotten herself all worked up about the prospect of a relationship and all that was on the table was merely capital D desire? That was nothing to be afraid of. Especially if Dylan's reaction had more to do with respect and consent than disinterest.

"You're imagining having sex with her right now, aren't you?"

"That is absolutely not what I'm doing." Though it wasn't entirely out of her thoughts, either.

"If you aren't, then I'm guessing you're stuck in overthinking mode," Talise said.

"It's not overthinking if it needs to be thought through."

That earned her a disapproving look.

"I'm serious. How inappropriate would it be for me to hook up with Dylan while we're co-chairing Cider Week?"

Talise folded her arms. "I'm pretty sure no one cares."

That might be true in the grand scheme of things, but people loved to gossip. And she knew without a doubt at least a few members of the Cider Association board would like nothing more than to take her down a few notches. People like Don Farrell. It suddenly hit her. Is that why he maneuvered the two of them together in the first place?

"Now you're definitely overthinking."

Maybe she was. But she had a reputation to maintain, to expand. Especially if she had any intention of garnering respect in her own right and not merely living in the shadow of her parents. "I'm considering the fact that Dylan and I could be discreet."

Talise raised a brow, her smile full of satisfaction. "Sounds like you're a hell of a lot further along than maybe a maybe."

She spent so much time weighing the should or shouldn't of things, she often didn't even get to the could. Much less the would. If Dylan didn't object to keeping things between them private, was there any reason they couldn't indulge a mutual attraction? And was she willing to be the one to put that on the table?

Chapter Fourteen

Dylan climbed the steps to the front door of Mira's townhouse and rang the bell. She shifted from foot to foot, clutching a bottle of cider and trying to remember the last time she'd felt so uncertain. It didn't take long to realize how often she'd been afflicted lately. Mira had a way of keeping her unsure of what to expect next.

Take tonight. Who invited someone over after kissing them and then declaring said mind-blowing kiss was a bad idea and shouldn't happen again? Mira, apparently. It was like she wanted to tempt fate.

Or maybe she wanted to prove a point.

Hanging out just the two of them—at Mira's house, no less—practically begged a repeat of what happened in the production room at Forbidden Fruit. A repeat and more, with no chance of being interrupted or caught. But maybe that was Mira's way of proving that the kiss, mind-blowing as it might have been, was nothing more than a fluke. Or maybe not a fluke but an aberration, a temporary lapse in Mira's unflappable self-control.

Either way, she didn't like what that meant for the evening ahead. Would she be forced to pretend the epic chemistry didn't exist? Or would it sit there like a giant cartoon elephant in the room with them? Maybe less like an elephant and more like that experiment they did on kids, the one with marshmallows designed to test their capacity for delayed gratification. A bullshit experiment, it turned out, but the sentiment held.

Or, just maybe, the invitation and the flirty banter they'd been rocking for the last week meant Mira had changed her mind. The thought had her shifting again, though with a very different sort of anticipation.

Her thought spiral came to an abrupt halt when Mira opened the door. She stood in the doorway, bathed in rays of summer evening light that had her skin glowing like burnished bronze. "Hi."

Dylan pulled herself together, metaphorically collecting her tongue from where it had landed on the doormat. "Hi."

"Are you okay?" Mira's tone might have been sincere, but a smirk played at the corners of her mouth. Her exquisitely shaped, impossibly soft, utterly kissable mouth.

"Uh-huh." She cleared her throat and tried again. "Never better. You?"

Mira's expression turned quizzical. Not surprising, since Dylan's response sounded like the sort of thing she'd say at the mechanic. "I'm good. Come on in."

She stepped inside, trying to focus on the space and not the way Mira's ostensibly casual dress—different from the one she'd worn earlier at work—made her mouth water.

"Oh, I should have asked before. You're not allergic to cats, are you?"

As if on cue, a gray and white tabby strolled in from the kitchen and gave her legs a cursory rub before darting up the stairs.

"I'm not. I'm technically a dog person, but I enjoy furry friends of all kinds."

"All kinds, huh?" Mira seemed amused by the assertion.

"I've had cats, dogs, hamsters, and guinea pigs. Love them all."

"Fascinating."

"I take it you're feline exclusive?" A fact that wouldn't surprise her in the least.

"By default more than design. I didn't have pets growing up and a cat seemed the most reasonable place to start since I'm gone so much."

A perfectly reasonable reply, even if it left her wondering again about Mira's parents. Mira's childhood. "I like your place."

"It's a little generic, but it suits my needs," Mira said like it was a line she'd used before.

"If it works for you, there's nothing wrong with it." Even if she'd done the opposite, buying a clunky old house for just herself.

"I like that I can decorate it how I want, but don't have to think about maintenance."

Mira's unabashed practicality didn't surprise her anymore. And rather than sparring with her about it, which Dylan had been compelled to do in the beginning, she found herself appreciating the juxtaposition to her own tendencies. Wondering, maybe, if they might rub off on each other, if only a little. "A feature I would have enjoyed last February when I was replacing my hot water heater after it burst in the middle of the night and flooded my basement."

Mira's eyes got big. "They burst?"

She couldn't help but chuckle. "Well, not a spectacular explosion or anything. One of the seals goes and the water goes with it."

Mira shuddered. "That still sounds horrifying."

"You don't get any warning, so some people just replace them after so many years. I'm sure you could call someone to give yours the once-over and give you a recommendation. I'm not an expert, but I think there's usually an install date marked on it somewhere so you at least have a sense of when you're on borrowed time." She had no idea why she was going into such great detail about something Mira hadn't technically asked her about, but she couldn't seem to stop.

Mira didn't appear bored, but she didn't look all that interested either. "I'm going to do that."

She nodded and instantly felt like a bobble head, so she stopped and cleared her throat. "Yeah. So, anyway."

"Is that for me?" Mira lifted her chin toward the bottle still in Dylan's hand.

"Oh. Yes. We don't have to drink it. I just, you know, didn't want to show up empty-handed."

"That's very nice of you." Mira smiled again, which didn't help Dylan relax but did manage to switch the source of her unease back to how gorgeous Mira was and how difficult it would be to spend an entire evening together and not kiss her again.

"Well, it felt like the least I could do after you offered to make dinner."

"Thank you for indulging me. I don't often get to cook for guests." The casualness of the comment didn't match the flirty look in Mira's eyes.

"I'll come over any time. Assuming you let me reciprocate, of course." She wasn't at all sure what game they were playing, but if Mira could play it, so could she.

"You cook?" Mira asked.

"You sound surprised."

"Sorry." Mira dropped her head for a moment. When she lifted it, the smile returned and her lids trailed by half a second. The result was a serious case of bedroom eyes, and Dylan's entire body responded with enthusiasm.

"Don't be sorry. I like keeping you on your toes."

Mira's lips parted slightly, but she didn't speak. If she was trying to make Dylan want to kiss her again—and then some—she was doing a hell of a job. If Mira wasn't trying, well, Dylan didn't even want to imagine what sort of powers she had the potential to unleash.

Rather than allow herself down that path, Dylan cleared her throat. "So, work first or dinner?"

"How would you feel about a working dinner?"

The question might as well have been a bucket of cold water. "Sure."

Mira lifted a shoulder. "Then we can, you know, hang out?"

Hang out? Was that code for things consenting adults might do after dinner? Or was it merely the combination of an overactive imagination and wishful thinking? It was a good thing she managed to keep Mira on her toes at least a little because the opposite was absolutely true. Since she had no idea which Mira meant, she settled in for an evening of wait and see. Perhaps with a little cat and mouse of her own.

❖

By the time Mira cleared the dishes and waved off Dylan's offer to help clean up, her body practically hummed with anticipation. From the moment Talise backed her into a corner—the corner where she admitted wanting to take Dylan to bed—she'd essentially built a case for why it was the logical, self-empowered thing to do. Okay, maybe it was also a tiny bit reckless and irresponsible, but she never got to be either of those things and she'd damn well earned herself a sexy diversion.

What would Dylan say if she knew that was the trajectory of her thoughts? That she'd all but planned the evening as a seduction? If the flirty looks and casual touches were anything to go on, Dylan might simply say she was on the same page. Not knowing for sure was killing her. Well, that and the nagging voice in the back of her mind that kept up a running commentary of how it would feel if she put herself out there, made the first move, and found herself roundly rebuffed.

No. She wouldn't go there. One, because it would turn her into a decidedly unsexy sack of nerves. Two, because she wasn't in the business of second-guessing herself. Not at work and not in life. She might not be bold and brash like Dylan, but she took calculated risks in which she could reap the rewards or survive the fallout. Tonight was no different. Not really.

She returned from the short trip to the kitchen and found Dylan poring over the leather notebook she seemed to always have with her. Charming in theory if not practice. "I'm dying to know what all you keep in there."

Dylan looked up. "A little science and a lot of magic. Oh, and lists. Lots and lots of lists. To-do and otherwise."

"Of course." Not unlike her laptop, though she didn't believe for a second it kept Dylan as organized or efficient as she could be. Then again, maybe Dylan didn't see that as the point.

"Is there anything else we need to take care of? It feels like we're ahead of the game, but you're the one who's done this before."

She still wasn't used to Dylan deferring to her. Though, to be fair, it happened only selectively. "I think we are, in fact, ahead of the game."

"Are you finally at the point where you don't regret getting saddled with me?"

Nothing about the phrase was inherently sexual, but it didn't stop Mira's mind from going in all sorts of sexy directions. Some involving leather. And riding. She cleared her suddenly parched throat. "Something like that."

"For the record, I think we make a good team."

They did, weirdly enough. Even though things weren't going to be exactly how she wanted them—as far as the gala was concerned at least—they were going to be good. Good for a broader swath of their fellow producers and customer base. That's what mattered at the end of the day. "I concur."

Dylan grinned. "So, now what?"

Another innocent question that sent her thoughts to some not so innocent places. "Are you in a hurry to head home?"

Her own version of an innocent question, one that let Dylan read all sorts of things into it. If she wanted to.

"Not terribly."

Her default would be to suggest a movie. It would give them something to do, get their bodies in closer proximity than the dinner table. But Talise's reference to Netflix and chill had her second-guessing herself. Not that she had a lot of other ideas. Not ones that didn't involve dragging Dylan straight to bed.

"Movie?" Dylan lifted a shoulder, expression playful. Like she could read Mira's mind.

"Sure." Whether she meant movie or "movie," it gave them a plan and got them on the sofa.

"You can tell a lot about a person based on their movie preferences," Dylan said as they moved into the living room.

"Is that so?" She gestured to the couch and let Dylan get settled before joining her—close but not too close.

"Oh, absolutely." Dylan made a show of looking her up and down. "I'm guessing you're a classic rom-com kind of woman. Smart but easy, reliably happy ending."

She might be trying to get into Dylan's pants, but she couldn't hold back the snort of laughter. "Um, no."

"Really?" Dylan shifted her body until they were facing each other. "Do tell."

She lifted a shoulder. "I like thrillers."

Dylan pressed fingers to both her temples and narrowed her eyes. "Thrillers?"

"Yes. I'll take a good heist or a spy movie, but psychological thrillers are my favorite."

It was fun and more than a little satisfying to watch Dylan shake her head in disbelief. "I should have known you'd go against type."

"You might not mean that as a compliment, but I'm taking it as such."

"No, no. It's a compliment. I swear." Dylan shook her head with more vigor.

Mira tapped her index finger to her chin. "Let me guess. You're... sports movies."

"Ha ha."

"No?" She hadn't been kidding.

Dylan winced. "I'm actually a die-hard rom-com fan. I thought it might be something we had in common."

She pressed her lips together to keep herself from laughing. "Go figure."

"I'll watch a thriller with you as long as it's not too scary. Not to be dramatic, but the disturbing ones honestly and truly keep me up at night."

She resisted a joke about keeping Dylan safe, if for no other reason than it implied a bit too directly they'd be spending the night together. "I'm sure we can find a compromise."

They settled on *Ocean's Eight* even though they'd both seen it. Because Sandra and Cate didn't need a reason and it was nice to have that opinion in common. And maybe because it was the sort of movie she'd put on if her intention was to make out more than watch. Which left her wondering—yet again—if Dylan's thoughts were in the same vicinity. She stole glances through most of the scheming, then stretched and settled into a position a few inches closer. God love her, Dylan did the same. The shift had Gloria abandoning her spot between them with an indignant meow.

By the time the heist started, she was borderline desperate for Dylan to make a move. Only, Dylan wasn't going to because she'd been the one to put the brakes on. If this was going to happen, it was up to her to light the fuse.

She slid a hand onto Dylan's thigh, giving her plenty of time to tense or move away. Dylan stayed put. She leaned in more, bringing her lips close enough to brush the skin of Dylan's neck below her ear. Dylan did move this time, turning her head and bringing their mouths into perfect alignment.

What happened next was a blur, but she'd swear on her life it was mutual. Lips and hands and entire torsos seemed to join the party at once, all heat and wanting and pent-up energy with nowhere else to go. Dylan's hand covered her breast just as Mira inched hers under the hem of Dylan's shirt, the need to touch skin as essential as breathing.

The next thing she knew, Dylan was over her, the glorious length and weight of her covering Mira's body completely. No words, just the spark of pure chemistry. All the waiting and wondering and worrying seemed so silly now. Dylan wanted her as much as she wanted Dylan. And, in that moment, she wasn't sure she'd ever wanted anyone as much as she wanted Dylan Miller.

Chapter Fifteen

Dylan pulled back and scrubbed a hand over her face. "I thought we agreed we shouldn't do this."

Mira continued to work at the buttons of Dylan's shirt, hoping to keep the pause momentary. "Aren't you the one who's all about breaking the rules and doing what you shouldn't?"

Dylan sat back but kept her hands on Mira's thighs. "Not with sex, though. Not with feelings."

Mira pressed her lips together. A sheep in wolf's clothing was about the last thing in the world she'd expected from Dylan. "Really? You're going to be the voice of reason now?"

Dylan had the grace to offer a sheepish smile. "It's not for lack of wanting you."

It could have been a line, but she believed Dylan meant it. Which put her in the unfortunate position of deciding whether to agree or try to convince Dylan otherwise. "What if I promised not to hold it against you after the fact?"

Dylan frowned. "That's not what I'm worried about."

"Isn't it?"

Dylan took a deep breath and blew it out. "Okay, maybe a little. I like you. More than that, I respect you. We've finally become friends and I don't want to mess that up."

She appreciated that on principle, even if it felt like a cockblock in the moment. "I'm a big girl. I don't need you looking after my feelings."

Dylan looked her up and down. The hunger remained in her eyes, so that was something. "That doesn't mean I'm going to disregard them entirely."

The unexpected chivalry threatened to get on her nerves. Maybe that should have been a red flag, but it only served to spur her on. Going to bed with Dylan was about getting her way now. However she felt about Dylan, she felt very strongly about getting her way. "What if my feelings are squarely in the want to get in your pants category?"

Dylan laughed then. "I'd ask you one more time if you were sure this is what you wanted."

"And if I said I'm certain it is?"

"I'd kiss you."

Dylan closed the space between them, covering Mira's mouth with hers. Unlike before, when the kissing got lost in the sensation of Dylan's body against hers and the promise of skin on skin, this kiss was all-consuming. All the wanting, all the adrenaline—distilled into pure desire. Exploring tongues, a gentle nip. The brightness of apples and the warmth of whiskey. Time slowed and their surroundings faded, and all that existed were Dylan and the kiss and a resounding yes to the would they, wouldn't they question that had been hounding her for weeks.

When Dylan finally eased away, a smug smile played at the corner of her mouth. Like the deference before, it had the potential to irritate the hell out of her. But it meant Dylan was finally on the same page and she wasn't about to get her panties in a bunch over winning. "And then what?"

"I'd look to see if your eyes matched your words."

She had no doubt her arousal was written all over her face. "And?"

"And I'd take one look and say, 'where were we?'"

She liked to think a clever comeback leapt to the tip of her tongue, only to be swallowed by Dylan's mouth covering hers. The reality was that Dylan left her speechless. Fortunately, kissing Dylan gave her lips something better to do.

Dylan's hesitation vanished. In its place, an intoxicating mix of confidence and skill. Dylan waged an artful assault on her senses. Her mouth moved from Mira's lips to her throat, across her collar bones, and along the line of skin exposed by the neckline of her dress. Her hands managed to hold Mira in place and roam over her at the same time.

Meanwhile, Mira's hands—that had stilled during their brief negotiation—resumed the task of ridding Dylan of her shirt. The rest of Mira vibrated in anticipation. Of the promise of doing something truly impulsive and a little reckless. Of knowing Dylan wanted her as much as she wanted Dylan. Of knowing that want was about to be satisfied.

"Would you like to move somewhere more comfortable?" Dylan asked.

Mira blinked her eyes open and forced them to focus. "Huh?"

Dylan, shirt now open to reveal a snug A-shirt that accentuated her erect nipples, smiled. "I asked if you'd like to move somewhere more comfortable. Like a bed. Not that I'm opposed to hot and heavy on the sofa. It just doesn't strike me as your style."

Nothing—not a single blessed thing—about this was her style. In a way, that was the beauty of it. But she didn't want Dylan to think she had weird hang-ups about her bedroom. Or think she was too horny to make it the fifty or so feet. Besides, bed offered lots of nice options. If she was going to do this, she was going to do it right. And for as much of the night as Dylan's stamina allowed. "Excellent suggestion. Come with me."

"Happily." Dylan took her outstretched hand and followed her upstairs.

Mira got to her doorway but paused. "Even if we're being impulsive, we should be responsible. Have you been tested recently?"

Rather than balk at the question, Dylan smiled. Like maybe she was relieved that Mira asked it. "Six months ago, after my girlfriend of about a year and I broke up. You?"

She nodded, absorbing the relationship history as much as sex. "It's been over a year for me, but it was after my last male partner. I've had one encounter with a woman since, but it was, um, let's just say extremely low risk."

Dylan raised a brow.

"Did you not know I'm bi?"

"No. I mean, I didn't know, but it was the extremely low risk part that made me curious."

Mira winced and glanced at the ceiling briefly before making eye contact. "She asked for a hand job then fell asleep before asking what I might want."

Dylan cleared her throat but had the decency not to laugh. "Well, not to be arrogant or anything, but that isn't what's going to happen tonight."

"If I had any notion it might be, you wouldn't be here."

"I'm glad your bar is higher than that."

Mira swallowed. "I should be clear, though. This isn't 'hey, let's see where this might go' sex. I'm not looking to make more of this than is there."

A shadow seemed to pass through Dylan's hazel eyes, but it vanished as quickly as it appeared, and she smiled. "I'm pretty happy with exactly what's on the table."

A cryptic response, but she wasn't in the mood to split hairs. Or, rather, the point of taking Dylan to bed was not to obsess about every possible implication or outcome. The point was to be in the moment and do whatever the fuck she wanted for once. "Good."

In her room, she flipped on the lamp that sat on her dresser. The natural linen shade let light through but softened it. She finished ridding Dylan of her shirt. And her undershirt. And her pants. Dylan made a joke about keeping up as she dispensed with Mira's dress.

"Damn," Dylan said.

She'd argued with herself about wearing good lingerie, what it said about her intentions or whether it might jinx things. But the look on Dylan's face assured her matching lace was never the wrong decision. Mira basked in Dylan's appreciative stare. She guided them toward the bed, but not before Dylan flicked open the clasp of her bra and slid it down her arms. They tumbled onto the mattress side-by-side, all roaming hands and hungry mouths.

Dylan caressed the swell of her hip. She traced the curve of Dylan's shoulder blade. Legs tangled. Urgent but playful, satisfying on its own and yet not nearly enough. It reminded her of college—when going all the way wasn't a given and a half naked make-out session could be an end unto itself.

She lost track of time. Like, truly lost track. Kissing Dylan was hypnotic and what had probably been a few minutes could just as easily have been two hours.

As arousing as that might be, it also proved unsettling. The goal was to let loose, not lose herself. So she did what she did best. She took control.

It took minimal effort to roll them both, straddle Dylan's thighs, and barely break the kiss. She felt instantly better and markedly more aroused. She tore her mouth from Dylan's long enough to make sure the feeling was mutual.

"I was wondering how long that would take." Dylan's expression was playful.

She sat up, squeezing Dylan's hips between her knees. "How long what would take?"

"You needing to be on top."

She could take offense on principle, but she was having too much fun. She arched her back slightly and gyrated a few times. "Are you complaining?"

Dylan didn't speak, but she rolled her head side to side with the sort of slow exaggeration that said more than any words could have.

"Good."

"Unless you're one of those no touch, stone types. I'd respect it, but I'd be incredibly sad," Dylan said. Her hands came up and her expression shifted. "Wait. You made a comment about your last hookup not asking what you wanted. I'm thinking that means you want something at least."

The declaration registered as sincere and suggestive at the same time. "You'll get your turn. Eventually."

Dylan didn't argue. But she did kiss, caress, squeeze, and pinch in all the right places. Particularly impressive given Mira's best efforts to make her incapable of coherent thought. The switch finally flipped when Mira slipped her hand into Dylan's snug boxer briefs. Dylan's clit was hard and hot, and her wetness coated Mira's fingers.

Dylan groaned. Mira groaned a little herself. And while Dylan's hands didn't still or fall away, they took on the restless movement driven more by wanting than intention. Confident she'd pushed Dylan to the edge, she slinked down Dylan's body, tugging her briefs off and nudging her legs apart as she went.

"Wait, wait." Dylan's head came up first, then her shoulders, and she propped herself on her elbow.

"Is this not okay?" She hadn't pegged Dylan for fastidious, but she hadn't pegged Dylan for plenty of things, so it wouldn't be the first time she'd been wrong.

Dylan offered a half-shrug and an almost bashful smile. "No, no. All teasing aside, I'm more of a, you know, ladies first kind of person."

If her face wasn't hovering mere inches from Dylan's clit she might have laughed. Or smacked Dylan on principle. But her face was that close. So irresistibly close she could breathe in the musk of Dylan's arousal. She pursed her lips and cocked her head slightly, not breaking eye contact. "I guess you'll have to make an exception."

She didn't wait for a reply. She slid a hand under each of Dylan's thighs, curling her arms around them and grasping the tops of Dylan's hips. She took a second to enjoy the fact that Dylan was literally dripping for her before slicking her tongue into Dylan's wetness.

"Fuck." Dylan's body tensed and her head fell back.

"Too much?" She really hoped it wasn't.

"Not too much. Just really, really good."

In lieu of a reply, she returned her mouth to Dylan's clit. Long strokes, lazy circles—as much for her own pleasure as Dylan's, at least for now.

"I can feel you smiling, you know. There's no need to be smug."

She wouldn't say she'd forgotten how playful sex could be. More that playfulness in general wasn't her style. But Dylan's coltish tone made her smile in earnest, and there wasn't a reason in the world she couldn't play along and be whoever and however she wanted. At least for tonight.

She didn't lose track of time, but she did get lost in how satisfying it could be to pleasure someone. When Dylan came, she called Mira's name with something resembling awe. It stirred something in Mira's chest that she promptly brushed aside. She crawled up the bed to lie beside Dylan.

"If you do that, you can always go first." Dylan rolled to her side, lids heavy and a drunk looking smile on her face.

Mira opened her mouth to dispute the implication of always, but Dylan swallowed the assertion with a kiss.

"You set a high bar, but I'm going to do my best to rise to the occasion." Dylan kissed her again, then came onto her knees to remove Mira's panties. After tossing them aside, she positioned herself over Mira. But rather than straddling Mira's thighs, she nestled one of hers between.

"I..." Whatever thought she had—retort, agreement, request—vanished with the friction of Dylan's thigh against her clit. "Fuck."

"We'll get to that."

The gentle tease exuded confidence. It turned her on as much as the movement of Dylan's body over hers did. Not her typical response—to teasing or arrogance. But Dylan didn't mean it in an arrogant way. She could tell. And for some reason she couldn't explain, she had absolutely no doubt Dylan had both the skills and the attentiveness to deliver.

And damn did Dylan deliver. She worshipped Mira's breasts with her mouth. Kissed across her ribs. Scratched ever so lightly along her sides. Hypnotic massaging circles with her thumbs, down Mira's thighs and back up. All with relaxed focus and not even a hint of being in a hurry.

Somewhere between that and Dylan's tongue pressing into her, she gave up trying to make sense of it and gave herself over to how good it felt. Her body hummed under Dylan's touch. Hummed and then revved, like an engine hitting the open road. Higher and higher, until her brain and her body united in a singular and almost desperate search for release.

It came. She came. Not all at once but in waves, radiating through her and back again like an echo, leaving her sated and sweaty and breathless.

She lifted her head long enough to make eye contact with Dylan before letting it fall to the pillow. "Damn."

Dylan crawled up to where she was, draping an arm over her in a way that calmed her frenetic pulse without coming off as possessive or sentimental. "I was just thinking the same thing."

❖

Dylan could have basked in the afterglow of being with Mira for the rest of the night. No surprise, Mira didn't work that way. Not ten minutes after coming, she sat cross-legged on the bed, face serious but with her gorgeous breasts still on perfect display. "Okay, we probably shouldn't do that again."

Dylan took a deep breath, too full of sex endorphins to take it personally. "Is this where I remind you that doing it in the first place was your idea?"

"No." Any sharpness in Mira's reply got lost in the sly smile that came with it.

She propped herself on her elbow. "All right. Should I ask why or dive right into the reasons we absolutely should do it again?"

"I might need to hear the reasons."

She sat up and mirrored Mira's position. Because she was teasing but not. "First, because sex that good should never be a one-time thing."

Mira folded her arms. "Maybe it was that good because it was a one-time thing."

"I don't believe that, so we definitely have to do it again to see who's right."

Mira closed her eyes for a moment and shook her head. "Do you take anything seriously?"

Not the first time a woman had asked her that. "I take you very seriously."

That got her an eye roll.

"I mean it. Finding sex with you incredibly fun doesn't mean I'm careless about it. Or flip. It just means it's really fucking fun."

The last bit was risky, but it got Mira to crack a smile again. "You're right."

Since she was on a roll, she decided to take a chance. "God, it's sexy when you say that."

Mira swatted her but without any force.

"Again, I'm being completely serious," Dylan said.

Mira frowned. "Okay, well, so am I then. Forget what I said."

Well, it was nice while it lasted. "The part about me being right?"

"No. The part about not doing it again."

Not where she thought Mira was going. Though, her brain was pretty addled by sex, and double negatives tripped her up sometimes. "So, we can do it again?"

Mira leaned forward, coming onto her knees. "Can." She pressed her lips to Dylan's. "Could." Another kiss. "Should."

If a small part of her mind needled her to press, to figure out exactly what Mira was thinking and feeling and wanting and needing, the rest of her effectively told it to go fly a kite. Mira's position—on her knees and with her hands braced on Dylan's thighs—left her breasts practically in Dylan's lap. Ignoring them felt like an insult to the universe and whatever goddess of sex had decided tonight was going to happen.

She grazed her fingers along the impossibly soft undersides before cradling each perfect mound in her palms. Mira's nipples hardened on contact and the sensation of hard and soft, the warmth and the weight of them, sent Dylan's momentarily sated body into overdrive. She groaned and Mira chuckled.

"You're easy," Mira said.

"You're perfection." Maybe it was a line, but she meant it.

Mira shifted forward again, making a not so subtle suggestion that Dylan lie back. The move was confident, assertive, and hot as fuck. Normally, three of Dylan's favorite things. But given how they'd spent the last hour or so, there wasn't a chance in hell she was going to let Mira top her again.

She wrapped her arms around Mira's waist and twisted, flipping their positions on the way down so Mira was on her back, and she was braced on top. Surprise flashed in Mira's ebony eyes, but desire quickly followed.

"Hi," Dylan said.

"Hi." Mira blinked slowly and licked her lip.

"I hope that was okay." She wanted to keep Mira on her toes, not cross any of her boundaries.

Mira nodded.

Dylan thrust against her. "And this?"

Another nod.

She shifted most of her weight onto her knees, freeing one hand and slipping it between them. She grazed her fingers along Mira's still swollen clit. Mira's eyes fluttered closed, only to open when Dylan eased two fingers inside her. "And what about this?"

Mira smiled then, just as her hips rose to meet the thrust of Dylan's hand. "Yes. Absolutely yes."

Dylan allowed her own eyes to close for a moment. To revel in the way Mira clamped around her, pulled her in. The way Mira's lush and lithe body felt under hers.

So unexpected. And somehow so much better than she expected. Like everything with Mira, it seemed.

When she opened her eyes, Mira's gaze fixed on hers. The look on her face had gone from playfully sexy to downright hungry. "More?" Dylan asked.

"More."

She added a third finger and Mira groaned. There was a rawness to it. A sound of uninhibited pleasure distinct from the indisputably sexy sounds she'd made earlier.

It wouldn't take much to become addicted to that sound. A worry for another day. For the moment, she had more pressing things to attend to. Like making Mira come undone. And proving that doing it again—and again and again and maybe again after that—was unequivocally the right call.

Chapter Sixteen

Not only did she and Dylan have sex again, they met up and had sex four nights in a single week. And three the week after that. They didn't make plans, exactly. But by mid-afternoon, one or the other of them was texting a *Free tonight?* or an *Up for dinner and...*

It wasn't sustainable—and not only because they lived an hour apart—but Mira couldn't bring herself to put a stop to it. Dylan didn't seem interested in letting up either, at least as far as she could tell. Even though it meant ridiculously early mornings for at least one of them every time they spent the night together.

As impractical as the whole arrangement was, it was the most fun she'd had in as long as she could remember. Pizza and old movies at Dylan's. Vietnamese food and heckling house hunting shows on her couch. And dear God, the sex. So much sex. Parts of her ached from it all and the rest of her felt more limber and alive than if she was going to the gym every day.

If part of her worried about the what next, the rest of her— maybe for the first time ever—embraced the notion of enjoying the moment and dealing with the consequences when she had to. She'd expected the whole thing to give her anxiety, but it turned out to be quite freeing.

Like tonight. The Cider Association board meeting was down the lake toward Watkins Glen, more Dylan's neck of the woods than hers. They hadn't even discussed it, but she packed a bag of essentials in anticipation of winding up at Dylan's.

Had she confessed hooking up with Dylan to Talise? Yes. Had she told her all these other details? Not a chance in hell. She'd let her hair down, but she had a reputation to uphold.

Which was why, when she arrived at Blackbird Cider, she made a point of chatting with board members she hadn't seen in a while and took a seat next to Autumn, one of the few female cider makers besides Dylan and her. By the time Dylan extricated herself from what appeared to be a lively, if slightly one-sided, conversation with Frederick, the meeting was about to start and the only open place to sit was on the opposite side of the room.

She offered a playful shrug, not wanting to give the impression she did it on purpose, but also not minding a little bit of distance. It was a business meeting after all, and she didn't need anyone catching a glimpse of her hand straying to Dylan's thigh under the table. Not that she couldn't resist, but at this point, she wasn't entirely sure she could.

The meeting started and she channeled her most professional self, not letting her gaze settle on Dylan or her mind wander to what she'd rather be doing. The fact that it took effort made her feel like a teenager with a crush, but she was surprisingly okay with that. Especially since she'd harbored her fair share of crushes in both high school and college and didn't let them keep her from a perfect grade point average. She hadn't been sleeping with said crushes, but oh well.

The flash of a notification on her screen caught her attention and she glanced down.

I'm definitely imagining you naked right now.

Her gaze darted to Dylan, who regarded her with a raised brow and a mischievous smile. Dylan looked down just long enough to type something into her phone. A second later, another notification popped up.

Crawling into my lap and riding me.

She looked at Dylan again, this time with a we-are-in-a-meeting glare. Dylan lifted a shoulder, all innocence. Then she started typing again.

Are you into strap-ons? Looking at you right now has me wishing I was packing.

Mira gasped, then tried to cover the gasp with a cough. She snatched her phone from the table, grateful Autumn's attention remained on Frederick and the budget report. *Will you control yourself? We're in a meeting and you're making me wet.*

I have a hard time controlling myself around you. Followed by: *And you didn't answer my question.*

Her sense of propriety, honed as it was, proved no match for the effect Dylan had on her. A handful of words and she was hot, bothered, and horny as hell. *Maybe I'm keeping you in suspense.*

Pretty sure that's an implicit yes. How do you like it?

Mira stared at her phone, now sitting in her lap. Was she really sexting during a work meeting? Apparently she was. *I like to be on top.*

She had the pleasure of watching Dylan's reaction, of knowing she'd put that look on Dylan's face from twenty feet away. *Shocker.*

The winky face Dylan added took any sting out of the comment, but spurred her on nonetheless. *But if you play your cards right, I'll let you bend me over.*

This time, it was Dylan's turn to cough. And not some subtle clearing of her throat. She got a case of that awkward persistent cough that happens when a tiny tickle becomes an all-consuming force that won't subside, leaving a body out of breath and unable to make it go away.

She felt a little bad. A little.

"Mira?" Don looked at her expectantly.

"I'm sorry?" Did he have to catch her every time she wasn't paying attention? It was like he went out of his way to try to make her look foolish.

"We're discussing the partnership with our downstate counterparts and wanted to know how your conversation with their marketing team went." Don's ever so slightly condescending tone only reinforced her suspicions.

She cleared her throat, relieved that once again, being prepared saved the day. "They're completely on board with our plans for cross-promotion and are open to a joint gala next year, especially if we entertain a venue in the Catskills."

Don's lip curled. "Quite a hike for our friends out near Buffalo."

"Yes, but a compromise and less of a hike than for their members on Long Island. Again, we're still in the early talks about that, but I think the exposure to both consumers and potential retailers in and around the city would make it more than worthwhile."

"Brava, Mira." Frederick clapped his hands together. "We'll all reap the benefits from your powers of persuasion."

Most of the group murmured their agreement and conversation shifted to the lobbying committee, who were cautiously optimistic about proposed modifications to sales tax requirements that would streamline both collection and reporting for sales across county lines.

I'd like to request a private audience with your powers of persuasion.

Since she shouldn't even be looking at her phone after all that, Mira replied with an eye roll. Not mature, exactly, but something resembling restraint.

Seriously, though. Way to put Don in his place. What a tool.

She didn't need credit for holding her own, but it was nice for Dylan to notice, to appreciate it. It made her look forward to spending the night at Dylan's place even more. But first, she needed to get through the rest of this meeting, without letting herself get any more distracted.

❖

When the meeting ended, Mira seemed intent on speaking with everyone in the room except Dylan. It didn't bother her at first. Mira was a master networker, and she made a point of not just making connections but maintaining them. Hell, it was a trait she admired and would do well to emulate.

But as the minutes dragged on and Mira wouldn't even make eye contact with her, she struggled to take it any way but personally. She lingered, obviously, and attempted some networking of her own. It didn't help her shake the sense that something with Mira was off, but it made the time pass.

Mira finally made her way over, seeming to effortlessly end a conversation just as Dylan did. "Hi."

"Hi." Mira's face looked relaxed and happy, but the ship of suspicion had already sailed. "Was the sexting too much?"

Mira's eyes narrowed and her head tipped, confusion apparent on her face. "No. It was distracting but fun."

"Did I do something else to piss you off?"

"Of course not." Mira offered what appeared to be a playful smirk. "Well, not that I'm aware of at least."

Huh. "Then why did you spend the last hour acting like you could barely stand me?"

"You're exaggerating."

"Am I?" From where she sat, Mira had given her more of a cold shoulder today than when they'd actually disliked each other.

"I was being professional."

On the surface, it made perfect sense. Keeping their personal involvement private would shield it from the sort of gossip that flitted through professional circles of any ilk. The innocent, nosy sort of gossip as well as the kind that included phrases like quid pro quo and conflict of interest. She certainly didn't want any part of that, and she imagined Mira would find the very idea abhorrent.

Still. Something in Mira's tone struck her as more than Mira the consummate professional. More, even, than Mira's strait-laced, borderline uptight tendencies might produce. It struck Dylan as personal. Like Mira would shun that sort of innuendo in general, but the prospect of being romantically linked to Dylan would be a particular affront.

Dylan lifted both hands. "Hey, I was just asking. It wouldn't be the first time a woman was upset with me without my knowing."

"Why does that not surprise me?" Mira rolled her eyes. Again, it could have been playful. But it didn't feel that way.

"Do you want to grab a bite while we're here?" Given their text exchange during the meeting, she'd had every intention of asking if Mira wanted to go home with her, dinner be damned. Now, she wasn't so sure.

Mira smiled. "I'd love that. But I have to talk with Frederick about some board stuff. How about you grab a table and I'll join you in a little while? Shouldn't be more than ten minutes or so."

A perfectly reasonable answer, but it did little to sooth Dylan's frayed—what? Nerves? Ego? Whatever the feeling was, she wasn't used to it. And she absolutely didn't like it.

She did as Mira suggested and got a table. Only to look out the window and spy Mira talking with Frederick in the parking lot. Was she seriously about to be stood up?

They talked for a couple of minutes and exchanged hugs. Mira headed in the direction of her car, hovering at the driver's side door and offering a wave as Frederick pulled away. As soon as he did, she headed right back to the restaurant. Any relief over not being stood up got lost in the irrefutable evidence that Mira didn't want Frederick to know they were having dinner together.

A moment later, Mira slid into the booth, complete with bedroom eyes and a come-hither smile. The look, and the promises behind it, left her tempted to drop the whole thing. It would bug her all night, though, and she wasn't known for hiding her feelings. "Are you embarrassed to be seen with me?"

"What? No. That's ridiculous."

"I saw you walk out with Frederick and go all the way to your car until he pulled away. You clearly didn't want him to know you were staying to have dinner with me." There was no plausible non-shifty explanation.

Mira cringed. "If Frederick knew we were staying, I would have felt obligated to invite him. Nothing against Frederick, but that's not the kind of dinner I had in mind."

Okay, so there was a totally non-shifty explanation. Dylan let her shoulders drop.

"Do you wish I'd have asked him to join us?" Mira asked.

"Oh, no. Not at all."

"Then why do you look deflated?"

Should she own being irrationally insecure? Probably not. "It just felt weird. It's fine. And, I mean, I get being discreet. We don't officially work together, but no point raising eyebrows, right?"

Mira smiled. "Exactly. I'm glad we're on the same page."

Were they? Well, close enough. "Yeah."

"I should be up front though. I'm not going to let on that I'm sleeping with someone who is technically both a colleague and a professional rival, but I'm also not into PDAs as a rule. It's not about you."

Well, it was, but at least not in the ways she'd let herself think. A consolation, even as it made her feel a bit foolish. "Is it the public part or the display of affection part?"

Mira chuckled. "It's fine if I'm with someone and we're with other people we know. But walking down the street is different. I'm not going to hold your hand, but I don't hold anyone's hand."

In her mind, holding hands was one of the most innocuous ways of showing affection. Second only to hugging, perhaps. Though, truly, how often did she do it? And with whom? Not friends, for sure. And not really women she dated casually. "Do you hold hands in private?"

The nose wrinkle was brief but telling. "I mean, I'm not opposed. It's just so…"

Since Mira genuinely seemed to be searching for the right word, Dylan offered the unexpected one that popped into her mind. "Intimate?"

Mira smiled. "Yes. Intimate. Exactly."

They may have been fucking for the last two weeks, but they were a long way from intimate. At least the kind of intimate she was implying. "I'll keep that in mind."

Mira nodded, effectively closing the topic. They perused the menu, did some friendly haggling over a few small plates to share, and placed their order. Conversation flowed easily. Nothing terribly deep or revealing, but they swapped stories about everything from freshman year college roommates to favorite books and dream vacations. It mostly managed to put her mind at ease, even if it left her wondering what it might be like to cross the line into that other category of intimate.

By the time they paid the check, Mira's bedroom eyes had returned, and Dylan focused her attention on enjoying the sort of intimacy they did have. "Would you like to come back to my place?"

Mira lifted a shoulder, more flirtation than indecision. "I packed a bag."

"You did?" That delighted her perhaps more than it should have.

"I figured I could save myself the trip home and sleep until six instead of five."

Utterly practical. And yet, maybe a little, straying into girlfriend territory. They might not be talking about it in those terms, but she wasn't about to complain. "I like the way you think."

Mira smirked. "I'm going to remind you of that next time you disagree with me about something."

The fact of the matter was that they hadn't disagreed about much since those initial meetings. Not about work and not about anything they were doing outside of work. But she wasn't about to correct Mira on that now. And, again, she wasn't about to complain.

Chapter Seventeen

Mira pulled into Dylan's driveway, cut the engine, and smiled. She'd spent the better part of the twenty-minute drive thinking about all the things she'd like Dylan to do to her and she was more than a little turned on. Dylan got out of her truck and waited for Mira to join her before heading to the side door. Not chivalry, exactly. And certainly not the over-the-top displays she'd experienced, particularly from male suitors hoping to get laid. No, it was more of a casual consideration, one Dylan probably didn't even think about.

For some reason, it struck her. And threatened to stir something in her deeper than the unrelenting physical desire she'd accepted—come to expect, even—from hooking up with Dylan. Something in the feelings department.

"So, where's this strap-on I've been promised?" They hadn't even gotten inside, but the need to shift her focus back to the physical got the better of her.

Dylan unlocked the door but turned before pushing it open. "Someone's impatient tonight."

She smirked, falling safely back into her comfort zone. "Someone's been making me think about sex for the last three and a half hours."

Dylan hummed her approval. "Well, we can't have that going to waste."

Inside, Eloise greeted them with a single bark and an exuberant dance that came mostly from her rear end. Mira bent to pet her, reminded that dogs might be more work than cats, but they made up for it with enthusiasm and affection. "Hi, pretty girl."

Eloise pranced under the praise, twisting herself in hopes of getting butt scratches instead of head. Dylan chuckled and scooped food into her bowl. "Go on then."

For all her basking in Mira's attention, the allure of food won out and she darted to her bowl. "I love her joie de vivre," Mira said.

"Oh, she's got the joie all right." Dylan closed the lid on the bin of food and turned to face Mira. "Now, where were we?"

She stepped into Dylan's outstretched arms. "You were telling me all about this strap-on of yours and what you were going to do with it."

Dylan's expression turned innocent. "Was I, now?"

"I'm pretty sure you were. You should take care of anything that needs taking care of, though. I have a feeling it's the kind of conversation that will be hard to stop once we get started."

"It's so sexy when you're practical."

She'd made peace with Dylan's teasing about her tendency to be boring and logical, in part because she'd already turned that premise on its head by instigating their affair in the first place. "I have some spreadsheets we could go over while we fuck, if it would turn you on."

"Rawr." Dylan made a cheesy, exaggerated biting gesture. Then she grabbed Mira and nipped at her neck in earnest.

Mira squealed, in surprise as much as being tickled. Dylan squeezed her tighter, interspersing cartoon gobbling noises with her kisses and bites. The whole thing was spontaneous and silly. And, in a weird way, sexy. "You need to take me to bed now."

"Your wish is my command." Without letting go, Dylan leaned around her, flicking the lock and turning off the outside light.

"Be careful or I might hold you to that."

"In bed. Your wish is my command in bed," Dylan said.

An important distinction, but an appealing prospect nonetheless. "I'll take it."

Dylan's arm slid around her waist. "Is this where I tell you the prospect of you being super demanding in bed is hot?"

She smirked, but the truth of the matter was that she loved the push and pull she and Dylan had. Dylan had toppy energy, but she didn't need to be in charge. And as much as Mira liked being in charge—was accustomed to it—Dylan playing both sides made things fun. And sexy as fuck. "Yes. Yes it is."

Dylan's other arm came up and pulled her close. "I want you to tell me exactly what you want."

That, she could do. "Mm-hmm."

"And I want you to tell me exactly how you want it."

"Right at this very moment, I want you to stop wasting time teasing me in your kitchen and take me to bed."

Dylan stepped back and grabbed her hand. "Like I said, your wish is my command."

They'd spent enough nights together that going to bed was no longer marked by a frantic stripping of each other's clothes and a desperate tumble into bed. Well, most nights.

Dylan led them to the bedroom but let go of her hand and went to her nightstand. She snagged a black bag from one of the drawers. "I'll be right back."

"I'll be right here."

Dylan crossed the hall and the bathroom door clicked shut. For some reason, she liked Dylan wanting a moment of privacy to get ready. Dylan was such a mix of bravado and restraint, swagger and subtlety. Mira wouldn't have thought such a combination would appeal to her. But instead of frustrating her, it kept her on her toes. She couldn't remember the last time a sexual partner had done that. More, she couldn't ever remember a time craving it.

She reminded herself to enjoy the novelty rather than analyze it. She wasn't looking to marry Dylan. They were simply having a good time. And having a good time—without overcomplicating it—was the whole point.

With that settled, she unzipped her skirt and slid it down her legs. She folded it neatly over the chair in the corner and did the same with her blouse and stockings. Underwear, too, but she decided to leave her slip on so she wasn't standing around waiting for Dylan naked.

She sat on the edge of the bed and switched her thoughts to the matter at hand. Specifically, what she wanted Dylan to do to her. And exactly how she wanted it done.

❖

Dylan took the moment alone to get the cock adjusted and the harness tightened just how she liked it. She also took a few deep breaths, centering her arousal and setting aside all the other stuff that had crept into her mind throughout the evening. Mira wanted her. For now, that's what mattered. She—they—would sort out the rest when the time came.

She returned to the bedroom and found Mira perched on the edge of the bed, legs crossed. She'd stripped down to nothing more than a black slip, and the way her body filled it out was enough to make Dylan's mouth water. And yet Mira's foot, bouncing with restless energy, gave her pause. "Nervous or impatient?"

Mira stood, her gaze lingering on the cock before she made eye contact. "What do you think?"

The slip clung in all the right spots and fell softly over the rest of Mira's body, the hem barely grazing the tops of her thighs. Her right hip jutted slightly; her head angled the other way. She was, in short, perfection. "Is there anything on this earth that makes you nervous?"

Mira looked at the ceiling for a couple of seconds, and a sly smile played at the corners of her mouth. "Anything in the millipede or centipede family and people who cry at the drop of a hat."

Dylan chuckled. "How do you manage to utterly surprise me and yet not surprise me at all?"

That earned her a raised brow and a full smirk. "I'm a woman of many talents."

"And, I might add, sexy. So, so sexy."

"What are you going to do about it?" Mira asked.

An invitation, sure, but there was no mistaking the challenge that accompanied it. And if there was one thing Dylan couldn't resist, it was a challenge. "I have a few ideas."

Mira lifted her chin. "Good."

She crossed the room and encircled Mira's wrists, one in each hand. Not too tight, but with purpose. "And you? Any ideas?"

Mira's gaze traveled the length of her, pausing once again at the cock. "I don't think you should take your time."

"Mmm."

"And I don't think you should worry about being gentle."

What was that about Mira surprising her? "No?"

Mira shook her head exactly once. "No."

She tightened her hold on Mira's wrists, felt Mira instinctively test her grip. Mira leaned in, chest first. Her already taut nipples strained against the silk and lace. Dylan kissed her—her mouth, her neck, the gorgeous expanse of exposed skin between her collar bones and the swell of her breasts. Mira's whole body arched, expressing without words exactly what she wanted.

Without releasing Mira's wrists, Dylan walked them back toward the bed. When Mira's legs bumped the mattress, Dylan let go and gave her a shove. Not typically her style, but the situation seemed to call for it and Mira didn't appear to mind.

Mira sprawled across the duvet, her luscious body on perfect display. Dylan took a moment simply to appreciate it. Mira cleared her throat. Dylan took the hint. "Right, right. I'm not supposed to take my time."

Mira opened her mouth with what Dylan could only assume was a clever comeback. But instead of giving her the chance, she blanketed Mira's body with her own and covered Mira's mouth with a kiss. She'd only meant to stifle the retort, to make a case for her ability to act swiftly, but she lost herself in the way Mira's body moved under hers, the way Mira's tongue teased and tempted and tortured.

Mira's legs parted, inviting her in. Mira's hips thrust provocatively, pressing into the cock and creating a disarmingly perfect amount of friction against her clit. Urgency took hold and any need to make her case became moot.

She kissed her way down Mira's body, sucking and biting her nipples through the fabric. There wasn't much else in her way, but she inched up the hem of the slip, exposing Mira's hips and the patch of trimmed hair at the apex of her thighs. "God, you're gorgeous."

Mira lifted her head. "You're pretty gorgeous yourself."

"I promise I'll fuck you halfway to next week if you want, but I need to taste you first." It came out like a line, but she meant it. She felt like an addict who couldn't get enough, and Mira's body beckoned her—promising euphoria more intense than any drug.

She dropped a line of kisses along Mira's inner thigh, where her skin was softest. Her labia were dark and slightly swollen, already slick with wetness. Dylan breathed deeply, taking in the faint musk that was utterly unique to Mira and had invaded more than a few of her dreams.

Mira cleared her throat again, but it came out almost as a whimper. She wouldn't admit it to Mira, but it was the sort of sound that turned her insides to jelly. The kind of sound that made her want to give Mira anything—everything—she wanted.

Since she knew exactly what Mira wanted in that moment, Dylan gave it to her. She licked. She sucked. She reveled in how deliciously hard Mira's clit got and the way her whole body tensed as she both chased release and tried to keep it at bay. She took that as her cue, shifting onto her knees and positioning the cock. "Do you want me to grab lube?"

Mira laughed. "That won't be necessary."

She eased one finger into Mira and then a second. The way Mira tightened around her made her shudder. She'd been with her fair share of women, but something about Mira's body, the way it responded, felt like magic. She removed her fingers and slipped the tip of the cock inside. Mira let out a soft moan that made her entire body clench with desire, and she was pretty sure she'd never wanted a woman more than she wanted Mira in that moment.

"Please." Mira's request could have been begging, but it felt more like a command. And she was only too happy to oblige.

She slid the cock deeper, starting with shallow thrusts to give them both a chance to acclimate, to settle into a rhythm. Mira's body rose to meet her, taking more of the silicone in each time. The movement made for the most deliciously erotic pressure on her clit. She closed her eyes and let herself sink into the sensation.

When she opened them, Mira's gaze locked on hers. Mira's hands gripped her thighs and, for as much as Mira was technically the bottom in this scenario, there was nothing remotely submissive about it. "I need to feel more of you."

Before she could ask what that meant, Mira wiggled herself away and rolled over. She shifted onto her hands and knees and shimmied her body back until her backside was directly in front of Dylan. The sight of it, the sense of Mira serving herself up on a platter, just about did her in.

"Is this okay?" Mira tossed a playful look over her shoulder that said she already knew the answer.

Words refused to form, so Dylan merely nodded. She eased the tip of the cock in, only to have Mira thrust back and take the entire length in at once. Mira let out a sound somewhere between a purr and a moan. Dylan groaned, the pressure on her clit suddenly straddling the line between pleasure and agony.

She set her hands on Mira's hips, using Mira's movements and her own desire to create a sensuous rhythm. It didn't take long for things to escalate to one of those moments she both didn't want to end and almost desperately needed to. She reached around to stroke Mira's clit.

"Yes. Fuck. Yes."

Mira's words reverberated in Dylan's ears and sent her over the edge. Her body tensed and tightened as she rode the orgasm. Just as it crested, Mira let out a sound Dylan hadn't heard from her before, and she gushed into Dylan's hand. The intensity of it had a ricochet effect. A second orgasm crashed through Dylan, bouncing around inside her and hitting every muscle and nerve.

Mira collapsed onto the bed. She followed suit, landing to Mira's left. "Wow."

Mira lifted her face from the pillow, her hair disheveled and partially covering her eyes. "Yeah."

Dylan brushed her fingers across Mira's forehead, nudging a couple of curls to the side. "That was really hot."

Mira nodded before letting her face fall into the pillow once more.

"You okay?" She'd sort of lost herself at the end and needed to be sure.

"Mm-hmm." Mira's answer was muffled by the pillow but conveyed her meaning just fine.

Dylan flopped onto her back and let out a contented sigh. The cock bobbed around, as though announcing its willingness to go again. She loosened the harness and slipped it off, pretty sure Mira was as done as she was. Mira rolled onto her side and ran her fingers through Dylan's hair. Her limbs seemed heavy, and she had sort of a half-drunk smile. A decidedly good look on her.

"I'm sorry about your sheets."

Sated as she was, Dylan couldn't resist the urge to kiss her. "I'm not."

Mira smiled and her eyes drifted shut. "It was really good."

She was generally fifty-fifty when it came to cuddling after sex, but all Dylan wanted to do was gather Mira into her arms and drift off. "We can change them and take a shower, or you can come over here where it's dry."

Mira scooted herself over and draped an arm over Dylan's chest. "I'm good with whatever."

In no hurry to move, she wrapped her arm around Mira and simply enjoyed how good it felt. She must have lost track of time because the next thing she knew, Mira's breathing had evened out with sleep. The realization nudged her own body in that direction, so she pressed a kiss to Mira's shoulder and allowed herself to follow.

Chapter Eighteen

Dylan wrapped a towel around her waist and took a moment to enjoy Mira drying herself off. "Can I make you breakfast? Do you have time?"

Mira secured her own towel across the top of her breasts. "If you don't try to tempt me back into bed, then yes."

"I always want to tempt you back into bed, but I'd rather see you eat a real breakfast, so Scout's honor."

Mira bumped Dylan's hip with hers. "Yogurt is a real breakfast. Especially for those of us who don't spend our days doing manual labor."

She ignored the comment and headed to the bedroom to grab her clothes. "Omelet and toast? Gee, I think that sounds great, too."

Mira grumbled but laughed and followed her.

Since it took her about thirty seconds to throw on clothes for the day, she left Mira to get ready and headed to the kitchen. She fed Eloise, then poured herself a cup of coffee from the pot Mira insisted they start before showering—because it was more efficient that way—and opened the fridge. Hers might not be as elegantly stocked as Mira's, but it did the job.

By the time she heard Mira on the stairs, she'd sautéed a red pepper and some spinach and was adding it to her pan of eggs. "Swiss or provolone?"

She didn't turn from the stove but caught Mira's answer from the hall and topped the veggies with slices of Swiss. Mira walked in, looking every bit like a corporate glamazon: fitted dress, flawless makeup, and every curl arranged to look effortlessly polished. All the more impressive given the small overnight bag Mira had come with. Even though Dylan loved casual Mira best, the professional look suited her. And it gave Dylan extra satisfaction to think about being the one to muss her up at the end of the day. "You're looking particularly boss babe today."

Mira smirked. "It's the monthly video call with the heads of all the company divisions."

Which she'd learned was code for seeing—and thereby wanting to impress—her father. "You know you'd slay in a potato sack, right?"

"Yeah, but what's the fun in that?"

She didn't press because she'd learned that, for Mira, her clothes and makeup and hair were as much a source of pleasure as they were professional armor. "Toast?"

"I got it." Mira grabbed the multigrain bread Dylan had bought to be nice but was starting to like and slipped slices into the toaster. "Juice?"

"Sure." Dylan rarely drank juice that wasn't on its way to becoming cider, but she'd noticed that Mira kept a jug of grapefruit on hand and, well, why not?

It wasn't the sort of leisurely affair they might enjoy on a weekend, complete with tag-teaming the crossword like they'd done the Sunday before. But it was cozy and comfortable, and it wouldn't be hard to imagine doing it every morning.

"Are you bringing a date to the gala?"

Dylan froze, cup of coffee halfway to her lips. It had to be a trap. She just wasn't sure what kind. She set her coffee down. "Was I supposed to ask you to be my date? Like, formally?"

Mira gave her an exasperated look.

"What? I'm serious. I didn't think that sort of thing mattered to you." She pointed a thumb back at her chest. "But I will full-on promposal your ass if it would make you happy."

The muscles in Mira's jaw tightened ever so slightly. "I don't mean me. I meant someone else."

For a second, Dylan thought she'd misread Mira having a moment of vulnerability. Insecurity, even. Then it hit her. "You don't think we should go together."

Mira took a deep breath, like she was weighing what to say that might make Dylan feel like less of a fool. "It's just, we've gone pretty far out of our way to keep things between us private."

Which was making less and less sense to her, if she was being honest. "Yeah."

"I'm not saying it always has to be that way."

"No?" Sure as hell felt like it.

"There's so much going on during Cider Week. Launching the reparations package, both needing to speak at the gala, being prepared to talk to the press. It's a lot."

She couldn't argue that. Though, in her mind, that made going together more logical than dragging a date along.

"You're mad."

Dylan shook her head. "I'm not."

"I can tell. Your face isn't very good at hiding how you feel."

"Do you want to bring a date to the gala? Is that what this is about?" They hadn't talked about being exclusive, but as far as she was concerned, this was a shit way to suggest they see other people.

Mira huffed out a breath that did nothing to mask her irritation. "No. I thought we should discuss it. Have a plan."

It always struck her when she could pinpoint the moment a conversation tipped into argument territory. Well, in real time. It was plenty easy to find it in hindsight. The thing was, she didn't want to argue with Mira. At least not about their relationship. For all their sparring in the beginning, and all the things they still disagreed on, being together had proved almost shockingly easy. She didn't want that to change. Even if Mira's mental gymnastics to keep things on the DL got under her skin. "Okay. What's the plan?"

Mira folded her arms, clearly reading the question as passive aggressive. "That's what I was asking you."

She didn't want to escalate the situation, but she wasn't about to lie. "I'd like to be your date. I get what you're saying, though, and I won't argue about it. I guess my second choice would be not to have a date at all, so I can at least shoot you knowing looks across the room and not feel skeevy about it."

Mira smiled. "And so I can go home with you at the end of the night."

It was the exact right thing to say. It smoothed Dylan's feathers and reminded her of what was important: at the end of the night, Mira wanted to go home with her. Maybe the original question came from a place of vulnerability after all. She returned the smile. "I always want you to come home with me at the end of the night."

A flash of surprise passed across Mira's face before she focused on the omelet in front of her. Only then did Dylan realize what her words technically implied. Which, ironically, was the absolute truth of her feelings. But she knew better than to say so. At least right now.

Hopefully, things would settle down after the gala. Their time together would be inarguably relationship territory and not about working on a project. They could talk about what that meant, what they wanted it to mean. And even though she'd never been the one to want too much commitment or talk of the future, she was having a hard time thinking about a future without Mira in it.

❖

Mira strode into the Pomme offices just after nine—technically late but still with more than an hour to spare before the quarterly conference call. Talise, who happened to be standing at Margo's desk, looked her up and down. "Look who decided to join us."

Margo, who'd been at Pomme for only about six months, looked slightly horrified, but Mira merely laughed. "I'm trying to model better work-life balance. It's not a corporate value if the people touting it don't live it."

Talise nodded slowly. "Nice recovery. I'm impressed."

"Thank you. And as a show of good will, I won't write you up for insubordination." Since that got her little more than a withering look from Talise, she turned her attention to Margo. "I'm kidding. We don't do that here."

Margo responded with a nervous nod and a hesitant smile. "Actually, I'm glad you're here. Your father called already this morning and wants you to call him before the meeting. He said ten minutes should be plenty."

She was accustomed to being summoned, so the request—and the six a.m. West Coast timing—didn't faze her. "Will do. Thank you, Margo."

She headed to her office, Talise hot on her heels. "Please tell me you're late because you were having morning sex. I want to live vicariously through you."

"No one is stopping you from morning sex, you know. You're the one rocking throuplehood. Something tells me you could have sex every morning."

Talise let out a beleaguered sigh. "Poppy is sort of a morning person, but AJ is not."

She laughed because anti-threesome Talise had so quickly become casual about it. "Maybe if the two of you woke her up with sex, she'd become a morning person."

Talise seemed to consider this possibility. "Maybe. But you still need to answer my question."

"Not today. Dylan made me breakfast."

This time, the sigh was wistful. "Breakfast might be even better than sex."

Her mind flitted to what she and Dylan had been up to the night before. "If it is, I think you're doing it wrong."

Talise smirked. "Fine. Still, breakfast is nice. Is she a good cook?"

"She can whip up an omelet just fine." And other things, actually, even if she didn't want Talise to know exactly how many times Dylan had cooked for her.

"Omelets on a weekday morning. Maybe you should marry her now. I'm not sure it gets any better."

She hadn't gone so far as to imagine marriage, but she'd started to accept that she and Dylan were in a relationship. Capital R relationship. Even if she'd spent their breakfast conversation talking about the possibility of bringing someone besides each other to the gala. "You need to raise your standards and I need to prep for my meeting."

Talise shrugged, her way of conceding the point, and left Mira to her own devices. Mira settled at her desk, did a quick survey of her inbox, and returned her father's call. As expected, it was one of his usual reminders to do something she'd already taken care of. She thanked him and assured him everything was under control. And despite knowing that day needed to come soon, she decided today was not the day to exert her autonomy.

The meeting started and the various division heads gave their updates. No more boring than usual, but her mind wandered, and she was grateful to be a passive participant for the bulk of it. About half an hour in, she caught the flash of a notification in her peripheral vision. Since no one would be the wiser, she let her gaze drift down to the screen.

What's a sexual fantasy you have but have never been able to explore?

She cleared her throat and ran a hand up the back of her neck, stealing a glance at her computer to ensure she didn't look as hot and bothered as she'd suddenly become.

Please don't say threesomes.

Fortunately, she was on mute, so the guffaw went unheard by the rest of the meeting attendees. She unlocked her phone and held it just below the sightline of her camera, faking eye contact with whoever was talking and keeping her engaged, resting half-smile firmly in place. *I'm in the middle of a meeting.*

Kinky. Then: *I wouldn't have pegged you as an exhibitionist.*

OMG. Stop. It's a virtual meeting but I have to look like I'm paying attention. She shifted the angle of her head and nodded a few times as Nigel ran through the financials for overseas sales and distribution.

So, that's a no on the public sex? Too bad. I'm imagining sliding my hand up your thigh under some glossy conference table.

It became increasingly difficult not to laugh. At Dylan's over-the-top lines but also the fact that she'd somehow become the person who sexted during work meetings. *Did you want me to spread my legs and pass you a note that says I'm not wearing panties?*

Dylan's reply was instant. *I do now.*

Since she had a few minutes before her slot on the agenda, she decided to play along. *I'll tell you one, but you first.*

You drive a hard bargain.

Her practiced half smile gave way to a real one. *You like it.*

I really really do. Okay, so...

As much as she wanted to know what Dylan would say, she couldn't risk being caught with her head in the clouds. *Have to present. Back in a few.*

Not trusting herself not to look, she turned her phone face down and double-checked that her deck was in slideshow mode and ready to screen share. Her father did his usual praise and pontificating before calling on her. She flashed an I'm super prepared and excited smile and launched in.

Only about fifteen minutes passed between setting her phone aside and the meeting ending, but by the time Mira snatched it and unlocked the screen, she practically buzzed with anticipation and arousal. Ridiculous? Absolutely. Did that mean she was going to stop? Absolutely not.

Dylan's message was long. It filled the chat window and then some. She scrolled up to start at the beginning but stopped, holding the phone to her chest. Were they really discussing sexual fantasies?

She shook her head and laughed. Given what they'd been up to the last few weeks—last night included—the metaphorical pearl clutching seemed plethoric. Still. She'd never done that with a sexual partner before. A fact that made her feel awfully boring all of a sudden.

She pulled the phone away from her body and focused on the screen. No time like the present.

I was joking about being an exhibitionist, but not entirely. Not full-on public sex, but maybe somewhere we might be caught. A supply closet. A dark office after hours. That sort of thing. It's not the danger so much as the impulsiveness. Wanting each other so badly we can't wait another minute.

Mira let out a shaky breath. Absolutely, one hundred percent not her thing, yet Dylan had a way of making it sound hot.

I'm not implying we should. Just saying it's something I fantasize about.

She appreciated the caveat. *You make it sound enticing. Even if the mere thought makes my rule-follower-self anxious.*

She hit send, then it struck her that Dylan might be disappointed. Or think she was uptight. She chuckled. That ship had sailed. Dylan knew full well she was uptight. This was different, though. They'd thrived on the opposites attract thing, but the idea of real incompatibilities in bed made her sad.

Now you have to tell me yours.

Dylan's answer pulled her from the threat of an insecurity spiral, dropping her nicely back in the land of fantasy. And a whole new kind of anxiety set in. *Um.*

Come on. I promise it's extra sexy coming from a super polished, put together type.

Again, she laughed. To think she'd once found Dylan's confidence, her gregariousness, off-putting. The truth of the matter was it had been her own self-consciousness, her own fears, that triggered that reaction. Now that she'd let Dylan in, she'd let some of it rub off on her. And it made her brave. *Spanking. Wax play. Bondage.*

It was hard to say whether sending multiple ideas—without explanation or context—made it easier or harder to wait for Dylan's reply. *Giving or receiving?*

A snort of laughter—part relief, part delight—escaped. *Receiving.*

The text back consisted of three flame emojis and nothing more.

You don't think it's cliché that the powerhouse femme secretly wants to be topped?

Only seconds passed before the answer came through, but it felt like an eternity. *Not if I'm the one doing the topping.*

Chapter Nineteen

An away message for a Friday afternoon off was probably overkill, but Mira put one up anyway. If nothing else, it would assure staff she took time off, something Talise nagged her about regularly. Just like coming in late every now and then. It wasn't sufficient to encourage work-life balance; one had to model it.

She changed clothes in her office, not wanting to take the extra time to swing home, then crept down the back stairs. Not because she didn't want to be seen leaving but because she didn't want Talise to comment on her change of outfit. Which was silly, really. She wasn't going to show up for an evening of outdoor music and bonfires in a business suit, and no way in hell would she be caught in the office wearing jeans. It was the latter Talise would tease her about. Well, that and the fact that she'd gotten herself signed up for a weekend with Dylan's sister and the sister's fiancé instead of kinky escapades.

The invite had actually come hot on the heels of their foray into discussing fantasies and Dylan had joked about how meeting the family required consent, too. It softened the blow of having to delay the weekend of sex she wanted and made the prospect of meeting some of Dylan's family a little less daunting. It also helped to think of it as a casual thing with Dylan's sister. That carried a lot less weight than meeting the parents would.

She checked her hair and makeup in the rearview mirror, then started the drive to Forbidden Fruit. When she got there, she had a text from Dylan saying she'd gone to pick up Emily and Jason from her house so they could drink without worrying about driving. Rowan was out by the stage, chatting with the band who'd arrived to set up. That left her to head inside and make herself comfortable. As comfortable as she could be, of course, not knowing at all what to expect.

She perched on a stool at the bar and watched the staff of three arrange glassware and wipe down the laminated menus customers would use to pick the ciders in a tasting or flight. Not unlike the bar at Pomme, really, though the fact that they all wore jeans and dark green Forbidden Fruit T-shirts gave the scene a more relaxed vibe than her tasting room.

Kind of like Dylan. At first, she'd bristled at Dylan's casual energy. It struck her as immature, not serious. But the more she and Dylan got to know each other, the more she realized it was simply a different way of doing things, a different way of being. Dylan worked just as hard and cared just as much for the things she was passionate about.

While she hadn't meant to think about sex, thinking about Dylan and passion sent her mind careening down that path. The way Dylan wielded a strap-on. The look of fierce determination on her face after Mira swore she'd come as many times as humanly possible. Wondering what it would be like to lie pliant under Dylan with her wrists bound to the headboard. The mental images had her squirming and wishing she could get Dylan to herself for an hour before all the required socializing.

"You must be Mira."

At the sound of her name behind her, Mira started. By the grace of God—or maybe the years of ballet and Pilates classes—she didn't fall off her chair. She turned and found a pretty brunette beaming at her. "I am."

"I'm Audrey, the business manager." She tipped her head and offered a playful smile. "And Rowan's girlfriend."

"Oh. Right." She slid from the stool and extended a hand, hoping to come off as both friendly and composed. "It's nice to meet you."

"Likewise. I've heard lots about you. Sorry to sneak up on you like that."

She wondered what Audrey's emphasis on the word lots implied but didn't have the chance to ponder it for long. Dylan came in with a beefy Scandinavian-looking guy and a petite, more feminine version of herself. Introductions and hugs and handshakes took up all the space for a few minutes, only to be repeated when Rowan came in from outside. It was all so jovial, and she didn't feel like an outsider, as she'd worried she would. She did feel a flutter in her stomach when Dylan kissed her—the kiss itself the culprit more than having an audience—but that was something to worry about later.

Rowan ushered the group outside to one of the half dozen fire pits situated on the expanse of grass between the building and the orchard. "It's not chilly yet, but I took the liberty of getting one started for us," she said.

"My hero." Audrey kissed Rowan with even more abandon than Dylan had kissed her, which reminded her that PDAs in front of friends could be nice.

Dylan and Rowan slipped into host mode, taking drink orders and encouraging everyone to settle into the cedar Adirondack chairs arranged around the fire. In an amusing twist on bro code, Jason followed so he could check out the bar. Audrey snagged the seat on one side of her, and Emily took the other, both promising to vacate when Dylan returned.

Emily set her elbow on the arm of her chair and propped her fist on it. "So, you're the boss lady at Pomme d'Or."

The phrasing made her laugh. Well, the phrasing and relief that Emily led with that and not some variation of so, you're dating my sister. "I am."

Dylan, Rowan, and Jason returned with glasses of cider, but Dylan and Rowan were needed to help at the bar during the rush before the music started and Jason volunteered to help carry cases to and fro. Though Mira couldn't help but wonder if he felt more at ease with Dylan and Rowan than being left behind with the more obvious girls.

The conversation that ensued surprised her. Maybe because it flowed so freely. Between Emily's taking over the family restaurant and Audrey's background as a Big Four accountant, they had a million things to talk about that had nothing to do with sex or relationships. Which wasn't to say those things didn't creep in eventually, but it felt natural and not like some forced intimacy that would leave her feeling uncomfortable or, worse, like a stick in the mud.

The band was better than she expected. So was the fried chicken from the food truck that had set up shop for the night. There was dancing and laughter and, as the temperature dropped with the setting sun, all the fire pits came to life. She wasn't the sort of person to think of an evening as magical, but that's exactly what it was. If it hadn't been for the prospect of going home with Dylan, even with two other people in the house, she'd have been downright sad to see it end.

❖

Dylan watched the light shift from the pale gray of dawn to the soft gold of early morning. Mira remained half in her arms and half splayed across the bed. In the quiet, and with Mira sound asleep, she allowed herself to trace circles on Mira's skin and bask in the perfection of being wrapped up together. The sort of basking that would likely throw Mira into brisk efficiency—getting up and making coffee and starting the day. Because, she'd begun to learn, that's how Mira operated. But also, maybe just a little, because keeping busy meant she didn't have to sit still and feel things.

It provided a small consolation that it seemed to be Mira's way of moving through the world and not something particular to their relationship. Would Mira even call what they had a relationship? Not that she was the sort to press, but she'd definitely caught feelings and it would be nice to have more to go on than a hunch and a hope.

She was borrowing trouble. It wasn't like she wore her emotions on her sleeve, or even had big swelling ones all that often. Well, except when it came to cider. Honing her craft, getting Forbidden Fruit off the ground and on the map—that took up all the mental, physical, and emotional energy she had. Romantic relationships might be a nice enhancement to her life, but they certainly weren't the focus. Having feelings for Mira didn't change that. In all likelihood, Mira was in the same boat.

Since arguing with herself rarely amounted to anything good, she slipped from bed. Mira moaned, but otherwise showed no signs of waking. She pulled on a pair of sweats and a faded blue Henley and went to see if anyone else was up.

She came downstairs to find Emily already puttering around the kitchen, the aroma of coffee beginning to waft. "Well, good morning."

Emily stepped back from the refrigerator and closed the door. "Good morning to you, sunshine. I fed Eloise. Don't let her tell you otherwise."

Eloise plopped herself right in front of Dylan, tail wagging. Dylan scratched her ears. "You're cute, but you're not getting second breakfast."

Emily regarded the dog with affection. "I told you she'd believe me over you."

Eloise sniffed and Dylan shrugged. "Are you looking for cream or plotting breakfast?"

Emily pointed to the carton of half-and-half already on the counter. "Breakfast."

"I can make breakfast, you know. I'm not as good a cook as you, but I'm competent. Just ask Eloise." Eloise sniffed again and let herself out through the doggy door. "Okay, don't ask Eloise."

"You're competent all right. Maybe I wanted to do something nice to thank you for such a great little getaway. I didn't think Jason and I needed it, but clearly we did."

"Aw." She crossed the room and gave Emily's shoulders a squeeze. "Are things feeling hard?"

"No, no. Nothing like that. It's just that between our work schedules, wedding planning, and house hunting, our time together hasn't been down time, you know?"

"I do know." She had no complaints about the amount of sex she and Mira were having, but between that and talking shop, she wondered if they'd get to a point where they could simply relax together. Like whole afternoons—taking drives or poking around farmer's markets.

"Speaking of knowing things, you owe me lots of details and a big ole apology."

The details part she got, even expected. "Why an apology?"

"Because the last time I saw you, you insisted there was nothing to tell."

"Well, there wasn't. We hadn't even slept together yet." She glanced at the ceiling and did some quick calendar math. "We hadn't even kissed."

Emily huffed. "And clearly all that has changed."

"I texted you that we were dating, that she'd be here this weekend." A weak comeback and they both knew it.

"I'm pretty sure your text messages didn't go beyond 'we're dating' and 'she'll be here this weekend.'"

"Both those things are true." She so wasn't helping herself here. At the rate she was going, Emily would be insulted and not just irritated.

Emily leaned against the counter and crossed her arms. "You have it bad for her, jerk face. And if my keen powers of observation are anything to go on, Mira's got it just as bad for you."

Part of her wanted to believe that. Believe that she and Mira had more than a project in common and epic sexual chemistry. But Mira always seemed to be holding back a part of herself. Maybe it had to do with time and how long they'd been dating, or with her worries over professional propriety and discretion. Whatever it was, she couldn't pretend it wasn't there. "I don't know."

"Of course you don't. You're a bit of a blockhead when it comes to love. I see a lot of couples come into the restaurant and trust me, I know when they're in love and when they're not."

Dylan made an X gesture with her hands. "It's been like two months. Let's not get carried away."

Emily rolled her eyes. "I'm not saying propose tomorrow kind of love or grow old together love. I'm saying that whatever is going on between you and Mira is way more than casual."

She could lie, but what would be the point? "Yeah."

"Mom is not going to be pleased."

"Wait. Why?" Her parents were beyond supportive of the gay thing. And both she and Emily had dated people of different ethnicities. Her parents might not win the inclusive language game, but they tried.

"Because unless I've missed something, you haven't added her as your plus-one to the wedding."

"Oh. That. Yeah."

"Yeah, that." Emily gave her the sort of exasperated look only a younger sister could. "She was so disappointed when you broke up with Brianna."

"She never even met Brianna."

Emily shrugged.

"I sort of hoped I could fly under the radar for at bit longer before making it a thing."

"Are you embarrassed of us? Is that it?" Emily asked.

"Obviously. I mean, have you seen you?" The tease was instinctual and not off brand for their relationship, but Emily frowned, putting Dylan on the defensive. "Kidding. Mira comes from money, but she's cool. If anything, I think she might feel out of place. Not because of money but because I think her relationship with her parents is kind of transactional."

"Huh." Emily nodded slowly, like it made sense but such a thing never would have occurred to her. "You should definitely invite her."

It wasn't like she hadn't thought about it. "I will. But don't tell Mom yet. I want to make sure she says yes first."

Emily looked her up and down. "I'll give you a week."

"Deal."

"Now, pour me some coffee and tell me where you keep the mixing bowls so I can whip us up some waffles."

Chapter Twenty

M ira stood with Dylan on the front step and waved as Emily and Jason pulled away. It struck her as an awfully domestic sort of moment but strangely, she didn't mind. Just like the casual breakfast for four—made entirely by Emily—took the edge off her headache and didn't leave her uncomfortable about not doing much to help. It could have made her feel like a guest, but it sort of made her feel like family.

Maybe it was the remains of her hangover talking. It might have been mild by most standards, but she wasn't used to hangovers of any kind. She also didn't get tipsy, though that's exactly what she'd been last night. A little loose. Almost giggly at times. And so busy getting into Dylan's pants she hadn't bothered with the water and painkiller regimen she relied on anytime she indulged in more than a glass or two of cider.

So not her. But for all that it was out of character, she couldn't remember the last time she'd had so much fun.

Audrey was a woman after her own heart, friend material. Rowan was sweet—a mellow foil to Dylan's more outgoing personality. Even Emily and Jason were great. Jason took being the only guy in stride way better than some of the men she'd dated and Emily's capacity for giving Dylan a hard time proved both formidable and entertaining. For as many double dates as she and Talise had orchestrated through the years, it had never felt like that.

She hadn't realized it was something she wanted. Something that was missing.

"You look so serious right now. I want to ask what you're thinking, but I'm kind of afraid to."

She gave Dylan an exasperated look, though she wasn't truly annoyed. "I'm thinking I should probably head home myself."

Dylan slipped an arm around her waist and squeezed. "But it's only Saturday."

"But I have laundry and grocery shopping to do."

"Adulting is overrated." Dylan kissed her with enough purpose to send most of her coherent thoughts scattering, including any thoughts of adulting. "Besides, if you stay tonight, we won't have to be quiet."

The memory of trying not to make any noise—and failing spectacularly—had a wave of heat creeping into her cheeks. "They heard us, didn't they?"

Dylan didn't hesitate. "Oh, for sure. Though, for the record, I think there was more giggling than anything titillating."

She squeezed her eyes shut and made a face. "I'm not sure that makes me feel better."

"Does the fact that they were getting it on, too?"

She hadn't considered that. "Maybe."

"Jason works a lot of overnights. If they're tumbling into bed at the same time, I'm certain they're making the most of it."

"Yeah." She'd dated an ER doctor once. She considered it a noble profession, but scheduling time together proved an utter nightmare.

"Are you thinking about my sister having sex or did you just agree to spend the day with me?"

"Dylan." She smacked Dylan without thinking, then realized she'd done it with more force than she intended. "Sorry."

Dylan merely smiled. "Oh, Emily does much worse. And that says nothing of when she's really mad at me."

"Still." She didn't worry she'd inflicted harm, but she didn't make a habit of spontaneously smacking people, either.

"I'll forgive you if you answer my question." Dylan's eyes danced with humor.

"I was thinking about what it was like to be with someone who worked weird hours."

"Oh, really?" Dylan's brow arched, more playful curiosity than please disclose your relationship history. At least she hoped that's the sentiment Dylan was going for.

She trailed a finger down Dylan's chest, between her breasts and all the way down to the drawstring at the waist of her sweatpants. "Even worse than dating someone who lives an hour away."

"I think we manage to make good use of the time we carve out."

Thoughts of laundry and groceries and the work she usually did for at least a few of her weekend hours faded. In their place, wondering how many hours she and Dylan could spend in bed before having to come up for air or food. "Indeed we do."

"Besides, don't you want to try out the sex candles I got when we have a gloriously free evening and nowhere to be the next day?"

So many parts of that question caught her attention, but she decided to start with the obvious. "Sex candles?"

"You requested wax play, did you not?"

It hadn't been a literal request. Merely one item in a string of fantasies she'd shared during their last round of sexting. Dylan said she hadn't done it but was game. Mira interpreted that as more of an "in theory" sort of statement than a "let's do that soon." "I mean…"

Dylan lifted both hands. "No pressure. But it sounded hot."

She raised a brow, unsure if Dylan meant the double entendre.

"Hot and also hot." Dylan tipped her head back and forth, a playful expression on her face. "And I did my homework, for the record. I don't take that sort of thing lightly."

She wouldn't. For all that Dylan came across as happy-go-lucky, she possessed intense focus when it came to things she cared about. "Well, if you went to all that trouble."

Dylan's demeanor sobered. "No pressure on the timing, either. I absolutely want you to stay, but I don't want it to be something you regret come Monday morning. And I want you to be relaxed and in the right frame of mind if we, you know, experiment."

It wasn't the first time it felt like Dylan had read her mind. This time, though, it felt intimate. A case of Dylan really understanding her, really paying attention. It sent emotions rippling through her along with the arousal. "I'd like to stay."

"What if we spend a couple of hours on the sofa first. I know you've got your laptop with you, and I could do a little work, too."

Not a concession, exactly. More a continuation of that understanding. "You don't have to butter me up. I already said yes."

"Ha ha."

She smiled, allowing herself to love how easy it all felt. "Which isn't to say you should never butter me up."

"Another kink?"

She laughed. But unlike Dylan's ha ha, it came out as a decidedly unsexy snort. "I'm going to go with no on that one."

"Okay, okay." Dylan nodded like she needed to file that fact away for future reference.

She considered smacking Dylan on the arm again but grabbed her hand instead. "Let's go in. It's chilly out here."

Dylan obliged and even got a fire going before grabbing her ubiquitous leather-bound journal and joining Mira on the couch. "Buttering up aside, I do have something to ask you."

Mira, who'd barely gotten her inbox loaded, looked up from the screen. "What's that?"

"Emily wanted to know why I hadn't invited you to the wedding yet."

"Oh." She didn't know what she'd been expecting, but it wasn't that.

"It's not that I wouldn't. Or didn't want to." Dylan spoke quickly and it was kind of adorable to see her squirm.

"But?"

"But I wasn't sure if a rowdy, big family wedding was your kind of thing."

To be fair, it wasn't. But she prided herself on being able to adapt to any social situation with grace if not ease. And she now considered Emily a friend. "Do you want me to go with you?"

"Yes. I think we'd have a blast. I just didn't know if you'd think it was fun." Dylan winced. "Especially if my mom gets ahold of you."

"Gets ahold of me?"

"She's, um, a bit more eager for me to settle down and get married than I am."

"Ah." She had visions of meddling middle-aged mothers sizing up their children's future prospects, but her reference points came from movies more than real life.

"So, as long as you don't mind comments about being a nice girl and questions about where you see yourself in five years, I'd love for you to be my date."

For some reason, the mention of being a "nice girl" planted a seed of discomfort in her stomach. Maybe because Dylan's family seemed pretty traditional, and Black and bisexual didn't necessarily translate in that setting. "What if she doesn't think I'm a nice girl. Or, not the sort of nice girl she wants for you?"

Dylan looked her up and down, then planted a loud, showy kiss on her lips. "You should be so lucky."

Not exactly the response to ease her anxiety, but a perfectly reasonable one. And it wasn't like she wanted to field questions or hints about whether another set of nuptials might be on the horizon. In fact, it was probably for the best if no one in Dylan's family had any ideas like that at all because she liked what she and Dylan had, exactly as it was.

❖

Dylan went up to her bedroom, leaving Mira to finish a few straggler emails. They'd managed a little bit of work, a nice walk, and a light dinner—the kind of leisurely day that kept its head above lazy and left her feeling both happy and relaxed. Well, as relaxed as one could be while thrumming with anticipation.

She'd read the instructions on the set of play candles at least a dozen times, but she read them again anyway. She lined them up by color—supposedly the least intense heat to the most—before lighting the dozen regular votives she'd arranged on the various flat surfaces of her room. The latter was a familiar task, though she hadn't done it with Mira yet. Mostly because stripping each other's clothes was about all they usually managed before tumbling into bed.

Tonight was different.

Different as in novel, obviously. She'd never dripped hot wax onto a lover before. But it was more than that. It was about being intentional with one another, sensual. She wanted Mira to feel that, to bask in it.

She'd no sooner blown out the last match when Mira strode in with all the purpose of an executive walking into a business meeting— an amusing juxtaposition to the leggings and Stanford T-shirt. Mira stopped short. "Hi."

Dylan smiled, willing Mira's brain and body to slow, if only a little. "Hi."

Mira made a circular motion with her finger, indicating the entire room. "This is fancy."

"I wouldn't say fancy, but I wanted to make it nice."

She expected a retort, but Mira's expression turned almost bashful. "You didn't have to do that."

"I wanted to."

Mira bit her lip. Not uncertainty, exactly, but it was in the vicinity. "I was coming in to say I wanted to take a quick shower."

"All right." Mira's penchant for getting clean before she got dirty never failed to send a surge of arousal coursing through her. "Would you like company?"

Mira smirked, her usual confident demeanor back as quickly as it had gone. "Always."

"I'll grab fresh towels and meet you there."

Mira disappeared and Dylan finished setting the scene, complete with an old sheet over the bed so neither she nor Mira would waste a thought on errant drips. She grabbed a pair of towels from the hall closet and headed to the bathroom. The water was already running, and steam billowed over the top of the curtain. Mira hummed what sounded like a Janelle Monae song, which made Dylan smile and calmed the nerves she hadn't expected.

She stripped off her clothes and stepped in, sending all her senses going at once. The fragrance of Mira's bodywash enveloped her as much as the steamy spray. And Mira's body, wet and shining and slick with suds, was as much a treat for her eyes as the fingers she grazed over Mira's skin.

Mira's eyes blinked open. "I was starting to worry you'd gotten lost."

"Just a quick detour."

"Ah." Mira stepped back to make room for her under the showerhead.

She turned to wet her hair and was treated to the press of Mira's breasts into her back. The moan that escaped was involuntary, not that she'd have tried to stop it. "How is it you feel that good?"

Mira laughed. "Magic. Is it wrong that I sort of want to call off the whole thing so we can get right to the fucking?"

She turned again, this time to face Mira, and wrapped her arms around Mira's waist. "If that's really your preference, it's your call to make."

"Oh, no. I simply wanted you to know how much I wanted the fucking. But I also want everything that comes first, especially after you went to all that trouble."

Mira's tone was light, but the comment made Dylan wonder if Mira's partners often didn't go out of their way to make things special. Or, maybe more accurately, Mira didn't let them. Whatever the case, she didn't take for granted how much Mira trusted her. And she planned to appreciate each and every minute of it. "And technically, we have all night."

She did a quick once-over with the three-in-one shampoo, conditioner, and bodywash that Mira made fun of, then they took turns getting handsy while the other rinsed. After cutting the water, she handed Mira the second towel and conversation lulled as they dried off. Mira hung her towel and the bonnet she used to keep her hair dry. "Do you mind if I moisturize quickly?"

Mira was as adamant about her lotion as she was her showers. Dylan didn't think she was supposed to find it as sexy and charming as she did, so she settled for an "of course" and headed back to her room, thinking it was the sort of routine she wouldn't mind getting used to.

In the bedroom, the candles bathed the room in both a faint coconut fragrance and romantic light. The nerves returned but were joined with the buzz of anticipation. Mira appeared in the doorway. Whether it was the hot shower or the fact that she was now completely naked, Dylan didn't know, but she moved more slowly than before. Not hesitant, but with an entirely different sort of intention.

"Ready?" Dylan asked.

Mira nodded.

"Would you prefer I do your front or your back?"

"Mmm. Back, if you don't mind."

She'd figured that would be the answer, but her research told her some women preferred the other. "Your wish is my command."

Mira smirked. "I do love it when you say that."

Normally, the comment invoked teasing about not getting used to it, or that it only applied to things in bed. Tonight was different, though. Tonight involved a power exchange, and she didn't take that, or Mira's trust, lightly. "Tonight, it's completely true."

Mira walked to the bed and crawled in. She looked at Dylan over her shoulder. "Well, then, I put myself in your hands."

The comment sent Dylan's already thrumming desire soaring. She picked up the first candle and took a deep breath. All the while, willing time to slow and her mind to commit each and every detail to memory.

Chapter Twenty-one

M ira took a deep breath and shifted her body, settling into the mattress and enjoying the cool sheets on her skin. She could do this. She wanted this. And she could ask Dylan to stop if she decided she didn't. They'd negotiated it all, up to and including a safe word, even though it wasn't really that sort of play.

Why was she so nervous?

From all her research and reading, it wouldn't hurt, at least not all that bad. If anything, it was the sort of sensation she craved—moments of intensity followed by a radiating warmth. Like spanking, which she'd done before without any trepidation and enjoyed immensely. And really, wax play didn't come with the power dynamics or potential shame triggers that spanking did, so it should be no big deal.

Again, why was she so nervous?

Because it hadn't occurred to her until that moment how intimate it would feel. How intense it would be to be the absolute center of Dylan's attention. Slow, methodical, intentional. Oh, and entirely one-sided. No reciprocating, no playfully pushing each other closer and closer to the edge. Her role was to lie there, to be present, and to take it all in.

Fuck.

"Why are your fists clenched?" Dylan brushed her fingers over Mira's knuckles.

"They aren't." She relaxed them as subtly as possible.

"Are you having second thoughts?"

"No," she said too quickly.

"It's okay if you do, or if you change your mind altogether."

She nodded, grateful to be lying on her stomach and unable to look into Dylan's eyes. An armor of sorts, though the only thing threatening to take her down in the moment was a barrage of emotions she didn't know what to do with. "Thank you."

"Are you ready?"

"Yes." She inhaled deeply once more and let it out slowly.

"Try to relax. I think it's easier to absorb sensation that way."

It made her wonder exactly how much research Dylan had done. The thought of Dylan reading up and trying to learn—so that she could do it well but also do it specifically for her—sent a shimmer of warmth through her that had nothing to do with the hot wax she was about to experience. "I'll do my best."

Dylan chuckled softly. "I know you will."

She closed her eyes and rested her cheek on the pillow of her folded hands. Without sight, her other senses swelled, and the strike of a match practically echoed in her ears. A moment later, the sound of Dylan blowing it out and the almost sweet sulfur smell. She wiggled slightly, then stilled. Waited.

"I'm starting with the one that's supposed to burn the least hot. I'm going to ask you to say more, less, or just right."

They'd already agreed to these words, sort of a tamer version of the green, yellow, and red commonly used in kinkier play. Just like wax play itself, the communication felt like a way to ease in, to test the waters. "I will."

The first drip landed right between her shoulder blades. Warm, but nothing more. "More please."

The next drips came in rapid succession and seemed to be falling from a place closer to her skin. A momentary sting with each, but the final one rolled along her skin, warm and sensual. "How's that?"

"Somewhere between more please and just right."

Dylan continued dripping wax—down her spine, along the curve of her shoulder blades. Singular drops interspersed with longer pours. She lit a second candle, the one meant to burn hotter, and alternated them. "I can't even begin to describe how beautiful your skin is in this light, and against the pink and purple of the wax."

"Will you...will you take a picture for me? When we're done, I mean?" It felt like a silly thing to ask for, but she wanted to see and didn't know how else she would.

"Of course. How are you? Do you want more?"

"Yes, please."

"I confess, I'm a little bit in love with you using that phrase."

She chuckled, thinking she could get used to it, too. At least in this context. The chuckle became a hiss when a particularly hot drip landed on a patch of bare skin.

"Too much?" Dylan's voice held both apology and concern.

The sensation had already mellowed. She let out the breath she'd sucked in. "Just right."

"Mmm." Dylan's reply seemed more to herself than to Mira, which made her smile.

Dylan continued, changing out the candles and playing with the height from which she let them drip. Not knowing when each drip would land, not knowing exactly how it would feel, freed her mind somehow. Anticipation gave way to regulating her breath, to letting the more intense pricks of heat land without flinching.

As difficult as it had been to think about being the singular focus of Dylan's attention, Dylan made it easy for her to sink in. To experience each sensation, the way pleasure flirted with pain. She'd expected the whole thing to be kind of playful and super hot. Not that it wasn't those things, but it all unfolded slower than she expected. More sensual. More intentional. And, again, deeply intimate.

"I've created quite the abstract work of art here." Dylan's voice coaxed her from the trance she hadn't meant to fall into.

"Have you now?"

"Give me one second. Are you okay?"

"I am."

Dylan's weight shifted and Mira imagined her grabbing her phone. "I'll only get a shot of your back. You know, for privacy."

Even as she trusted Dylan, she appreciated the consideration. "Thank you."

She lifted her head as Dylan rejoined her in bed. Dylan brushed a piece of hair from in front of her eyes. "How are you feeling?"

"A little bit like I'm the one who melted."

"Wait. Is that a good thing?"

The concern in Dylan's voice melted her even more. "Very good. I promise."

"Oh, good. Do you want me to start taking it off?"

She was a little sad she couldn't do that part herself but nodded.

Dylan propped herself on one elbow but didn't sit all the way up. She danced her fingers slowly over Mira's back. The play of sensations over skin and through the wax pulled Mira back into that state of hyper awareness the wax had given her in the first place.

Dylan worked slowly—single drips and big, irregular collections of drops. For as new as the experience had been, the gentle tug, the friction of the wax peeling away from her skin, felt strangely familiar. Like all the times she dipped her finger into the candles she lit while studying in college and grad school. Her roommates poked fun at her bizarre way to zone out, but it never deterred her. She loved the hot wax enveloping her skin, the perfectly smooth texture as it cooled. And, best of all, the slow and methodical act of peeling it off and starting over.

Just like with dripping the wax on, having someone else remove it felt hypnotic. Her senses shifted, tuning in and out. Intense focus gave way to the feeling of drifting, both physically and in her mind. Not unpleasant but also not entirely within her control. Novel, for sure. Enticing. And maybe the tiniest bit unsettling.

In what felt like no time at all, Dylan settled next to her. "So? What's the verdict?"

She pressed her lips together, suddenly shy. "Slower than I expected. More sensual. Does that make sense?"

Dylan smiled. "Were you expecting it not to be sensual?"

How could she explain? Or rather, how could she explain without getting hokey and emotional? "I guess I think of kinky play in general as kind of an onslaught. Sensation that's intense enough to command all my attention and shut my brain off."

"And that didn't happen this time?"

"It's not that it didn't. It's more like…it's like it was differently intense. Like it forced me to slow down and feel each sensation singularly." And to be inescapably aware of her body and who was on the other end of those sensations.

Dylan trailed fingers over the newly uncovered skin. "Is it okay if I like the sound of that?"

"Of course." Even if it freaked her out slightly. "But I'm hoping I can talk you into fucking me into oblivion before we call it a night."

"That can definitely be arranged."

She considered admitting she needed that reset, that being with Dylan like this stirred up feelings that didn't go with the arrangement they had, but she thought better of it. "Oh, good."

Dylan stood to set the bowl of discarded wax on the dresser and used the moment of physical separation to collect herself. Something between them had shifted. Like the tumblers of a safe lock clicking into place so that the treasure inside might be revealed. She felt it and she'd bet money Mira felt it, too.

But then Mira asked to be fucked into oblivion. Not that she had any complaints about such a request. The fact that Mira wanted her as much as she wanted Mira was one of her favorite things about their relationship.

And yet.

The way Mira asked felt like a step backwards. Or, maybe more accurately, like Mira was holding firm, grasping the status quo rather than letting that shift happen. Spinning the dial so Dylan had to try to sort out the combination from the beginning.

Dylan shook her head. She was hyperbolizing. Mira had let her do something that entailed a massive amount of trust. That kind of vulnerability would obviously feel like a precipice, and it made perfect sense for Mira to seek solid ground. Even if she wanted Mira to leap. Even if she already had.

It was that. Her own heart was in a state of free-fall.

Wanting Mira's to be right there with her was all well and good, but it wasn't what they'd agreed to. Maybe that was a subject she could broach—would need to broach—at some point, but doing it before the gala seemed foolhardy. Doing it tonight felt even more feckless.

She returned to the bed. Mira rolled onto her back and regarded Dylan with an inscrutable expression. Dylan cleared her throat. "So, you liked that? You're feeling okay?"

Mira nodded. "Very much."

"And how's your skin? Is it sensitive?"

Mira squirmed this way and that. "Maybe a little."

"Hmm." She'd been careful, but maybe she'd gotten closer than she should have.

Mira blinked a couple of times, all innocence. "Or maybe I'm just saying that so you'll let me be on top."

The combination was simply too much. Dylan didn't stand a chance. "I thought we'd established I'm perfectly happy to have you on top."

"Right, right." Mira nodded slowly.

"Would you like me to grab the cock?" It would feel amazing, even if part of her longed for nothing between them. Not even that.

"Mmm. Only if you want it. I mostly want to get my mouth on you and your fingers inside me."

A simple request as far as things went, but it turned her insides molten and allowed desire to supplant the swirl of emotions. "Yes, ma'am."

The ma'am got her a pithy look, but Mira didn't waste time complaining. She sat up and pointed to the bed. "You, there. Make yourself comfortable. I plan on taking my time."

She'd joked in the beginning, but she'd come around to finding Mira's assertive side particularly hot. Especially after Mira had so willingly put herself in Dylan's hands. "Yes, ma'am."

She crawled into bed and Mira wasted no time straddling her. "There. That's better."

"This reminds me of the first night we had sex." She wondered if Mira remembered that, if she thought about it as often as Dylan did.

"You mean the night you teased me about needing to top you?" Mira circled her hips suggestively.

"The night I learned I had zero complaints about you topping me."

Mira smirked. "Let's be honest. You're really the top."

"I like to think we're good at taking turns."

"Yes. That."

She placed a hand on each of Mira's hips. "But if you keep torturing me like that, I might have to flip you after all."

Mira wiggled. "Like this?"

She gritted her teeth. "Like that."

Mira moved down Dylan's body, nudging her legs apart and settling between them. She ran her tongue lightly over Dylan's vulva, not touching her clit but making it spring to almost painful attention. "And this?"

Dylan tried for an "uh-huh," but it came out more like a grunt.

Mira repeated the move and every muscle in Dylan's body tensed. "Well, we can't have that."

With that, she pressed her tongue into Dylan's wetness. But rather than the slow build Mira usually employed—coaxing her to the edge only to draw her back and do it all again—this was a no holds barred blitz. Mira bombarded her with sensations and didn't let up. Raw, possessive, and so very close to too much. But instead of overwhelming her, Mira somehow walked the line of exactly how much Dylan could take.

And then, without hesitation, she drove Dylan to the most blindingly intense orgasm of her life. Mira rested her head on Dylan's thigh and Dylan heaved out breath after breath, trying to bring herself back from the sexual stratosphere into which Mira had launched her.

She lost track of how long they stayed like that, but Mira's movements brought her back to the mattress and the sheets and the fact that she had bones and muscles and the like. "Um."

"Mmm. I like rendering you speechless." Mira came up the bed and knelt beside her.

"That was so good I don't even mind you being smug about it." It helped that smug happened to look especially good on Mira.

"And here I thought you were going to insist on fucking that smug look right off my face." Mira shifted her body slightly, opening a space between her knees that all but invited Dylan's hand.

"I'm not saying I don't want to do that, too." The heat radiating from Mira's pussy was almost as intoxicating as the wetness that coated Dylan's knuckles after barely touching her.

"You definitely should." Mira thrust against her, a move that managed to be equal parts seduction and challenge.

Since Mira was all but dripping onto her hand, she didn't hesitate to plunge two fingers into her. "Like that?"

Mira gasped, rocked her body back and forth to take Dylan deeper, then looked right into Dylan's eyes. "More."

She added a third finger and groaned at the sensation of Mira clenching around her. She turned her wrist slightly, shifting the angle of her thrusts and positioning her thumb to stroke Mira's clit. It was swollen and hard and she was pretty sure she didn't imagine Mira's pulse thudding through it.

"Yes. Fuck yes. Harder."

She obliged, loving that she had the power to drive Mira as high as Mira drove her. Mira rode her hand and her words dissolved into the sort of primal sounds that had Dylan wondering if she could orgasm simply from listening to them. Maybe if her clit wasn't still thrumming from the last one.

"Dylan." Mira practically screamed her name and came in a flood. It pooled in her hand and ran down her wrist. Dylan might not have come again, but her body tensed and rode a wave of pleasure that wasn't too far off.

Mira collapsed next to her. "Oh, my God."

Dylan rolled to her side. "Something like that."

Mira wrinkled her nose. "Sorry about the mess. You keep making me do that."

She couldn't suppress a smile. "I'm not."

"Still. Sleeping in a puddle is far from sexy."

No arguments there. "We can change the sheets easy enough. Or, better yet, go sleep in the guest room and deal with it in the morning."

Mira propped on an elbow and trailed a finger down Dylan's torso, right between her breasts. "Have I told you lately you're a genius?"

She might crave big feelings, but it was impossible to deny how much she loved this lighter side of Mira. "I'm pretty sure you've never told me I'm a genius."

"Hmm." Mira tapped her finger to her lips. "Well, you are tonight."

"I'll take it." She got up and extended a hand, then led them to the spare room.

Once they were tucked under the covers and Mira had settled into the crook of her shoulder, she kissed Mira's brow. Mira lifted her head, like she wanted a real kiss good night. Only instead of a kiss, Mira gave her a solid poke to the ribs. "Just don't get too used to it."

"Used to what?" Silly to ask, since she already knew the answer.

"Me calling you a genius. It'll go right to your head and then you'll be unbearable."

She might have protested, but Mira's mouth silenced her with a firm, deliciously emphatic kiss. When she pulled away and situated herself back into their snuggle, it was Dylan's turn to poke. "You keep kissing me like that and you can call me anything you want."

CHAPTER TWENTY-TWO

Mira turned this way and that, taking in her appearance from as many angles as possible. She rarely passed on the chance to dress up, enjoying the opportunity to take her hair and makeup to more glamorous places and wear elegant—more than flattering but professional—attire. But even by her standards, she'd gone overboard.

Not an evening gown, because that would have been over-the-top for even the fanciest cider event of the year. But a new dress, one that cost more than the handful of gowns she kept stashed in the closet of her spare room. The copper-colored silk felt exquisite on her skin and while she wasn't one to fixate on her figure, the cut hugged every curve just right. Sexy, but subtle enough to be classy.

She told herself it was a treat for organizing her first Cider Week Gala as COO, but the lie didn't get much traction. It was absolutely, completely, one hundred percent for Dylan.

She tried another pose, reminding herself it wouldn't be the first time she'd dressed to impress a date. Not that she and Dylan were technically each other's dates. Only they totally were. She'd even bummed a ride from Talise so she could go home with Dylan without having to deal with her car.

Was it wrong to think of Dylan as her date? To be thinking about going home with her before the evening even started? A couple of months ago, she'd have said yes. Because being with Dylan blurred professional lines, and she didn't do that. But also because she'd been so certain Dylan wasn't her type. Even when they'd started sleeping together, she'd chalked it up to a moment of reckless indulgence. Well, many many moments.

But somewhere along the way, she'd caught feelings. The kind of feelings that made her wonder what would happen if they kept seeing each other. If they stayed together. Could they make it work in the long run? Where would they even live?

A text from Talise announcing her arrival spared her the rabbit hole of those thoughts. She grabbed her coat and purse, told Gloria not to have any wild parties, and let herself out. Talise waved from the driver's seat. She returned the greeting but directed her attention to the woman in the passenger seat—a full-figured brunette with a dazzling smile. Only when she got to the car did she realize someone sat in the back seat as well. This woman wore a suit and tie and had a smile that was a bit crooked, but no less charming. She slid into the empty seat behind Talise. "Hi."

She caught Talise's grin in the rearview mirror. "I couldn't settle on one date, so I brought two."

She hadn't met the members of Talise's throuple but knew Talise had invited them both, so she simply returned the smirk. "The more the merrier, right?"

"You can borrow AJ if you want to pretend to arrive with someone." Talise offered a wink before backing out of the driveway.

"Happy to oblige." The butch in the back seat next to her extended a hand. "And nice to meet you."

She laughed because she had a feeling Talise had explained her reasons for tagging along. "Likewise."

"And I'm Poppy." The woman in the front seat pivoted to face her.

"Mira. And I'm glad you both could make it tonight. It's a bit far, but a fun event."

Poppy waved a hand. "Oh, we went ahead and booked a room at the hotel so we could have a good time and not worry about getting home."

Not for the first time, she had a flash of envy for how adventurous and carefree Talise could be when it came to relationships. But on the heels of that came a surge of very specific longing for Dylan. More visceral than she could remember feeling about anyone she'd dated before and this strange hybrid of sexual desire and emotional—what? Was it longing? Connection? Promise?

It unsettled her to feel things she couldn't explain.

She didn't like to think of herself as the sort of woman who kept relationships at arm's length. It simply worked out that way. Dating as pleasant diversion and professional convenience. And because it was generally a mutual sentiment, it never felt shallow or stunted. Until now.

Until Dylan.

"You okay back there? You're awfully quiet."

Conversation had swirled around her, and she had no idea how long she'd been lost in her thoughts. "Yes, yes. Just going through my speech is all."

"So, Talise says you put this whole event together. Is that true?" AJ asked, clearly tossing her a softball.

"That's been the case for the last few years, but this year I had help."

"And that's the person who is your date but isn't, right?" Poppy asked.

The question made her feel silly. "Um, yes."

Poppy nodded. "I love that you two got together while you were working on a project. That's how AJ and I met."

"Really? What do you do?" Hopefully, bouncing the conversation back to them would get her off the hook. Or at least free up some of her brain space to wonder again if Dylan thought her request to not officially be each other's dates was irrational.

Poppy gave AJ an affectionate smile. "We both work for nonprofits. I do work aiming to eliminate food insecurity and AJ does advocacy for survivors of domestic violence. We teamed up on a project to support families moving from shelter to transitional housing."

AJ grinned. "It was all very professional until it wasn't."

Poppy reached back to slap AJ's knee before looking at Mira. "The work part stayed utterly professional. Always."

"Except when she got bossy, and I had to remind her I was working with her and not for her." AJ winked.

Poppy didn't seem offended. "Well, someone had to keep her in line. So, will you two be out after tonight, then?"

She couldn't remember the last time someone had asked if she was out. It proved quite jarring and felt inherently judgmental. But then she remembered the conversations with Talise about her own identity—being out as a lesbian to her family but not poly. It gave her a modicum of comfort to know she wasn't alone in feeling like things were complicated sometimes. "Maybe."

Poppy offered a reassuring smile. "Not that you asked for advice, but in my experience, as long as you're not making out in the middle of board meetings, most people won't care much one way or the other."

It was a hypothetical but cut so close to the reality of her situation, she had to laugh. At the comment but also at herself. God, she could be uptight sometimes. "I'll keep that in mind."

❖

"I think your date has arrived." Audrey angled her head toward the entrance of the ballroom.

Dylan turned instinctively, without thinking or worrying about being discreet. And it was a good thing she wasn't terribly worried because the second her sights landed on Mira, everything and everyone else in the room disappeared.

"Close your mouth, dude." Rowan elbowed her lightly.

She did, but elbowed Rowan back.

"She is stunning, though." Audrey sounded almost wistful.

"Hey, I thought you preferred masc of center." Rowan made a show of sticking her hands out and looking offended.

"Yeah, but a corpse could appreciate that." Audrey didn't even pretend to stop staring and added a back-and-forth motion to signify the whole of Mira.

Rowan looked exasperated more than threatened. "Would you feel the same way if I'd said that?"

"Yes." Audrey turned to Rowan and planted fists on her hips. "One, because it's objectively true. Mira is gorgeous. Two, because I think it's healthy and normal to find other people attractive and super insecure for partners to keep that sort of thing from one another."

Rowan took a moment to reflect on that before turning to Dylan. "In that case, damn, dude. Your girlfriend's a knockout."

"She certainly is." She could have bantered back and forth, but she had more pressing matters to tend to. Specifically, saying hello and letting that gorgeous girlfriend know just how much of a knockout she was. She crossed the room, willing herself not to slide her arm around Mira's waist or press her lips to Mira's neck right below her ear. Instead, she focused on Talise and the two other women who seemed to be part of their group and tried not to jump to any conclusions about Mira bringing a date after all.

Rogue date or not, Mira's eyes lit up at the sight of her—not something she could fake. "Hi."

She smiled and put her attention back into not kissing Mira. Because, to borrow Rowan's phrase, damn. "Hi, yourself."

"Have you been here long? Is there anything that needs to be done? You look fantastic, by the way."

She had to laugh at Mira's unyielding efficiency, even dressed to the nines and ready for a party. "Only a few minutes. Not a single thing to do and I confirmed that with Helen. And I have nothing on you. You're stunning."

Talise tucked her tongue in her cheek and smirked, while the two other women looked amused, like they were all in on a private joke. She tried not to be bothered and hoped someone would let her in on whatever it was. Eventually, Talise reached out and gave her shoulder a squeeze. "I'm not sure whether to say Mira's found someone who can keep up with her or that she's finally met her match."

That got a withering smile from Mira and chuckles from the other two. Dylan shrugged. "I'm not sure those are mutually exclusive."

Talise tipped her head in concession. "You have a point there."

Mira cleared her throat. "If you'll allow me to pause the make fun of Mira fest, I'd like to do introductions."

The couple appeared slightly cowed. Talise, not so much. Dylan bowed slightly. "Please."

"Dylan, you know Talise, of course, but may I introduce her dates for the evening? Poppy and AJ."

Her brain tripped but recovered quickly enough, recalling Mira's comment about Talise being poly and dating a married couple. She extended a hand. "It's a pleasure. I'm glad you could make it."

AJ shook her hand first, then Poppy. Poppy beamed. "We do love a chance to get dressed up."

"Especially when it's a gala we're not the fundraisers for," AJ said.

"They're both in the not-for-profit sector," Talise said.

"Ah. Well, then I'm doubly glad you can kick back and have a good time." She wagged a finger at Mira and Talise. "Don't let either of them put you to work."

Any additional small talk was cut off by the arrival of Frederick and his husband, along with a few other members of the Cider Association board. It wasn't long before the doors opened, and other guests started pouring in. She got pulled into one conversation then another, losing sight of Mira in the process. Cider flowed and waiters with hors d'oeuvres began making the rounds. She snagged a mini corndog and chuckled over the disagreement she and Mira had over the suitability of such a thing for a fancy gala.

She caught glimpses of Mira here and there. Without fail, Mira would be wrapped up in one conversation or another, laughing and smiling. People seemed to bask in the glow of her attention. Like she'd been born for events like this. It reminded her how much she wasn't, that she could charm her way through most situations but didn't move through elegant or formal spaces with comfort.

The realization threatened to leave her hinky, but more than once, she caught Mira stealing glimpses of her. Not casual glimpses either. No, Mira regarded her with something resembling hunger. Those looks kept any potential insecurity at bay and stoked her desire.

As desperately as she wanted to grab Mira by the hand and drag her to a darkened coat closet to cop a feel, the stolen glances and surreptitious smiles sustained her.

About an hour into the evening, the band took a break and Mira took the small stage. After her gracious words of welcome and encouragement to sample the ciders and support the cideries that made up the Finger Lakes Cider Association, she launched into her speech about the fundraising efforts of the association and some of the past beneficiaries. Dylan hardly believed it possible, but Mira spoke even more elegantly and more passionately than when she'd rehearsed the day before.

"This year's gala supports Acres of Equity, a nonprofit based here in upstate New York whose mission is to support Black and Indigenous-owned businesses and individuals in the pursuit of sustainable agriculture and land stewardship. Acres of Equity provides acreage, training, and grants to diversify agricultural production and to offer reparations to the communities displaced and disenfranchised by the original spread of European settlers throughout the state."

Mira paused, cuing the screen behind her to drop and the house lights to dim. Dylan had seen the rough cut of the promotional video Talise and Jamal worked on together, but seeing it on the big screen—polished up and perfectly edited—got her a little choked up. About the cause, but also because she had this almost parental pride in how much Jamal had learned and grown in the last couple of years.

The video ended and the crowd applauded as the lights came up. Mira turned back to the microphone. "In addition to tonight's ticket sales and the silent auction, the Cider Association is proud to launch its first ever Reparations Package, an exclusive collection of ciders featuring over a dozen upstate New York producers. It will be available starting tonight and through December, with all proceeds benefiting Acres of Equity."

Another round of applause and Dylan made her way to the edge of the stage as they'd discussed. Mira introduced her, just as they'd rehearsed, and Dylan joined her. She did her part, explaining the package options and how to purchase it, and handed things back to Mira, who reminded everyone about Downstate Cider Week kicking off and encouraged everyone to enjoy the rest of the evening. When they exited the stage, both she and Mira were swarmed with well-wishers, members of the local press, and a handful of purveyors offering to promote the package even if they weren't the ones selling it. It might have been business as usual for Mira, but Dylan couldn't remember a time more people had wanted to talk to her at once.

It was magical. It was affirming. It was exhausting.

When the crowd finally thinned, she found Mira huddled with Talise and her dates. She'd no sooner joined the conversation when a man she didn't know approached them. His focus went immediately and fully to Mira. "Ms. Lavigne, I couldn't let the evening pass without introducing myself. Connor Fortin, Hudson Valley Cider."

It didn't surprise her at this point that Mira drew attention—and admirers—like a magnet. But she couldn't help feeling miffed that he didn't even glance at her. Especially since she'd literally been on stage with Mira as a fellow cider maker and person involved in the gala. She caught AJ shooting her a gagging gesture behind Connor's back, which mollified her slightly.

Mira, of course, turned on the full charm. "It's such a pleasure to meet you."

"Fantastic event tonight. I love your partnership with Acres of Equity." His smile—flawless and confident—reminded Dylan of so many guys she'd gone to college with. Frat guys. A little too polished and a little too moneyed to give people like her the time of day, even if they worked in the same industry. Oh, and a little too straight.

"Thank you. It's a project I'm passionate about, but also one I think will benefit the cider industry in the long run." Mira flashed an equally perfect smile back at him.

"I'd love to talk with you about it more." His eyes seemed to say more than his words, which made Dylan's skin crawl.

Mira reached into the small clutch that matched her dress and pulled out a card. "Absolutely. Let's set something up."

He took the card but seemed to study Mira more than the information on it. "I'm actually staying here tonight. Would you be interested in joining me for a drink at the hotel bar?"

Dylan didn't even want to think about the face she must have made, but Mira's smile didn't falter. "I'm pretty sure I'm going to turn into a pumpkin by the time we finish here."

Not the clear dismissal she would have preferred, but Connor seemed to take the hint. "That's too bad."

"Give me a call, though. I'm always happy to talk shop and good causes." She offered him a wink that Dylan was pretty sure could be read any number of ways.

"I most definitely will." He returned the wink with a knowing lift of his chin and bid her a good night.

When he was safely out of earshot, AJ rolled her eyes before giving Mira an appreciative nod. "Smooth."

Mira shrugged when Talise and Poppy concurred. Since Dylan didn't want to come off like a jealous asshole, she joined in. It bugged her extra that Connor hadn't even acknowledged her, and Mira didn't seem remotely bothered by it. Still, Mira had brushed him off. That counted for something.

Either way, she'd had about enough for one evening—sharing Mira's attentions but also having the very existence of their relationship be a secret. But rather than grumble about it, she took Mira's hand in a way that could totally pass as platonic and leaned in to whisper, "Please tell me I get to take you home soon."

No one but Mira could have heard, but her meaning was clear to Mira's friends. AJ offered her a conspiratorial nod. "Ladies, I think that's our cue."

AJ stuck out her elbows, and Talise and Poppy each took an arm. Talise immediately let go, though, to give Mira a hug. "Don't do anything I wouldn't do."

Mira stepped out of the hug and smirked. "Pretty sure that's a blank check."

Talise looked Dylan up and down. "With that one? Yes."

Dylan sputtered, then did her best to cover it with a cough. She'd known Mira and Talise were friends outside of work, but she hadn't realized they were that close. Though she wasn't about to turn down such a vote of confidence. Especially after Connor. "Thank you."

Mira rolled her eyes but laughed. She wished the threesome a good night before looking to Dylan. "How about we each make the rounds and start shooing people out of here?"

Something told her anything even resembling shooing guests out of an event was a stretch for Mira. So as much as she would have preferred to sneak out the back and call it done, she bowed. "After you, my beautiful co-hostess."

Chapter Twenty-three

Dylan unlocked the door and pushed it open so Mira could step inside. Mira did but dropped a playful smirk as she passed. By the time Dylan followed and locked the door behind her, Mira had already shed her coat.

"Thank you for hitching a ride with Talise so I could literally take you home with me."

The smirk remained and Mira paired it with a slow, appreciative once-over. "Thank you for bringing me home with you even though I didn't want to officially be your date."

The initial sting had faded, helped along by logic and reminding herself that getting to end the night with Mira mattered more than beginning it. Mira making eyes at her anytime they weren't engrossed in other conversations helped. As did the slow dance she talked Mira into. Even if the arrangement left Mira open to advances and her without recourse. "I may not have liked it, but I get it. And you're here now."

"I am." Mira's features softened into a smile.

Unable to resist the romance of standing together—in for the night but still all dressed up—she took Mira's hand. "I know I said this already, but you're breathtaking in that dress."

"Well, I didn't say it before, but I will now. I bought it, wore it, for you."

It could have been a throwaway comment, meant to titillate or tease. But Mira's expression made it clear she was confessing something out of the norm for her. It helped to smooth any feathers that remained ruffled from the fact that men and women alike seemed hell-bent on hitting on Mira at every opportunity, and Mira's deflections didn't have a whole lot of force in them. "I love you in one of my ratty old T-shirts, but I'm not going to lie, you are especially stunning in silk."

Mira raised a brow, making Dylan realize the potential implications of her phrasing. "Is that so?"

If a small part of her wanted to seize that moment, to lay her heart at Mira's feet and declare "actually, I love you, plain and simple," the rest of her screamed that it was too soon. At the very least, not the right moment. They were riding the high of a spectacular end to Cider Week and she didn't want Mira doubting the veracity of her words. So she took a page from Mira's book. "Though I'm looking forward to getting you out of it as quickly as possible."

The faintest trace of a shadow seemed to pass through Mira's eyes. So faint and so fleeting, Dylan couldn't be sure she hadn't imagined it entirely. "Well, what are you waiting for?" Mira asked.

"Not a single thing."

In her room, she kicked off her shoes and Mira did the same. She draped her suit jacket on the back of the thrift store chair whose job it was to hold half-dirty clothes. Mira wasted no time undoing her tie and sliding it from around her neck. But when Mira went to work on the buttons of her shirt, she caught Mira's wrists. Not hard, but firmly enough to get Mira's attention. Mira raised a brow. "Changing your mind?"

"Just the pace." She guided Mira's hands to her sides. "And the order of things."

"Oh, really?"

She took a deep breath, tried for a winning smile. "Indulge me?"

Mira's smile was slow, laced with mischief more than hesitation. "I suppose I could."

She brought Mira's wrists to her lips, kissing the inside of one and then the other. "Thank you."

"You're not going to torture me all night, are you? I've been wanting you since the moment I laid eyes on you."

"No torture, I promise. As for the all night part, I guess we'll have to wait and see."

Mira's head fell back and she laughed. A sexy move in any—well, almost any—context. For a woman like Mira, though, the moment of carefree abandon had Dylan's insides twisting in uncomfortably giddy ways.

She took advantage of the beautifully exposed expanse of Mira's neck, kissing her way down Mira's throat. Across one collar bone, then back and along the other. Down to where the most delicious swell of cleavage peeked over the neckline of her dress. She released Mira's hands and they went straight to Dylan's hair, tugging gently until Dylan's mouth made its way back to cover hers.

Dylan eased the zipper down with one hand and traced along Mira's spine with the other. She pinched the clasp of Mira's bra, exposing more skin to her wandering hands. She broke the kiss long enough to say, "You have the most impossibly soft skin. I want to touch every inch of you with my fingers, then my mouth."

"I will let you as long as you let me return the favor."

"I think that can be arranged." Because as much as she wanted to take her time and worship Mira, she might not actually survive the night without Mira touching her back.

She stepped back just far enough to give Mira's dress room to slink to the floor. The bra went with it, leaving Mira in nothing but a pair of silk panties a few shades darker than her skin. She let out an appreciative sigh.

"Are you not going to let me undress you at all?" Mira asked.

"I shouldn't find it sexy when you pout, but I do."

Mira ran a finger from the top button of her shirt to her belt. "If you don't let me get you at least a little bit naked, you're going to see me do a lot more than pout."

Mira's tone was coy, but there was something sweet in it, too. Like she was maybe letting her guard down in ways she hadn't, even when she'd let Dylan drip hot wax on her. Dylan couldn't be sure, but she hoped so. "Go on, then."

She expected Mira to rush because even when she wasn't in a hurry, Mira embraced efficiency. But she took her time with the buttons, kissing her way down Dylan's torso with each one. She even went so far as to drop a kiss on each of Dylan's wrists when she undid the buttons there. When Mira slid the shirt from Dylan's shoulders, so it joined her dress on the floor, she smirked. "See? I can take my time."

Even if she wanted tonight to be sensual, she couldn't resist the chance to tease. "But it's killing you a little, isn't it?"

Mira's hands, poised over Dylan's belt, stilled. "That sounds an awful lot like a challenge."

Was it? Did she want Mira to take her time because Mira wanted to, or for Mira to prove she could? Did it matter? "Invitation, perhaps."

"Ah." Mira waited a beat, took a breath. Two could play at that game. She slowly undid the buckle, licked her lips in anticipation. Dylan's abs contracted with her intake of breath when she flicked free the button at Dylan's waist. "Like that?"

Dylan merely nodded.

She smiled. Dylan was in rare form tonight and she had zero objections. She loved that they were still discovering new sides of each other, new ways of being together. New levels and layers. "You know, someone once told me that good things come with patience."

"That person sounds really smart. You should probably listen to them."

She nodded. "They came across as quite brash in the beginning. I wasn't sure they practiced what they preached."

Dylan's pants fell to the floor. "And now?"

"A long, delightfully drawn-out night of sex has recently proven me wrong."

"Hmm." Dylan slid her hands up Mira's arms and back down. "I hear you hate being wrong."

She lifted a shoulder. "Sometimes it's worth it. Would you like me to show you?"

Dylan seemed to consider for a long moment. "How about we show each other? After all, we have all night."

With that, Dylan once again encircled her wrists. She guided them to the bed and gently nudged Mira onto her back. Mira lifted both arms, beseeching Dylan to join her. "Come here. I need to feel you."

Dylan obliged, bracing a knee between Mira's legs and a hand on either side of her shoulders. "Like this?"

She arched in an attempt to create as much skin-on-skin contact as possible. "Closer."

Dylan lowered herself, not entirely but enough for Mira to feel Dylan's weight pressing her into the mattress. "Better?"

She squirmed, reveling in the sensations that already had her on the brink of begging. "Much."

"Good. Now, where was I?"

Dylan resumed kissing her—her lips, her neck, her shoulders. She tried to do the same, but Dylan shifted downward. Any protest vanished in the ecstasy of Dylan's mouth on her nipples. She clutched at Dylan's shoulders, her body already writhing, seeking Dylan's touch and the singular bliss of Dylan sliding inside her. Dylan clearly knew what she wanted but had her own agenda. Caresses, kisses, the tiniest bit of friction of Dylan's thigh against her clit. But nothing more. "Please."

"All in good time. I promise."

It was a new side of Dylan. A sort of stubborn patience that made Mira yearn for release but also yearn for something more. Connection, maybe? Or completion.

Each time she implored, Dylan promised she would. Only not yet. Soon.

When Dylan finally slipped inside, her body erupted—figuratively and literally. She called Dylan's name, as much surprise as release. Every muscle tightened and with every fiber she had, she tried to pull Dylan closer, deeper. Arms, legs, pussy—everything she had held on. "Please don't go yet."

Dylan shifted her head, just far enough to look into her eyes. With her free hand, she stroked Mira's cheek with more tenderness than Mira thought possible. Definitely more than she could handle. "Oh, baby. I'm just getting started."

She started to shake her head but found herself nodding instead. Like Dylan had her under a spell and she was powerless to do anything but follow wherever Dylan led. It was the sort of feeling that should have made her panic. Only it didn't.

Dylan eased out of her but resumed the slow caresses and lazy kisses. Like touching Mira was her new favorite hobby and she simply couldn't get enough. Before long, Mira started to squirm. Aroused again, perhaps even more than before. Wanting gave way to needing and needing gave way to a fire she hadn't known she could feel. Dylan coaxed her to the brink, easing her over the edge rather than pushing. Cascades of pleasure that simply tumbled one into another. Over and over until she literally thought another orgasm might break her.

The stirring in her chest had nothing to do with her racing pulse. She didn't know what to do with it, but she wanted to give Dylan even half of what Dylan had given her. So she turned the tables—exploring every inch of Dylan with her fingers, lips, and tongue. She basked in the way Dylan arched for her. Opened for her. Whispered her name with something akin to reverence.

She coaxed Dylan to orgasm with her mouth and a second time with her hand. That second time, Dylan's body tensed and held. Not unlike the seemingly countless times she'd come before. And yet something about it felt different. Felt like—what? Surrender.

Dylan would likely laugh if Mira used that word. A joke about never surrendering or, perhaps, a crack about gladly surrendering anytime Mira felt inclined to work her magic. And yet that was the word that stayed with her as Dylan's body trembled with aftershocks. As Dylan pulled her close and stroked her shoulder, her arm.

As Dylan's body stilled and her breathing slowed, another word came to mind. Love. It should have scared her, but it didn't. Because even though Dylan hadn't said it, she was pretty sure they both felt it.

Love.

Could it be as simple as that? She rarely thought so, but maybe this time. Maybe this was how it was supposed to feel.

Mira burrowed deeper into Dylan's embrace and let herself begin the deliciously relaxed drift toward sleep. And as her mind quieted and her limbs got heavy, it was that one word that stayed with her.

Chapter Twenty-four

Mira stood at the stove, swaying to Sade. She'd been in a good mood since the gala, but it had nothing on the elation she had going now. If Cider Week had been a hot fudge sundae, today would be the cherry on top. And she couldn't wait to tell Dylan the news. At the sound of the front door, she gave her hips an extra shimmy. "In here."

Dylan appeared seconds later, looking like she'd spent the day harvesting. Not a look she'd have put in her top ten, but it looked damn fine on Dylan.

"Whatever you're making smells amazing," Dylan said.

"Thank you. I'm so glad you're here. You'll never guess who I got a call from today." She put the lid back on the pot she'd been stirring and crossed the room. "Also, hi."

Dylan slid both arms around her waist and pulled her close. "Hi. Also, who?"

Rather than waiting for the answer, Dylan kissed her long and slow. After making her weak in the knees, it made her think—not for the first time—how nice it would be to come home to each other every night. For maybe the first time, she let herself sink into the idea rather than worry about it. And when Dylan's hand slid over the swell of her butt and gave it a squeeze, she let herself imagine skipping dinner altogether and going directly to bed.

Dylan took her time pulling away. "Sorry. I had to do that. Who did you get a call from?"

Despite the hugeness of the news, she basked in the playfulness Dylan brought out in her, that still felt new and a little wondrous. "Don't you want to guess?"

Dylan pinched her side lightly, making her giggle. "You just said I never would."

She had. But instead of feeling foolish, the giddiness of it all and being able to share it with Dylan simply grew. "Because you won't. And because you've probably never heard of her."

"Okay." Dylan let the word drag, seeming to enjoy playing along. "So, who is she and why does she have you all aflutter. I don't need to feel threatened, do I?"

"I haven't met her yet, so I don't know if she's hot, but I'm going to go with no." Though it gave her a flutter to think about Dylan wanting her enough to even joke about that sort of thing.

"Oh, good."

"Though, if her boss hits on me, we might need to talk."

Dylan narrowed her eyes then, though she seemed more intrigued than bothered. "All right. The suspense is officially killing me."

"Calista Gorman."

Dylan blinked.

"She happens to be the assistant producer of *First Up.*"

Recognition gave way to confusion. "The morning talk show?"

"You mean the nationally televised morning talk show on the largest cable news network?"

Dylan laughed. "Yes. That one."

"You would be correct."

"And she called you because…"

"Because she saw the Cider Week press release and reached out to me to schedule an interview." Four hours since the phone call, and she still couldn't believe it.

"Wait. An interview on the show?" Dylan asked.

"Yes. Live and in person, even. They're flying me down next week. It's going to be part of their series on outside the box holiday gifts featuring small and minority-owned businesses." She couldn't have orchestrated a better national publicity hit.

"That's fantastic." Dylan smiled, but the enthusiasm didn't reach her eyes.

"It's an amazing opportunity. I'll be representing Pomme, obviously, but I'm going to be able to talk about you and Forbidden Fruit and all the businesses the Cider Association represents."

Dylan nodded and continued to smile. "For sure."

"What's wrong?"

"Nothing. I'm super proud of you."

The assertion proved even less convincing than the smile. "Something is wrong. Your words are saying one thing, but your body isn't even speaking the same language."

Dylan ran a hand up the back of her neck and blew out a breath. "I am proud of you. And excited for that kind of publicity."

"But?"

Dylan looked at the floor, made brief eye contact, then stared at the ceiling. "But I'm a little disappointed I didn't get that phone call."

She'd had a moment of worry Dylan might have that reaction but just as quickly talked herself out of it. Bruise to the ego or not, the exposure would be good for both of them. She wanted Dylan to see that, to trust it. And, maybe even more, she wanted Dylan—her girlfriend—simply to be happy for her.

"I'm sorry. I know that's not fair," Dylan said.

She appreciated Dylan's saying so, knowing it even if she didn't feel it entirely. "I get it. But it really is an amazing opportunity. For both of us."

"Totally." Dylan nodded.

"Do you want to come down with me? We could make a weekend of it. See a show, have a couple of amazing meals." It was the sort of couple thing she rarely did with people she dated, the sort of thing she realized she wanted to do with Dylan.

Dylan shook her head. "We're in the middle of harvesting and pressing. I can't just run off for a few days of fun."

"So, maybe it's good that I got asked to do the interview anyway?" A stretch, but she was trying to lighten the mood.

Dylan offered a half-smile, but at least it seemed genuine. "I wouldn't go that far."

"I promise I'll talk you up."

"I really am excited for you."

"But are you as excited for that as you will be for the apple pie I made you?" She'd simply been feeling celebratory when she got home, but mentioning it now came off a little bit like a bribe. Or maybe a consolation prize. She didn't know if Dylan would take it as such, and she didn't particularly want to be in the business of smoothing ruffled girlfriend feathers, but there was no taking it back now.

"I'll never say no to pie."

Dylan's response didn't offer clarity one way or the other, so she set it aside. Because ruffled girlfriend or not, her parents were thrilled, and she was pretty damn excited for such a big and unexpected feather in her cap. And that was what mattered.

❖

Dylan woke before she needed to, so she spent twenty minutes tossing and turning and feeling sorry for herself. In part because she hadn't entirely let go of the jealousy over Mira landing the interview and not her. She didn't like that about herself, but at least she didn't lie to herself on top of it. But the other part, maybe even the bigger part, simply missed sleeping and waking up with Mira by her side.

Silly, really. It wasn't like they spent every night together. Though she had started to wonder with increasing frequency how they might manage to spend all their nights together. Even if neither of their places felt like a reasonable compromise.

Because thinking along those lines made her even more agitated, she hauled herself out of bed and got dressed. That was a worry for another day. Today, she'd be happy for Mira and happy New York cider would be in the spotlight for the million or so viewers who tuned in to *First Up* as they started their days.

Since her streaming package didn't include the channel, she drove over to Audrey and Rowan's. It made her smile to pull in the driveway and realize she no longer thought of the house as Ernestine's. Not that Ernestine would ever be forgotten. No, it was more that Ernestine's wish for Audrey to love the farm and consider it home had come true.

She'd no sooner opened the back door than the aromas of coffee and spices enveloped her. "Please tell me that smell is coming from something I get to eat."

Audrey turned from where she stood at the counter. "Do you really have to ask?"

Dylan shrugged before crossing the room to plant a kiss on her cheek. "I try never to presume that a woman wants to have sex with me or has baked for me."

Audrey laughed. "A sound philosophy I suppose."

"It's kept me out of trouble more than once."

"I bet. Help yourself to coffee." Audrey angled her head toward the pot. "The pumpkin bread is already in the living room. Rowan said you didn't count as company, so she didn't have to wait."

She helped herself to a mug from the cupboard. "As long as she doesn't eat it all before I can get a piece, I'm okay with this practice."

A few minutes later, she sat on one edge of the sofa, eating breakfast and thinking how weird it was to get together with her friends to watch someone they knew on television. The segment got teased twice before it actually came on, and they had to sit through a cheese of the month club and ten tech gadgets under twenty dollars before an artfully staged collection of ciders appeared on the screen. Pomme, with its gilded label, sat front and center. But a Forbidden Fruit bottle sat right next to it, along with ciders from Eve's and Seneca Hill.

The camera cut away and Gavin Banks appeared on screen. "I have the pleasure to welcome Mira Lavigne, the woman behind Pomme d'Or, New York's best-known cider. Mira, thanks for joining us this morning."

The shot expanded to include Mira, sitting in a chair where any number of famous people had sat before, hawking this project or that. "Thanks so much for having me."

"Oh, she looks fantastic," Audrey said.

Dylan nodded. The emerald green dress looked both classy and festive and made her skin glow. And even if she preferred Mira barefaced, her makeup was undeniably flawless, and her hair even more artfully arranged than usual. Like she was made for TV appearances. The realization abruptly highlighted the fact that Dylan wasn't, at least not by any conventional standards.

"Tell us about your cider."

"We source apples from all over New York state, Vermont, and Pennsylvania, working closely with our growers to ensure a high-quality harvest with the unique qualities that produce the cider Pomme d'Or is known for."

Gavin nodded, seeming to hang on Mira's every word. His smile reminded Dylan of Connor, making her grumble under her breath. "Now, I confess I just learned this. Your cider doesn't come in six-packs and live on the beer aisle like some people might expect."

Mira touched her hair lightly and shifted the angle of her head. On someone else, the gesture might have been a tell of nerves. On Mira, it radiated relaxed confidence. "It doesn't. That sort of cider is great, but it tends to be on the sweeter side and drinks like a bubbly, alcoholic apple juice."

Gavin offered a playful shrug. "I've been known to enjoy a bubbly, boozy apple juice now and again."

"It has its appeal." Mira smiled and it read as utterly genuine. If Dylan didn't know better, she'd swear Mira didn't have an opinion on the subject one way or another. Or, even wilder, think she agreed.

Gavin leaned in slightly and pointed a finger at Mira in a way that was probably his schtick but could have easily been a come-on. "But yours is different."

Mira shifted in her seat, not mirroring the lean exactly, but reciprocating the open and inviting body language. "We use the traditional champagne method, and the result is effervescent but much drier."

"Like champagne." Gavin seemed impressed with himself for making the comparison.

"Yes. Exactly."

Gavin continued to ask questions, though it felt to Dylan more like flirty banter than an interview. Mira demonstrated the best way to open a bottle, noting the goal was to get the cider in the glass, even if bubbles spilling out the top looked fun. The segment closed with ways to order online and some of Mira's personal recommendations. Well, that and Gavin asking Mira if she needed a date for New Year's Eve. When Mira merely laughed, Gavin pressed a hand to his chest and sighed. "Let me guess, you're spoken for."

Mira didn't hesitate. "I'll make you a deal. Give me a call next time you're upstate. I'd be happy to roll out the Pomme d'Or red carpet."

"Are you fucking kidding me?" Dylan slammed her mug down harder than she'd meant, sending the contents sloshing over the top.

Rowan and Audrey both looked at her with a mixture of confusion and alarm.

She stuck out her hands. "That guy hit on her and she didn't even pretend to blow him off."

"It's TV." Rowan gave a dismissive flip of her hand.

She looked back at the screen to catch Mira put her hand on Gavin's arm before the show cut away to another segment. The jealousy she'd tried to keep at bay reared its head, joined by a gnawing feeling of inadequacy. "He asked her out and she basically offered him a personal invitation."

"Wow." Audrey clicked off the TV. "Let's talk about how you really feel."

"It was gross. The part at the end but the rest of it, too. You honestly don't think she came off as patronizing?"

Audrey shook her head. "Not at all. I thought she sounded very gracious."

"Seriously? Not rehearsed and arrogant and just a little too perfect?" She looked to Rowan for support.

Rowan's gaze darted from Dylan to Audrey and back like their conversation was a tennis match. Or maybe like she couldn't decide whose bad side she'd rather find herself on. "Uh."

"Exactly."

Audrey made a flicking gesture with her hand. "But she mentioned Forbidden Fruit specifically. That's national exposure. She didn't have to do that."

She didn't. But the way Mira chose to talk about it—a scrappy startup with creative flair—felt like the pat on the head toddlers got before being told to run along and play. How was she the only one who saw it that way? "Nice in theory maybe but condescending in execution."

Audrey frowned.

"You think I sound unreasonable?"

"I think you sound…" Audrey shot Rowan a look of something that resembled apology, then looked right at Dylan and shrugged. "Jealous."

"Jealous that she's my girlfriend but flirting with some random guy on national television? Damn right I'm jealous."

Audrey's look of apology morphed into one of pity. "That part wasn't cool, but I think she was trying to be gracious."

The snort of derision made her feel like an asshole, but she couldn't take it back or bring herself to apologize.

Audrey had seen enough of her bluster that she wasn't deterred. "But that's not what I meant."

"Oh? What did you mean?" She didn't even try not to sound snarky.

"I think you're jealous of Mira herself."

Dylan let out another snort. "I do not want to be Mira."

"Of course you don't," Audrey said quickly.

"But?" She didn't really want the answer but couldn't let it go.

"But, maybe, you want what she has? The recognition and the attention and the reputation." Audrey cringed, like she was sorry to be the bearer of bad news.

She meant to sigh, but it came out as a growl.

Rowan leaned into her line of sight. "Hey, don't shoot the messenger."

"Sorry." As much grumble as apology, but it was better than nothing. "I am jealous. And I kind of hate myself for it. It's just frustrating that she's getting the spotlight and she isn't even a cider maker."

Audrey gave her forearm a gentle squeeze. "It's okay to have some envy. It doesn't mean you're a bad person, or even that you begrudge Mira getting the spotlight."

That should have made her feel better. It didn't. She wasn't used to this swirl of negative emotion, and she didn't like it. And, in this moment at least, she absolutely didn't want to talk about it. "I'm going to go to work."

Rowan, who knew her better than probably anyone, stood. "Give me ten and I'll head over with you."

She appreciated the offer, but not enough to accept. She always teased Rowan about needing to be alone with her thoughts, but today she got it. "Take your time. I'm going to get some air and clear my head. I'll see you there."

If Rowan knew her well enough to offer, she also knew her well enough not to press. "It's all good. I'll catch up with you in a bit."

She thanked Audrey for the hospitality, gave Matilda a scratch under her chin and Jack a scratch behind his ears, and made her exit. She drove down to the cidery so her truck would be there later, but rolled the windows down and let the cold, damp air cut through her. Inside, she headed right for the tanks and started pulling samples. The task calmed her but also reminded her of why she did what she did. Spending time with Mira might feel amazing in a lot of ways, but it muddied the waters, too. She needed them to be clear, to focus on what mattered. And that was making cider.

CHAPTER TWENTY-FIVE

Mira pinched the bridge of her nose and read the email again. Not that a second read would change the contents. *Honorable Mention.*

Yes, it had been risky to put a brand-new cider into the competition. An impulsive decision born from her time with Dylan. From flirting with creativity and innovation and risk. A decision she hadn't even run by her father.

Yes, it was a step out of her comfort zone, both professionally and personally. A stretching of her wings that felt good enough to make her forget the risk of straying from the status quo.

Yes, she could choose to see it as a win, a recognition that she was launching a new era at Pomme. One that was fresh and new and future-facing and full of potential.

But what was it really? *Honorable Mention.*

Pomme had garnered no less than silver with its entry into the state cider competition in all but one of the last twenty years. It earned gold more often than not and even had a handful of double golds, all of which were prominently displayed in a beautiful glass case in the tasting room. The case—and everything its contents represented— were her father's pride and joy.

She was going to have to call her parents. Hopefully, she could get to them before they saw the results themselves and explain why it wasn't an insult or a blow to Pomme's reputation in the long run. She could do that. She might even manage to believe it herself. She reached for her phone, but it rang before her hand touched the receiver.

It could be anyone. She blew out a breath, knowing full well it wasn't. "Hello."

"I thought we agreed you were going to enter the Late Summer Harvest."

She closed her eyes and resisted the urge to scrub a hand over her face, if for no other reason than it would smear her makeup. "Hi, Dad."

"Well?"

Since the ship of pleasantries had clearly sailed, she got to it. "Actually, you suggested that. I chose to go in a different direction."

He let out a grumble of displeasure.

"It was a way to step outside business as usual, to show that we're evolving as a company," Mira said.

"Well, I hope you learned your lesson." A muffled click stood in for a good-bye and the line went quiet.

She ran her hands along the edge of her desk then placed them, palms down, on either side of her keyboard. It was fine. It was a misstep, not the end of the world. Not even bad news, really. Just a lack of anticipated good news. Right?

No, not right. Not even close. She let out a sigh and shook her head, pushing her chair far enough out to lean down and rest her forehead on the desk, just shy of the spacebar.

A knock at the door startled her to an upright position. Like her father had figured out a way to teleport so he could chew her out in person. But when the door opened, Talise stood on the other side. "How upset are you?"

She let her shoulders slump. "More than I was before getting Yves's 'I'm disappointed in you' speech."

Talise cringed. "Already?"

"A stern talking-to is best delivered first thing."

Talise closed the door behind her and sat in one of the chairs opposite Mira's desk. "Do you want to talk about it?"

"Not really."

"That sounds like Mira-speak for you need to talk about it." Talise offered a sympathetic smile, her tone more encouraging than sanctimonious.

She let out a dismissive snort.

"I'm not saying you have to. Merely pointing out the obvious," Talise said.

"I know. I'm just lodging my distaste with you being right." Which was pretty much always, at least when it came to Mira's tendency to stew when she really needed to process.

"Noted."

"I'm just mad. This whole thing started with Dylan's nudges to be more adventurous, try new things." Which was much easier for Dylan, who didn't have an established company to steer and a reputation to maintain in the meantime.

"Nudges? What kind of nudges?"

She ran through their many conversations on the topic of cider making. But what she came up with had a lot more to do with her own dissatisfaction with toeing the line than any genuine poking from Dylan's end. "You know. Just her aura. It's all about shaking things up and not following the rules."

"Weren't you having thoughts of shaking things up before Dylan came along?"

Had she? Maybe. Okay, definitely. But Dylan was the one who made her feel like she should. Like she could. "Yeah, but Dylan is the one that got me all riled up, made me impatient. She got into my brain."

Talise pressed her lips together. "You got into your brain. Or maybe more accurately, you got out of your brain for once. Dylan merely got into your bed."

The sigh that came out this time was more of a grumble. "I knew you were going to bring that up."

"Maybe it's worth considering whether one has anything to do with the other."

"Are you implying that I compromised my professional integrity because I was too focused on getting laid?" The prospect would have set her on edge no matter what. Paired with Dylan's weird and sullen silence since she got back from New York, it had her wanting to throw things. And she was not the sort of woman who did that.

"I'm implying that you've opened your heart and with that comes being open to Dylan's influence. I happen to think that's a good thing, at least when it means trusting your gut and taking chances. But maybe that influence is at odds with the influence of your parents."

Somehow, that sounded even worse. "When it comes to running Pomme, my heart shouldn't have anything to do with it."

Talise's look of sympathy crossed the line into pity. "I hope you're just saying that out of frustration and disappointment."

Before she could argue that those emotions didn't have a place in running a business either, her phone flashed with a text notification. Since it was the first she'd heard from Dylan in a day and a half, she snagged it to see what the message said. Whatever it was had to be better than this wringer of a conversation with Talise.

I know you're probably at work, but I need to talk to you. I'm on my way up and I hope you can fit me in.

Okay, she'd been wrong. Dylan's text was way more ominous than Talise's not so subtle hints about the slings and arrows of vulnerability. She thrust her phone at Talise. "What am I supposed to do with that?"

Talise grimaced. "Say okay?"

"Well, it sounds like she's going to show up either way. Because who cares about things like regular business hours?"

Talise took a deep breath. "Do you want my advice?"

"No." She grumbled. Then realized she had no idea what to do and anything would be a better starting point than nothing. "Yes."

"Figure out who you're really upset with and what you're really upset about."

With that, Talise got up and left, leaving Mira to sit in her own cauldron of roiling emotions. From where she sat, the biggest source of her current problems was herself. What to do about that was another matter entirely, not to mention far more elusive.

❖

If the rational part of Dylan's brain knew showing up at Mira's office was a terrible idea, she paid it no heed. Same reason she didn't tell Rowan and Audrey why she wasn't going to be at work that morning. They'd surely be on team rational brain, and she didn't want to hear it.

She'd hoped the drive up to Pomme would give her clarity, give her calm. What it gave her instead was a raging headache and a cocktail of anger and sadness that promised no good would come of attempting a conversation. But heeding that would fall to rational brain, which she'd banished for the day. Besides, Mira's terse reply that she could carve out an hour practically begged for them to have it out. And the sooner she got that over and done, the better.

Since the main doors wouldn't be open for a couple of hours still, she went to the side entrance Mira had told her about the first time she'd come outside of tasting room hours. The office suite was quiet, with the receptionist typing away at her computer and no one else to be seen.

She didn't bother with announcing herself or checking in to see if Mira was available. She did pause in the doorway to Mira's office long enough to knock. The formality of that felt disquietingly fitting.

Mira looked up at the sound. "Dylan. Come in. Is everything okay?"

She shook her head.

"Is it the Honorable Mention thing? We got one, too. Disappointing but technically the first time any rosés have been recognized, so that's saying something."

Mira's words made sense, but her brain was so far down another path, they didn't entirely register. "Huh?"

"I saw that your rosé got an Honorable Mention. Mine did, too. Is that what you're upset about, that I nudged you to enter something you weren't in love with?"

She closed her eyes to keep herself from rolling them. "No, actually. Some of us don't turn our noses up at recognition we don't consider fancy enough."

"What is that supposed to mean?"

She hadn't intended to draw that parallel, but Mira dropped it right in her lap. "It means you're not a week out of being interviewed on national television and you're pouting about the size of your trophy in some state competition."

"Those two things don't have anything to do with each other."

"Don't they? It's all about being in the spotlight, isn't it? And you hate it when that spotlight includes anyone but you."

Mira laced her fingers together, though she seemed to be death-gripping herself rather than trying to placate. "Is that what this is about? The fact that I was on television, and you weren't?"

Admitting it suddenly seemed petty. Or maybe Mira was looking to make her feel petty so she'd let it go. "You don't even make cider."

Mira stood, came around the front of her desk so they stood face-to-face. "Just because I don't get my hands dirty the same way you do doesn't mean I don't make cider. And for the record, I represent a cider that's been around since before you were born."

She resisted a comment about being the McDonald's of cider because it wasn't fair or, grudgingly, accurate. It was more like Pomme was the big box to her scrappy startup. She'd convinced herself that didn't matter when it came to Mira and her as people, but she'd been stupid to think she could separate the two. "So, you're just going to ride those coattails."

For some reason, that seemed to strike a nerve. "No, I'm pushing the envelope and making my father question whether he made a mistake putting me in charge."

Under other circumstances, she'd stop the conversation and focus on that. She might not know the specifics but whatever it was clearly had Mira upset. But these weren't other circumstances and her feelings for Mira had clouded her judgment and gotten in the way of what she needed to do, more than she should have let them. "Poor Mira. Her brand is so well-known she's in danger of tarnishing its image by dabbling in something new."

"Look, I don't know what side of the bed you got up on to be this much of an ass, but I'm not a fan. And I'm not going to spend my workday listening to you go off about not being the center of attention."

She'd lost track of her train of thought at this point, but the anger—at Mira and at herself—remained. And it had nowhere to go but out. "It's all about the attention. For Pomme, for yourself. You seek it out and soak it all up."

"My brand has been around longer and has more name recognition. I'm not going to apologize for that."

"That's not what I'm talking about."

Mira managed to look both genuinely confused and defiant. "Then what are you talking about?"

The image of Mira on screen, smiling and flirting at Gavin had been seared into her mind. Part of why rational brain no longer had room to operate. "You don't think the interview had anything to do with the fact that you're gorgeous and feminine?"

"What are you implying, Dylan?"

"I'm not even saying you mean to, but I think you fall back on straight privilege when it serves you." She definitely hadn't meant to say that—hadn't really been thinking it even—but it was too late to take it back.

"You're seriously going to throw privilege at me right now?"

She shrugged. It felt gross, but if the shoe fit.

"Do you have any idea how fucking white this industry is?"

She did. More white, even, than it was male-dominated. Shame replaced some of her anger, though it didn't make her any more levelheaded. "I'm sorry."

"Are you?"

"Well, for implying you don't have to deal with racist bullshit on a regular basis." If Dylan conceded nothing else, she had to concede that.

"But you're not going to apologize for being jealous and kind of a jerk since I did that interview."

She scrubbed a hand over her face, hating herself but hating everything about the situation even more. "Actually, I will. I've been jealous and a dumbass."

"Not exactly an apology."

"I'm sorry for both of us. How's that?" That's what it boiled down to. Being with Mira distracted her from what mattered, but it also apparently brought out the worst in her. She couldn't pretend otherwise.

"What is that supposed to mean?"

She could back down. Or, at the very least, say she needed some space and leave it at that. But as much as she was pissed off, she was sad. Sad and scared. The last week made her feel like she'd started turning into someone she didn't like and, worse, didn't trust. And even knowing that being with Mira was the root of all that, Dylan wanted her. Loved her. It was that knife twisting in her gut that had the train of reasonable conversation leaving the station. "It means I'm becoming a self-important asshole more interested in publicity and recognition than in making good cider."

Mira's features softened, if only slightly. "You're not that."

"I've been acting like it. You're rubbing off on me in all the wrong ways."

And just like that, the softness vanished. "If you're not happy with yourself, then do something about it. But don't barge in here and tell me I'm the reason you—"

"I can't be around you anymore."

"What?"

The genuine confusion in Mira's voice could have made her feel better. Instead, it drove home how much Mira didn't get it. "You're a cider heiress, Mira. I'm a cider maker."

"So, now I don't work hard enough? What the fuck, Dylan?"

"You work your ass off. But at the end of the day, you could be the face and brains of pretty much any company, and it wouldn't make a difference one way or the other. You're a suit. A beautiful, charismatic, insanely intelligent suit."

Mira's eyes narrowed. The fire that had burned in them a moment before turned to ice. "I think you should go."

She shouldn't. Walking out would leave a rift that might prove irreparable. Her heart screamed at her to remain. But even as it did, her brain—overstimulated and run by adrenaline more than reason—knew that staying might lead to compromises she'd regret even more.

So, she left. She strode out of Mira's office, through the reception area, and out the front door of Pomme. She got in her truck, started the engine, and drove away. And even though regret already burned in her chest, she did it without looking back.

Chapter Twenty-six

Talise strode in with only a cursory knock and handed Mira a folder. "These graphics need your approval, and we'll incorporate them into the spring campaign."

Mira took the file and flipped through the contents. In addition to the new logo—a subtle riff on the classic Pomme imagery—there was a collection of coordinated labels, all taking their inspiration from the inaugural rosé. They were fresh and modern without breaking entirely from the original. A week ago, they would have filled her with pure elation. Now? Ambivalence at best. "Are you sure we should be doing this?"

"Do you not like the rose gold? I know it's trendy right now, but it's so right for the brand, I feel like it's going to stand the test of time."

She studied the label again. The metallic lettering could have been overkill, but with the slate gray paper, it somehow looked both elegant and hip. It also looked great next to the cream and gold of the logo and labels that had been Pomme's signature look since its founding. "I mean the whole line. What if my father is right and this is the wrong step for the company?"

"Do you think your father is right?"

The simple directness of the question caught her off guard. Since it was only Talise and her in her office, she didn't hesitate or wring her hands over the answer. "No."

"Then what's this really about?"

"Oh, I don't know. Maybe the fact that I have no idea what I'm even doing?" She hadn't meant to snap but it came out that way, sharp and short-tempered.

Talise, to her credit, didn't flinch. "Ah. Does that mean I should assume all glumness and irritability for the foreseeable future to be Dylan-related unless you say otherwise?"

She glowered. "I didn't say anything about Dylan."

"You didn't have to. I know that's what has you all riled up."

"I'm not some emotional rollercoaster of a teenager who can't function after a breakup."

Talise took a seat. "I didn't say you were. But Dylan got you thinking differently, taking more chances. And now that you're not together, you can't seem to decide whether to stick with the new version of you or revert to the old."

She let her head fall back. "I'm not sure what's worse—feeling this way or being so obvious about it that you can armchair analyze me in under a minute."

"To be fair, the ability to analyze you comes from knowing you for more than a decade."

"Okay, so the worst part is feeling this way to begin with. I'm too old to be this wishy-washy and too young for a midlife crisis."

"Can I ask you a question?"

She folded her arms. "You're going to whether or not I say yes, so go ahead."

Talise angled her head, conceding the point. "Are you squeamish because you're afraid of pushing your father too far or because you're resenting and resisting anything that might make you even remotely like Dylan?"

"Could you please warn me when you get up on the therapist side of the bed? I'd like the chance to brace myself for the probing questions."

Talise smirked. "You should assume probing questions unless I say otherwise."

This time, the phrase made her laugh. "I object."

"Overruled."

"You can't overrule me. You're not a judge and, technically, I'm your boss," Mira said.

That got her a look of indifference.

"Fine. Given how abhorrent Dylan found the idea of being anything like me, no, I don't want to be anything like her."

Talise let out a dismissive sniff. "Dylan is so wrapped up in her own self-righteous, small-batch ego, she likes to pretend she's not running a business like the rest of us."

Since her arms were still folded, it left her with limited options to express how unimpressive she found that explanation. She settled on a huff of her own.

"I'm not saying it's great, but that would make it a different animal, no? More about planting her flag on Mount Cider than her actual feelings for you?" Talise lifted one shoulder, like she wasn't entirely convinced of her own argument.

"I don't see how. I have no interest in being with someone who is that short-sighted. Not to mention insecure." Though the ache hadn't left her chest since Dylan stormed out.

"Even if it was a momentary lapse and not a permanent state?"

She'd conveyed the specifics of their fight—in excruciating detail—so the last thing she expected was Talise making any sort of concessions for Dylan. "Why are you defending her?"

Talise sighed. "Because I saw the way she looked at you the night of the gala. The way you looked at her."

"And?" She knew where Talise was going with that but didn't want to give her the satisfaction.

"And I think she's even more in love with you than you are with her."

She let out a snort instead of a sniff. "Even if that's the case, she's got a hell of a way of showing it."

Talise laced her fingers together and brought them to her chest. "Okay, but—"

"What?" Part of her wanted a perfectly reasonable explanation, part of her sat poised to tell that perfectly reasonable explanation to go to hell.

"How many times in your life have you been in love? Like, truly in love?"

Forget reasonable explanations, she was about ready to tell Talise to go to hell. "Once. You know this. It was in college and I'm not sure I'd say truly in love by adult standards, but it sure felt like it at the time."

"So, you know it's pretty rare to be head over heels for someone."

Yeah, which made this whole thing with Dylan all the more tortuous. "Are you trying to make me feel better or worse?"

"Neither. I'm trying to tell you that sometimes, when you're in love with someone that does something really stupid, you have to decide whether you're willing to chuck the whole thing or give them the chance to own being an idiot and apologize," Talise said.

Definitely in the feeling worse category. "Which is moot in this situation because Dylan has neither admitted to being an asshole nor apologized."

"Yeah, but what if she does?"

"How about you wait until that happens to give me advice?" Mira asked.

Talise shrugged, then stood. "Okay."

She resisted asking what the catch was, if for no other reason than she had actual work to do. "Excellent. I want to run this collateral by my parents but consider them approved."

That, of all things, got her a brow raise.

"It's the answer you want, isn't it?"

Talise smirked. "It is."

"Well, then. Get out of here before I change my mind."

Talise took her time sashaying to the door, then turned. "You know she's going to come to her senses and apologize, right? I'd put money on full grovel."

She ached for that to happen but held absolutely zero hope. And still wasn't sure what she'd do if it happened. "I know nothing of the kind."

Talise pressed her lips together and angled her head. "I give it a week."

With Talise gone, she flipped through the materials once more. They were nothing short of gorgeous. And come hell or high water, they were going to see the light of day.

She had half a mind to call her father directly. After all, it was her father who'd chewed her out and questioned her judgment. But technically, both her parents shared ownership and with it, final say. The truth of the matter was that the conversation she needed to have with them had as much to do with being their daughter as it did being the person they'd put in charge of Pomme. But since it was a business conversation first and foremost, she typed up an email requesting a conference call with them both.

Not five minutes later, her phone rang. Great. "Hi, Dad."

"What's this about?"

"I'd like to meet with you and Mom to share the collateral for the new rosé line in advance of the division meeting."

"All right, then. It's a big step, you know. I'm still on the fence. Especially after that whole Honorable Mention debacle," he said.

Of course he was. "Well, I've signed off on the graphics and the labels. We're going to develop a full marketing campaign to launch in April and peak in June, riding the wave of association rosé already has with summer."

Dad cleared his throat. "I'd like to see those before you move forward. And I want to revisit the size of the production run for at least the first two years to minimize potential losses."

Capitulation sat on the tip of her tongue. It was, after all, his call to make. But something stopped her. Something that may have been tied to Dylan's unapologetic gumption rubbing off on her. Or maybe it was simply a matter of finally coming into her own. Either way, she was done giving in. "I'm happy to send you copies of anything you'd like, but I've made the decisions already."

Dad sputtered for a moment. "I'm not trying to undermine you, I—"

"Then don't. I have the knowledge, the skills, and the instinct to run this company. I'm pretty sure you agree, or you wouldn't have put me in charge in the first place. I'm not interested in keeping this job if you don't trust me enough to let me do it."

Rather than a reply, she heard rustling on the other end of the phone, followed by mumbling. If she had to guess, he was relaying her impertinence to her mother and asking what he should do. It somehow diffused the knot of anxiety in her chest.

After a minute that felt like an eternity, he came back on the line. "Your mother thinks you're right."

The knot loosened a bit more. At least she wouldn't be defying—or disappointing—both of them. "And you?"

"I'm not sure you're right on this decision, but you're right that it's your call to make."

It was a thousand times more than she expected, but she knew better than to celebrate. "Thank you."

"You'll present at the division meeting next week."

It wasn't a question, but it didn't need to be. "I will."

Instead of the gruff good-bye she usually got, Dad cleared his throat. "Your mother and I love you."

He wasn't one to withhold affection, but he kept it separate from business almost to the point of rigidity. Well, affection above and beyond what he'd show any long-serving member of the staff. It left her a little choked up. "I love you, too."

She hung up the phone but didn't move from her desk. She sat for a long moment. "That went well," she said, even though she was alone in her office.

It didn't do anything to solve the Dylan situation—neither her aching heart nor the fact that they'd have to figure out a way to be civil to one another in public—but it was a step in the right direction. For herself. For the person she wanted to be and the life she wanted to build. And for the company she wanted to grow.

❖

Dylan shook the last bit of pulp from the end of the hose and hung it on the hook next to the pressing rack. She folded the cloth over the lot of it and set the plate on top before engaging the press that would extract the juice from the skins and stems and flesh. She hopped down from the platform and watched the golden liquid collect at the bottom of the tray before funneling into the collection tank.

When the grinder motor cut off, she yanked off the noise-cancelling headphones that saved her hearing but made her ears itch and let out a sigh. She caught Rowan in her peripheral vision but didn't say anything, not even when Rowan stood directly beside her. The soft cascade of juice falling from the pressing trays didn't do much to fill the silence.

"Aren't you the one who always says cider picks up the essence of the people who make it?"

"Yeah." Not that Gavin Banks understood stuff like that when he was flirting with Mira on national television. Not that Mira understood it either.

"Well, your juju is so bad I can practically cut it with a knife."

She grumbled but didn't argue. Hard to argue blatant truth. "Well, the pressing needs to happen so unless you want to put Audrey on the grinder, you're stuck with me."

"I'm not looking to replace you. I just want to help you out of this funk." Rowan's encouraging tone somehow felt worse that a swift kick in the ass.

"I don't want help. I like being a miserable bastard."

Rowan folded her arms. "Is that really easier than admitting you were wrong?"

"I'm not wrong," Dylan shouted. She hadn't meant to yell, but like so many things these days, it happened anyway. "Sorry. I shouldn't take it out on you."

Rowan didn't seem moved—by the yelling or by the apology. "Even if I'm going to keep telling you you're wrong?"

She grumbled some more, but quietly. "I said some shit things. I'll admit that. But it doesn't change the fact that I don't like who Mira made me be."

"Do you want me to start with the fact that Mira didn't make you be anything or the fact that wanting publicity and recognition doesn't make you a sellout?" Rowan asked.

"Neither." She walked over to check the level in the collection tank, but Rowan followed.

"Then how about I start with the fact that being in love with Mira doesn't mean you're going to become Mira."

"How about we don't talk about that either?"

Since the press needed a good hour to do its job extracting every drop from the pomace, Dylan stalked over to the holding area that housed the dozen or so crates of apples awaiting a similar fate. Rowan followed again, but she made a slow meander of it, complete with hands in pockets and shuffling feet.

"Are you seriously going to follow me around all day?" Dylan asked.

"Not all day. Audrey is coming for lunch, so I was hoping to talk some sense into you before then."

"There's nothing to discuss. I was an asshole. Mira told me to go to hell. I'll apologize eventually so we can be civil."

Rowan nodded. "None of that is wrong, but it doesn't address the part about you being in love with her."

Once again, her temper flared. "It doesn't matter if I'm in love with her. Mira isn't Audrey. She's not finding herself. She knows exactly who she is, and I don't want any part of it."

"I'm not sure whether you're selling yourself short, or her."

"It doesn't matter." She'd wasted hours trying to tease out the subtleties of right and wrong, give and take. And the only conclusion she'd managed to come to was that no matter how she sliced and diced it, she and Mira simply didn't add up. Since she had no illusions of Mira changing, it left her to. And from what she'd seen so far, she didn't like the way those changes looked on her. Much less the way they made her feel.

"Suit yourself. But if you think I'm a pain in your ass, wait till Audrey gets her hands on you."

Dylan mumbled a few expletives and something about people minding their own business, but Rowan had already returned to the pressing area to clean the grinder for the next batch of apples and didn't hear any of it. Just as well. Rowan might poke and prod, but none of it was her fault. No, she'd made this mess entirely on her own. Well, not entirely. Mira had played a starring role, whether she'd intended to or not.

It made her wonder if Mira had any regrets. If anything, she probably regretted hooking up in the first place. Not because she'd gotten her heart broken. No, Mira seemed to have no trouble staying calm, cool, and completely detached in all things. She might regret the inherent messiness of breaking up, not to mention the possibility of gossip, but that would be it.

Even as she hopped aboard the train of righteous indignation, Dylan's mind conjured Mira's face the afternoon they'd tasted and blended cider. And the playful sparring when they'd selected the menu for the gala. Of course, her imagination had a cruel streak and threw in images of Mira lying in her bed, colorful wax dripped all over her gorgeous back. And a few of Mira riding her—sensual, confident, perfect.

"Goddammit." She stalked to the side door, slamming it open harder than she meant to. On the other side, a startled and yet somehow not entirely surprised Audrey. "Sorry."

Audrey lifted both hands. "You're fine."

She most definitely was not fine. "Tell Rowan I'm taking a walk."

"You got it."

She stepped outside and immediately regretted not grabbing a coat. Not enough to go back inside and get it, but enough that she'd be even more miserable by the time she finished walking off some of her self-loathing.

"Hey, Dylan?" She turned, only to find Audrey regarding her with a mixture of pity and challenge. "Let me know when you're done sulking and ready to grovel. I've got some suggestions."

Audrey didn't wait for her reply, leaving Dylan to stare at the door Audrey had pulled closed behind her. A gust of wind blew and made her shiver, which made her swear. She hugged her arms tight around her chest and stalked in the direction of the orchard. "Grovel my ass."

Chapter Twenty-seven

Wedding rehearsals were not for the faint of heart. Or, maybe more accurately, not for the brokenhearted. Even the abbreviated ceremony got to Dylan and left her wondering—foolishly perhaps—about Mira and whether she ever thought about getting married.

Once they got to the rehearsal dinner part of the evening, she was able to distract herself, chatting with Emily's friends and getting introduced to the subset of Jason's people who were either in the wedding party or who'd arrived a day early. She even managed to sneak out during the salad course to visit the bar. Not for another drink, but to catch up with Barb, the woman who'd tended bar at her family's restaurant since before she was old enough to drink. A secondary grandmother of sorts, especially after her own grandmother retired from the job.

Only Barb didn't pour a strong one and regale her with tales. She cut right through the small talk and asked the sort of probing questions Dylan wanted to avoid.

"Aren't bartenders supposed to be good listeners?" Dylan asked.

Barb shrugged. "For strangers, maybe. You get the friends and family special."

"I'm going to take that as my cue to get back to the party."

"Suit yourself, sugar. You should come around more often, though. I miss your face."

For some reason, the casual endearment had her on the verge of tears. "I promise."

She slid off the stool and offered a salute before returning to the room where the dinner was being held. She plowed through her chicken cutlet, more because she'd barely eaten all day than she took any pleasure eating. Her parents were busy enough to leave her to her own devices and her brother's attention rested completely on his latest girlfriend, leaving her to stew as plates were cleared for dessert and coffee.

She took a swig of beer and resisted picking at the label. Instead, she drummed her fingers on the table and wondered what Mira was doing. Again.

Emily slid into the empty chair beside her and gave her a gentle kick under the table. "If you don't try to look a little less sullen, Jason's family is going to think you don't approve of the union."

Her fingers stilled and her shoulders straightened. "Oh, God. I'm sorry."

Emily laughed. "I'm kidding. Your socializing against your will game has improved. I just happen to know you really well and I can tell you're miserable."

Dylan cringed. "I'm not sure that's any better."

"Well, it makes you a sad sack more than an asshole, so it serves my purposes."

"Do you think I'm an asshole?"

Emily seemed to consider before answering. "Sometimes."

"Do you think I'm being an asshole about Mira?"

"I can't say. You haven't given me the whole story."

She should have known better than to expect unequivocal support. "You know, you could just take my side."

"Yeah, but what's the fun in that?"

"You're as bad as Rowan." Not that she'd expected otherwise. "And Mom."

"I'm worse than Mom because I've actually seen you with Mira and I know how bad you have it for her."

She'd spent the better part of two weeks convincing herself she'd been swept up in sex hormones, not really in love at all. And with that one simple statement—not even a mention of love—Emily sent her entire house of cards tumbling. "What am I going to do?"

"Have you considered telling her how you feel?"

Again, simpler than Rowan and Audrey's suggestion of groveling. And yet it cut right to her core. "No. Because whatever I feel for Mira, I also feel terrified of becoming someone I don't want to be. That has to be more important, right? Personal integrity?"

"That's bullshit."

Emily's retort aligned perfectly with their mother's arrival at the table. She smiled and pulled up a chair on the far side of Emily. "What's bullshit, dear?"

"Dylan is claiming fear of losing herself as grounds for her commitment phobia," Emily said.

"Ah." Mom nodded. "That does sound like bullshit."

Dylan scratched the back of her head, annoyed but not surprised at being double-teamed. "She's so unapologetically corporate. It started to rub off on me. You know how I feel about that."

Whether it was her defensive tone or the weakness of her argument, she couldn't say. But all she got in return was a pair of bland expressions. Then Emily and Mom exchanged looks, like they were deciding whose turn it was to read her the riot act. Emily angled her head ever so slightly. Mom gave an almost imperceptible nod. Even without speaking, they left Dylan feeling utterly managed.

Mom reached across the table and gave Dylan's hand a squeeze. Kind of an "I'm punishing you, but it's for your own good" gesture. "Honey, you are the most headstrong, individualistic person in this family."

Emily poked a finger at the table. "And that's saying something."

"So, you're saying I'm wrong and I'm too stubborn to admit it?" Which only made her want to dig her heels in harder, not that she'd give either of them the satisfaction.

Emily remained smug, but Mom's features softened. "I'm saying you are your own person and you always have been. You're not going to become a nine-to-five suit and tie because your girlfriend is."

It was funny. She'd literally called Mira a suit—to her face, no less. And yet, in this moment, her first instinct was to defend her. "She's not only that. She cares about her work."

"Of course she does. You wouldn't have given her the time of day otherwise."

Emily chose that moment to add her two cents. "And if the conversations I had with her when I came down were anything to go on, you've rubbed off on her more than the other way around."

She'd wanted to think so. But then Mira had gone on television and been so—what? Polished. Mira had been polished and poised and professional. And she'd flown into a fit of jealousy. Jealousy over Mira's success, her ease of moving through the world. Jealousy over the attention shown her by an equally polished TV personality whose suit probably cost more than the salary she took home in a month. "I'm an idiot."

Emily nodded. "I've been telling you this since I was old enough to use the word in a sentence."

"Before that, even." Dylan looked at Emily, then her mother. "What am I going to do?"

Emily lifted her chin. "Depends. Are you feeling brave?"

Brave had to beat pathetic, right? "Maybe."

Emily glanced at their mother before looking Dylan right in the eyes. "You're going to get out of here and go pull some movie-level romantic move."

That so wasn't her style. Mira's either, she was pretty sure. "Does showing up on her doorstep and asking her to forgive me count?"

Mom smacked her palm on the table. "It absolutely counts."

Emily looked down for a moment, took a deep breath. When she looked up, a shadow of worry shone in her eyes if nowhere else. "I'm all in on this move, but you'll be back, right? For tomorrow?"

"I wouldn't miss it, jerk face," Dylan said.

Emily smiled and blinked away what could have been tears, though she likely wouldn't admit it. "Well, get out of here then. Butthead."

"But drive safely," Mom said.

She eyed the beer she'd been nursing, grateful she wasn't the sort to drown her sorrows, and picked up the glass of water next to it. After downing the contents, she stood. "I love you both."

"We love you." Now Mom's eyes had gone teary.

Emily waved. "Have fun storming the castle."

She weaved through the tables and grabbed her jacket from the rack that had been set up at the entrance to the restaurant's party room. A glance back confirmed that Emily and Mom were whispering with their heads together and eyes on her. It occurred to her that not only was she about to lay her heart at Mira's feet, she'd all but invited an audience.

This was about to go either very well or turn into her most epic failure to date.

❖

Can we talk?

Mira rolled her eyes and set her phone down.

I want to apologize.

This time she grumbled and unlocked her screen. *Okay.*

Any chance you'd see me now?

As a person not known for patience, she appreciated the sense of urgency. But it was nine o'clock at night. She said as much to Gloria. *As in, right now?*

I'm outside. But it seemed aggressive to knock on your door unannounced.

She laughed before she could stop herself. It always bugged her in movies when the character who'd been the asshole showed up with some showy grand apology. Like, respect some boundaries, please. Talise called her a painfully unromantic curmudgeon, but she held firm. Not that she was keeping score, but this entrée earned Dylan points. *Come on, then.*

She opened the door and found Dylan on the other side, all dressed up and with a sheepish half smile on her face. "Did you put on a tie to apologize?"

Dylan let out a chuckle and ran her fingers through her hair in that way she did when she was distracted or nervous. "No, I just happened to be dressed like this when I decided to show up here."

In the five or so months she'd known Dylan, she'd seen her in a tie exactly once: the night of the gala.

"My sister's wedding is tomorrow, and the rehearsal dinner was tonight."

Oh, right. Dylan had asked her to go before things went to hell. "So, you left the rehearsal dinner to come over and apologize?"

"Yes. For the record, I have my sister's blessing. My mother's, too, for that matter. Actually, it was their idea."

So many thoughts raced through her mind. Was the rehearsal dinner in Buffalo, where Dylan's family lived? Had Dylan really driven an hour and a half without even knowing whether she'd answer the door? Did Dylan think it through or was this just one more example of act first, think later? And, maybe most alarming, how much did Dylan's family know about how badly their last conversation had gone?

"I mean, I didn't miss anything." Dylan offered a sheepish shrug. "Except dessert."

"Well, you came all this way, so come in." She stepped back so Dylan could, then closed the door behind her.

"I wasn't sure you'd answer, much less invite me in, so thank you."

"I consider myself a mature and rational adult." She wondered sometimes what it would be like to have a fiery temper. To be the woman who'd yell and slam the door in Dylan's face or throw Dylan's things out the window. It wasn't her style, though, and it never would be. Just the idea had her stomach twisting uncomfortably.

Dylan winced. "I deserve that."

She shook her head, stomach twisting for an entirely different reason. "I didn't mean it like that."

"It's okay if you did. I picked a fight with you, and I said some really gross things."

Gross wasn't the word she'd have used, but it fit. Each time she replayed the conversation in her mind, Dylan's words cut. Even when she slathered it with empathy, she kept coming back to the phrase "irreconcilable differences." And from where she sat, there was no getting around that.

"I don't want to make excuses, but I would like to explain. If you'll let me," Dylan said.

Irreconcilable or not, she couldn't ignore the fact that Dylan gave her agency to decide. So many people made apologizing about their own absolution and not about the person they'd harmed. There was also the matter of being—perhaps foolishly—in love with Dylan. "Okay. Let's talk."

Trusting Dylan would follow, she went into the living room and sat, opting for one of the armchairs instead of the sofa. Dylan perched on the sofa momentarily but almost immediately got up and began to pace. After a few lengths of the room, she turned to face Mira, taking a deep breath and blowing it out with force. "I was an ass and I'm sorry."

It was a start for sure. But it didn't give her any indication of whether it was going to be a no hard feelings, have a nice life sort of conversation or an I think we can make this work one. "Okay."

"The stuff I said about you having more privilege than I did was so over the line and completely insensitive. And like, I know better, you know? I got caught up in the moment of being upset about all the times I've been passed over and I went for the low blow. Which doesn't excuse it. I just—fuck, I'm stumbling over my words right now. I'm just trying to own that it wasn't okay, as opposed to that bullshit apology of saying I didn't mean it that way and I'm sorry I offended you."

Something about watching Dylan flounder affected her far more than a polished, articulate apology would have. "I know what you're trying to say, and I appreciate it. And I know there's a certain privilege in presenting as feminine and being assumed straight."

Dylan offered a half smile. "And gorgeous. Don't forget the fact that you're drop-dead gorgeous."

She rolled her eyes but returned the smile. "The point is, pitting the biases we face against each other wasn't helpful, in the moment or in the grand scheme of things."

Dylan nodded. "Yeah."

As nice as it was to clear the air of that, it didn't resolve the more fundamental issue. The one rooted in Dylan's emphatic declaration that she didn't want to be anything like Mira and therefore couldn't be around her. "So."

"So, that's number one on the list of things I fucked up."

"There's a list?" She certainly had one but wasn't sure Dylan would admit as much.

"Well, there's the matter of me calling you a suit," Dylan said.

Honestly, that had stung more than the bullshit about her privilege. "Yes."

"Just because your focus is on the business side of things doesn't mean you aren't passionate about cider. It was insulting to say otherwise."

"Thank you." She considered admitting that Dylan had helped her become more curious, more passionate, but decided to see how things played out first.

"But even if you cared more about the business side of things, there's nothing wrong with that. It's your life and your career. It's not mine."

"I'm not going to lie, that feels like a backhanded compliment at best."

Dylan shook her head vigorously. "It's not a compliment or an insult. It's a statement of fact that I managed to make all about me."

Even without knowing Dylan's end game, she appreciated the admission. "How so?"

Dylan paced the room a couple of times, then sat, like she realized she must look like a caged tiger. "Getting upset about the attention you and Pomme were getting made me feel like a version of myself I don't want to be. Does that make sense?"

It did. "Calling you self-serving and jealous probably didn't help."

Dylan hung her head. "You weren't wrong."

"It's okay to have some jealousy. I'm jealous of how creative and willing to take risks you are."

"It's only good when the risks pay off."

"I don't agree. You don't get the payoff if you don't have some missteps along the way." She thought about the conversation with her parents, finally staking her claim as the head of the company. That wouldn't have happened without Dylan. She took a deep breath and set a hand on Dylan's knee. "You taught me that."

Dylan looked at her with something she couldn't identify. Relief, maybe? With some wonder thrown in for good measure. But there was more to it. Something that made her chest tighten, that thrilled her even as it scared her a little. Something she'd been feeling but also kicking herself over. Something—

"I love you," Dylan said.

"You—"

"I know it probably isn't fair to lay that on top of everything, but I'd feel dishonest if I didn't say it."

The tightness in her chest intensified as her heart started to beat harder, faster, and more erratically than that time she attempted hot yoga on an empty stomach.

"The thing is, I've been falling for you for months. Only that's not what we agreed to. And I thought if I just held tight and things kept getting better, it would all sort itself out in the end. But then I fucked everything up and there's every chance I've lost any chance I had to be with you, so it seemed like the time to put all my cards on the table," Dylan said.

It was hard to pinpoint exactly when the tingling in her body turned into quivers of joy, but it definitely happened during Dylan's soliloquy. It was all she could do to keep a burst of laughter from escaping. "Will you stop talking for two seconds?"

Dylan, lips pressed together and eyes wide, nodded.

"The reason I was so pissed off about the insecure little tantrum you threw is the fact that I was falling for you, too."

"Insecure tantrum, huh? I guess I deserve that." Dylan cringed, then started, as though the second half of the declaration only just registered. "Wait. You were falling for me?"

"Yes. So, I was mad at you and mad at myself for falling for such an idiot."

Dylan reached out like she wanted to grab Mira's hand but caught herself. "Does admitting I was an idiot, and an ass, make it better?"

She nodded, not trusting that it could be as simple as that but desperately wanting it to.

"How much better?" Dylan asked.

She wasn't naive enough to think they could kiss and make up and not have to think about big, difficult talks ever again. Yet, for now, the idea of kissing and making up and agreeing to have those talks rather than running away felt like happiness and hope and a little bit of magic. "Enough that I'm hoping you'll stay."

"Stay? Tonight you mean?"

"Tonight, tomorrow, the day after that. Not here necessarily, but with me. However we decide we want that to look."

Dylan closed her eyes and took a deep—and what appeared to be fortifying—breath. "There is one condition, though."

"Oh?" She couldn't tell if Dylan was teasing or honestly putting a condition on the prospect of being together.

"I do have to be at the wedding tomorrow."

Was that all? "Of course. Really, my place is closer than yours, so it's probably more convenient for you to leave from here."

"It is." Dylan offered a smile that seemed almost bashful. "And it's not part of the condition, but I'd love it if you came with me."

If a lick of worry about meeting Dylan's family—after everything—coursed up her spine, she ignored it. Besides, if Emily and Dylan's mom supported Dylan showing up like this, they'd probably be disappointed if she didn't go. "I'd love to."

CHAPTER TWENTY-EIGHT

Dylan slid from bed and crept downstairs. The sun had just begun to peek through the row of trees that lined the back of Mira's compact yard. She smiled at the golden rays, at the coffee beans both going in and coming out of the grinder, and at Gloria, who'd heard the rustling and came to see if that meant breakfast. After filling the French press with water from the kettle, she opened a pouch and dumped the contents into one of Gloria's specially designated bowls. Gloria responded with a head butt and some purrs before diving in.

"And a very good morning to you, too."

She prepped a pair of cups with turbinado sugar and almond milk, chuckling at the fact that Mira had clearly disposed of any lingering half-and-half after their fight. Upstairs, she paused for a moment in the doorway, just to appreciate the sight of Mira fast asleep. She didn't consider herself particularly sentimental, but she was damn glad she had more mornings like this to look forward to.

As if sensing her gaze, Mira opened her eyes. Whether it was the sight of her or the prospect of coffee, Dylan couldn't say, but she immediately smiled. "Hi."

"Good morning."

Not one to waste time stretching or rolling around, Mira sat up and extended both hands. "A very good morning indeed."

Dylan handed Mira both cups and climbed back into bed. She accepted hers back and took a sip. "Why do you look as annoyed as when you got roped into having a co-chair for Cider Week?"

Mira's expression changed. "I wasn't annoyed."

"Yes, you were. I figured it was because you didn't like sharing the spotlight. But now I know you're not like that."

That got her an exasperated glare. "Just because I wear the limelight well doesn't mean I'm an attention whore."

She tipped her head slightly. "Hey, I said I stand corrected."

Mira lifted a shoulder. "I'm not a fan of group projects."

"Shocker."

"Besides, I thought you were a self-absorbed cider bro with a massive ego."

She cringed. "I deserve that. Even if the phrase cider bro hurts me a little."

Mira's features softened. "I'm glad to have been proven wrong."

"You're glad to have someone bring you coffee in bed."

"Well, that too." Mira took a long sip of her coffee and let out a contented sigh. "Definitely a both/and situation."

She loved that Mira, for all her busy-bee, get-up-and-get-going tendencies, had come to appreciate the luxury of coffee in bed. "I'm serious, though. I know why you were irritated then. Why are you irritated this morning?"

"I'm not irritated."

Mira's tone shifted, telling her there was something. It might not be irritation, but it wasn't nothing. "We spent all night making up and agreeing that we have to be open and honest if we're going to have a shot at making this work."

Mira's shoulders dropped and she sighed. "Are you sure this is a good idea?"

A lick of panic coursed up her spine. "What? Us?"

Mira smiled. "No, not us. Today. The wedding."

"Oh." Relief gave way to curiosity. "Do you not want to go to the wedding? It's okay if you don't."

"It's not that I don't. But it feels a bit like crashing. Plus the fact that your family will be inclined to dislike me if they don't already." Mira set her coffee down and folded her arms.

Genuine confusion set in. "I don't understand. What makes you think they don't like you?"

"You probably told them what we fought about since I was going to go with you in the first place and then didn't. They're your family so of course they'll take your side." Mira lifted her left hand and tapped a finger with each statement, like she was ticking items off a list. "And on top of that you left the rehearsal dinner to come see me. That screams high maintenance."

"Didn't we go over this last night? They wanted me to come here."

"Yes, but now I'm thinking clearly in the light of day. I really don't want to make things uncomfortable."

"Uncomfortable for me or uncomfortable for you?" She knew better than to admit it, but it was kind of fun to watch Mira squirm.

"Both of us. Either of us. Family can be weird under the best of circumstances. I'm pretty sure this is not that."

As much as she enjoyed teasing Mira—getting her to acknowledge she was being uptight and nudging her to relax—the handful of conversations they'd had about Mira's parents echoed in her mind. Ironically, it made her want to pull Mira into her family all the more. "I'll have you know my mother was on your side."

Mira dropped her hands. "What?"

"When I told my mother I'd be at the wedding stag, she asked what happened. I explained that we'd had a fight and probably broken up. So she asked me what we fought about, and when I told her she called me quick-tempered and short-sighted."

Mira's eyes narrowed. "You're making that up to make me feel better."

"I swear I'm not. You can ask her yourself."

"I'm obviously not going to do that." Mira's shoulders slumped, more dramatically than a moment before, but it seemed more playful exasperation than genuine anxiety, so that felt like an improvement.

"Fine, I will."

"Don't."

She shrugged. "It's not like I'll even have to. She's going to fawn all over you and her sentiments will be perfectly clear."

"Are you making fun of me right now?" Mira asked.

She set her coffee aside and took both of Mira's hands in hers. "No. Because I can tell you're truly stressed and not just being difficult on principle."

Mira scrunched up her face, but then she laughed. "I am stressed out."

"How about this? I promise I wouldn't ask you to come with me if I thought you'd be made to feel anything but welcome." She gave Mira's hands a squeeze.

"Okay."

"Okay, you'll come?"

"Yes. And for the record, I can hold my own. I'm not worried about that. It's your sister's day, though. I don't want to be the reason for any negative energy for her or anyone else in your family."

She resisted the urge to gather Mira in her arms and tell her that any mean or judgmental or otherwise not cool thing her parents had ever said to her didn't matter. Since she'd never actually met them, it felt like overstepping. Hopefully, she'd have the chance and, if needed, could remind Mira that she had someone in her corner, no questions asked. She liked the idea of being in Mira's corner, for all sorts of things and for a very long time.

❖

They got out of the car and Dylan tugged at the hem of her jacket. Mira smoothed her fingers over the lapels and smiled. "Stop. You look amazing."

Dylan's gaze raked over her, head to toe. "Pretty sure that's my line."

"Well, there's no rule against looking amazing together."

Dylan grinned. "There certainly isn't."

She wanted to kiss Dylan square on the mouth, but she didn't know who of Dylan's relatives might be lurking in the parking lot and didn't want to take any chances. Well, that and she didn't want Dylan to walk into church with lipstick smeared on her. "Come, on. Let's get you inside since you probably should be here already."

Dylan took her hand as they headed to the door and even though part of her wanted to protest, she resisted. Dylan had assured her it was a welcoming church. But more than that, Dylan had asked for her trust that the day would go well, and Mira had given it to her.

"You're sure you're okay on your own?" Dylan asked.

She would have lied but realized she didn't need to. "I'm sure."

The significance of that caught her as she slid into a pew about halfway up the aisle and Dylan went in search of Emily and the rest of the bridal party. She rebuffed Talise's teasing about it, but the truth of the matter was that she didn't trust people easily. Not with the big stuff.

And yet somehow, Dylan showing up at her door—and being truthful and humble and open—had done the trick. Well, tipped the scales maybe. She'd spent the last few months letting Dylan into her life and into her heart more than anyone else she'd ever dated. It had made the ugliness of their fight all the more wrenching, but it had also given them a solid foundation to land on, to recover from.

She'd never really understood the idea of strife making a relationship stronger, but she did now. She trusted Dylan more—now that she'd seen Dylan own her mistakes—than she had before things went sideways. Loved her more.

There was that word again. Love.

The procession began and the ceremony followed. Dylan made eyes at her from time to time; the minister managed to make the script feel familiar and somehow fresh. Emily and Jason exchanged vows they'd written themselves and even though she'd only met them the one time, their words for each other made her both laugh and cry.

The reception was at an old fire station that had been converted to an event space. In her opinion, it rivaled Pomme in both character and charm and had her thinking ever so vaguely about where she'd want her own wedding to be. Dylan's mother gave her one of the hardest hugs she'd ever gotten. Her delight in Mira being there, in everything working out after all, was so big and bubbly and bold, Mira couldn't have denied it if she'd wanted to.

After the meal, Emily and Jason had their first dance. Everything about it was sweet and romantic and gave her the kind of squishy feelings she rarely had. When it ended, the DJ invited other couples to join the bride and groom. Dylan extended a hand and eyed her hopefully. "Dance with me?"

She hesitated for a moment before remembering her mantra for the day. To let go a little. To enjoy the day. And most of all, to trust Dylan. "I'd love to."

A moment later, Mira stepped into Dylan's arms, and they began a meandering sway around the dance floor. Between parents and grandparents, cousins and childhood friends, the couples around them included pretty much every age bracket imaginable. More straight, white couples than not, but she couldn't detect any side-eye or even surreptitious glances.

"You okay?" Dylan asked.

She nodded and went for what she hoped was a reassuring smile.

"Are you sure? I promise everyone is cool, but if dancing together makes you uncomfortable, we don't have to."

She appreciated the offer. In fact, it assured her she didn't want to stop. "No, it's not that. I was just thinking."

"Uh-oh."

She angled her head, more amused than exasperated. "What makes you say that?"

Dylan shrugged. "I'm not sure I've apologized for everything stupid I said, so I'm fully expecting you to remember more things I need to be sorry about."

"Stop."

"I'm serious." Dylan's wolfish grin told Mira she wasn't. Not really.

"I was actually thinking that I wasn't entirely honest with you last night."

That got Dylan's attention. The grin faded and she visibly swallowed. "Oh. Is this a conversation we should be having somewhere other than the dance floor at my sister's wedding?"

She wasn't looking to make Dylan worry for nothing, but she didn't hate being able to get Dylan's attention so easily. "I think we're good."

"Okay." Dylan nodded, but her expression remained serious. "Lay it on me."

The choice of phrase made her smile. "Well, you know how I said I was so mad at you because I was falling for you?"

"Yeah."

"That wasn't entirely true."

"No?" Dylan looked genuinely worried now.

"No. The fact of the matter is that I'd already fallen for you. All the way."

"Is that so?"

Mira took a fortifying breath. "Yes. I should have said so last night, but I was feeling overwhelmed, and I didn't want to say it just because you did."

Dylan's brow arched. "Say what, exactly?"

She'd only said it to a handful of women in her life and only one man aside from her father. And yet it had never felt anything like this. New and exciting but also tested and strong. How glorious. "I love you."

The song hadn't ended, but Dylan stopped dancing. She did, too. The other couples on the floor, including the bride and groom, simply danced around them.

"You love me?" Dylan's voice held doubt, but it seemed less about not believing her and more like it might be too good to be true.

"I do."

"Even when you want to wring my neck?"

She sighed. "Even then."

Dylan's arms came around her even more tightly. "I'm so fucking glad."

She managed a smile before Dylan's lips covered hers. What maybe should have been a brief kiss—given their surroundings— went on and on. The music stopped. Someone started to clap, and others joined in. Romantic haze or not, she wasn't about to make out with Dylan in the middle of the dance floor when something obviously more important was happening, and there was every chance they were in the way.

She opened her eyes and looked to her left, then her right. People were staring. Not just people, either. Everyone in the room seemed to be looking at them. And most of them were applauding. She turned her gaze to Dylan, who stood there with a goofy smile on her face.

Emily appeared from nowhere and slung an arm over both their shoulders. "Had to steal my thunder, didn't you?"

Embarrassment gave way to utter mortification. "Oh, God. Emily, I swear that's not—"

Emily's eyes danced with amusement. "I think it's fantastic. I just have to give this one a hard time." Emily elbowed Dylan and Dylan elbowed her right back.

"You know, you technically don't have to give me a hard time," Dylan said.

"No, but I get to and it's a hell of a lot of fun, so why would I stop?"

Dylan shook her head and Mira laughed in spite of herself. She didn't think of Emily as family yet, but it wouldn't be a stretch.

Another song came on, one of those cheesy line dance songs that seemed to make an appearance at every wedding. A few people left the dance floor but even more joined in. And like before, everyone seemed perfectly content to dance around them.

Jason, who'd been sort of hovering off to the side, came over and joined them. "Given that kiss, I'm taking it you two made up."

Dylan smiled. "Something like that."

"Oh, good. Emily was hoping for that," Jason said.

The idea that Emily wanted them to be together gave her already full heart a top-off. She looked to Emily. "Really?"

Emily grinned. "Absolutely. I figure if Mom is needling Dylan to propose to you, she'll be too busy to pester us about babies."

Jason roared with laughter. Dylan squeezed her eyes shut and cringed. Mira, who felt like she was finally starting to get a handle on Dylan's family, merely smiled. "We'll see what we can do."

Chapter Twenty-nine

The following May.

Mira saved the sales report from the new line of rosé and smiled. If June's orders were anything to go on, she had a hit on her hands. Not that she'd ever tell her father *I told you so*, but it was nice to know she had grounds. She toggled over to her calendar and clicked the link for the Cider Association meeting. The faces of the usual suspects filled the screen, including Dylan's. She'd seen Dylan only a couple of hours before but indulged in staring at her anyway. She couldn't be sure, of course, but she had a feeling Dylan was doing the same.

Frederick called the meeting to order and ran through the boilerplate parts of the agenda. When it came time to discuss the planning team for Cider Week, Dylan volunteered first. They'd discussed it, but it still felt strange to bide her time. And remind herself it was that and not biting her tongue.

When Dylan said she hoped Mira would stay on as co-chair, Mira happily agreed. They'd planned that part, too. Dylan had teased her, but she liked having a plan. And even though she and Dylan weren't secretive about being together—or weren't secretive anymore, at least—she didn't need to go parading their coupledom around at board meetings.

"Dylan, do you want to stay on the line after the meeting so we can discuss?" Mira asked. Overkill, probably, but whatever.

"You don't have to pretend you're not going to do it over dinner," Steve said.

"Or coffee in the morning." Frederick added a wink to his comment.

She squeezed her eyes shut, more token embarrassment than any true discomfiture. Dylan had helped her see that her fellow cider makers were friends as much as colleagues. Well, most of them.

"You know, I feel like I should get some credit for this." Don waved a hand back and forth, presumably to indicate Mira and Dylan's relationship. "I'm the one who suggested you work together."

What was that about most of them being friends?

"Only if you admit you were secretly hoping we'd kill each other," Dylan said, drawing a laugh from pretty much everyone but Don. But even he cracked a smile.

"Not kill each other. Just make each other miserable."

"Don." Frederick seemed genuinely scandalized by the prospect.

Don shrugged and Dylan grinned. "Don't worry about it, Frederick. I'm not going to complain when I have the satisfaction of the last laugh."

She swallowed the suggestion that they get back to the agenda, if only because it would draw even more attention to her discomfort. And even if she'd never be the type to gloat about having the last laugh—at least not in a professional setting—she wasn't above enjoying that Don's machinations had backfired so spectacularly.

Don lifted his mug to the camera, whether in concession or congratulations, she couldn't be sure. Frederick cleared his throat and carried on with the agenda, though there wasn't much left to cover. When the meeting ended, she stayed on and Dylan did, too, even though the ship of playing it cool had sailed.

"That went well," Dylan said.

For some reason, the grin that accompanied Dylan's declaration made her think of that fateful meeting the year before. The one where Dylan had breezed on, soaking wet and seeming to take absolutely nothing seriously. She'd been so wrong, about Dylan but also about herself. About what mattered, what she really wanted. She didn't relish admitting being wrong, but she'd come around to acknowledging it could lead to all sorts of good things.

"You disagree? Did the teasing from the guys bug you?" Dylan asked.

"No, no. Not at all. I was just having a moment."

"Ooh. What kind of moment?" Dylan's brows wagged suggestively, and it was all she could do not to laugh.

"A sweet one, if you must know. I was thinking about how far we've come since the last time we agreed to co-chair Cider Week."

Dylan's features softened. "Aw. That is sweet. I'm glad you gave me a chance."

She wouldn't have said so at the time, but yeah. "I'm glad you gave me a chance, too."

❖

By the time Dylan finished with the Cider Association meeting, Jamal had finished boxing up the wild crab slated for pickup the next day. She had him help with labeling the most recent batch of rosé and sent him off to study for the business law final he'd been grousing about all week.

With Rowan out babying her trees and the tasting room adequately staffed for the afternoon, Dylan decided to knock off a little early. It would be a rare treat to get to Mira's and be able to start the evening together before six, given that one of them had to make the trek to the other's every night. Not untenable, but less than ideal. Something she felt more by the day.

They'd talked about moving in together, finding a place somewhere between Pomme and Forbidden Fruit that would be a good home base for both of them. There wasn't much in the way of towns to choose from, but she'd taken to scoping listings a couple of times a week. Which led her to an old Victorian in one of the hamlets that had promise. Because unlike Rowan and Audrey, neither she nor Mira had a whole lot of interest in plowing fields or tending animals. She'd scheduled a showing and hoped it might be the one.

She pulled into the driveway of Mira's townhouse about thirty seconds before Mira and had the pleasure of watching happy surprise play across Mira's face. "I didn't think I'd see you until seven."

"I worked extra hard so my boss would let me out early."

Mira laughed. She always did when Dylan joked about having a boss. Probably because Mira actually was the boss, responsible for the hundreds of people Pomme employed. "It's good for workers to feel some autonomy now and then."

"Well, this rogue worker is hoping she can convince her girlfriend to take a drive down the lake for a nice dinner."

Mira's brow arched. "Fancy. I figured you'd just try to get me into bed sooner."

"I didn't say that wasn't part of the overall plan." Though that might be pressing her luck after setting up the appointment to see the house without even showing Mira the listing online.

Mira smirked. "Noted."

"So, you trust me?"

A lighthearted question but one Mira seemed to really take to heart. "I do."

"Excellent. Especially since I have a small stop planned on the way to dinner."

"Now she tells me." Mira rolled her eyes but laughed.

"But I think you'll like it." She drove to the house, where the Realtor was already waiting for them. The For Sale sign in the front yard gave away her intentions, not that they were all that secret to begin with.

Mira got out of the car and looked it up and down. "But you don't like Victorians."

She'd made the mistake of saying so when they first started talking about the possibility of moving in together. And while she did prefer the cleaner lines of a Craftsman or even Colonial, she didn't care all that much about style if the substance was good. "I like this one."

After walking through every room—admiring fireplaces and agreeing the recent kitchen remodel had been done remarkably well— the Realtor locked up and left them on the front porch to discuss. Mira stood at the ornate gingerbread railing and studied the tidy yard. "It's not too fussy for you?"

"I'm not saying it's inherently my style, but the space is fantastic, it's in great shape, and the location is pretty damn near perfect."

Mira frowned. "Still. It's a big decision and I want us to be on the same page. Or at least compromise."

"I don't know. We've already established we don't have to think about cider or run our businesses the same way to be happy together."

Mira scrunched up her face but managed to make it look cute. "That's a pretty terrible line."

Dylan lifted her chin in playful challenge. "You disagree?"

"No, I'm simply pointing out that you're not always as suave as you think you are."

"You think I'm suave?" Dylan asked.

She expected that to earn her a smack to the arm, but Mira angled her head and smiled. "Sometimes."

"Like when I put Don in his place at the meeting this afternoon?"

That got her an eye roll but also a laugh. "Yes. Exactly like that."

"Does all this mean you like the house?"

Mira turned and regarded the front door, complete with stained glass transom. "You know I do."

"And if I swear on next season's harvest that I love it, too, will you believe me?"

"I believe you want to love it."

She reached for Mira's hand. "How's this? I love everything it signifies."

"And what, exactly, does it signify?" Mira's question was more invitation than interrogation.

"Us. A life together. Coming home to you every night and waking up with you every morning. Eloise and Gloria fighting over who gets the bigger bed. Your books and my books all smooshed together on the shelves. And a future, whatever we decide that should be."

She hadn't meant to make such a sentimental declaration, but Mira's eyes grew glassy with tears. "And you think we can have that here?"

"I wouldn't have brought you here otherwise." She hesitated to add the rest but decided Mira's more practical side would appreciate it. "And it's a solid investment should you ever decide to leave me and we have to sell."

"Seriously?"

"Hey, I'm hoping that never happens, but I know you think I can be fanciful sometimes."

Mira made a tsking sound. "You could leave me, too, you know."

"Or we could fall even more madly in love and live happily ever after. That's what I'm counting on."

Mira took a deep breath, lifting her shoulders and letting them fall on the exhale. "Then yes. Yes, yes, yes." Mira practically leapt into her arms, the joyful exuberance washing away any lingering doubt Dylan may have had. Mira kissed her and didn't stop kissing her for a long time. She imagined a lifetime of kisses just like that, standing just where they stood.

She and Mira both remained on the fence about being the marrying kind, but it felt a little like Mira had said yes to a proposal. She had, in a way. To a life together on their own terms. And Dylan couldn't remember a time she'd been happier.

About the Author

Aurora Rey is a college dean by day and a life coach and queer romance author the rest of the time, except when she's cooking, baking, riding the tractor, or pining for goats. She grew up in a small town in south Louisiana, daydreaming about New England. She keeps a special place in her heart for the South, especially the food and the ways women are raised to be strong, even if they're taught not to show it. After a brief dalliance with biochemistry, she completed both a B.A. and an M.A. in English.

She is the author of the Cape End Romance series and several standalone contemporary romance novels and novellas. She has been a finalist for the Lambda Literary, RITA®, and Golden Crown Literary Society awards, but loves reader feedback the most. She lives in Ithaca, New York, with her dogs and whatever wildlife has taken up residence in the pond.

Books Available from Bold Strokes Books

A Cutting Deceit by Cathy Dunnell. Undercover cop Athena takes a job at Valeria's hair salon to gather evidence to prove her husband's connections to organized crime. What starts as a tentative friendship quickly turns into a dangerous affair. (978-1-63679-208-8)

As Seen on TV! by CF Frizzell. Despite their objections, TV hosts Ronnie Sharp, a laid-back chef; and paranormal investigator Peyton Stanford, have to work together. The public is watching. But joining forces is risky, contemptuous, unnerving, provocative—and ridiculously perfect. (978-1-63679-272-9)

Blood Memory by Sandra Barret. Can vampire Jade Murphy protect her friend from a human stalker and keep her dates with the gorgeous Beth Jenssen without revealing her secrets? (978-1-63679-307-8)

Foolproof by Leigh Hays. For Martine Roberts and Elliot Tillman, friends with benefits isn't a foolproof way to hide from the truth at the heart of an affair. (978-1-63679-184-5)

Glass and Stone by Renee Roman. Jordan must accept that she can't control everything that happens in life, and that includes her wayward heart. (978-1-63679-162-3)

Hard Pressed by Aurora Rey. When rivals Mira Lavigne and Dylan Miller are tapped to co-chair Finger Lakes Cider Week, competition gives way to compromise. But will their sexual chemistry lead to love? (978-1-63679-210-1)

The Laws of Magic by M. Ullrich. Nothing is ever what it seems, especially not in the small town of Bender, Massachusetts, where a witch lives to save lives and avoid love. (978-1-63679-222-4)

The Lonely Hearts Rescue by Morgan Lee Miller, Nell Stark, Missouri Vaun. In this novella collection, a hurricane hits the Gulf Coast, and the animals at the Lonely Hearts Rescue Shelter need love, and so do the humans who adopt them. (978-1-63679-231-6)

The Mage and the Monster by Barbara Ann Wright. Two powerful mages, one committed to magic and one controlled by it, strive to free each other and be together while the countries they serve descend into war. (978-1-63679-190-6)

Truly Wanted by J.J. Hale. Sam must decide if she's willing to risk losing her found family to find her happily ever after. (978-1-63679-333-7)

A Good Chance by Ali Vali. Harry, Desi, and Desi's sister Rachel are so close to getting everything they've ever wanted, but Desi's ex-husband is coming back to get his revenge and rip apart their chance at happiness. (978-1-63679-023-7)

A Perfect Fifth by Jaycie Morrison. Streetwise pianist Zara Keller and Lady Jillian Stansfield couldn't be more different; yet their connection brings a new awareness of who they are and what they truly want in their lives—including each other. (978-1-63679-132-6)

Catching Feelings by Ana Hartnett Reichardt. Andrea Foster expected to catch a lot of pitches from the Alder Lion's star pitcher, Maya, but she didn't expect to catch feelings. (978-1-63679-227-9)

Defiant Hearts by Lee Lynch. In these stories, you'll find your lovers, friends, and lesbians you wish you knew—maybe even yourself. (978-1-63679-237-8)

Love and Duty by Catherine Young. All Princess Roseli wants is to marry her three lovers, but with war looming, she must instead marry Princess Lucia to establish a military alliance between their planets. (978-1-63679-256-9)

Murder at Union Station by David S. Pederson. Private Detective Mason Adler struggles to determine who killed a woman found in a trunk without getting himself killed in the process. (978-1-63679-269-9)

Serendipity by Kris Bryant. Serendipity brings jingle writer Annie Foster and celebrity pop star Bristol Baines together, and their undeniable attraction keeps them close, but will their different paths drive them apart? (978-1-63679-224-8)

The Haunted Heart by Jane Kolven. A ghost, a ring, and a quest to find a missing psychic—it's a spell for love. (978-1-63679-245-3)

The Rules of Forever by Nan Campbell. After reconnecting at their high school reunion, Cara and Lauren agree to embark on a textbook definition friends-with-benefits relationship, but trying to keep it uncomplicated is harder than it seems. (978-1-63679-248-4)

Vision of Virtue by Brey Willows. When virtue and desire come together, be prepared for sparks in this next installment of the Memory's Muses series. (978-1-63679-118-0)

Cherry on Top by Georgia Beers. A chance meeting leaves Cherry and Ellis longing for a different life, but when Ellis's search for truth crashes into Cherry's insta-filter world, do they have any hope at all of a happily ever after? (978-1-63679-158-6)

Love and Other Rare Birds by Angie Williams. Ornithologist Dr. Jamie Martin and park ranger Rowan Fleming are searching the Alaskan wilderness for a bird thought to be extinct and they're about to discover opposites really do attract. (978-1-63679-108-1)

Parallel Paradise by Mayapee Chowdhury. When their love affair is put to the test by the homophobia of their family, community, and culture, Bindi and Rimli will need to fight for a chance at love. (978-1-63679-204-0)

Perfectly Matched by Toni Logan. A beautiful Cupid named Hannah, a runaway arrow, and just seventy-two hours to fix a mishap that could be the best mistake she has ever made. (978-1-63679-120-3)

Royal Exposé by Jenny Frame. When they're grouped together for a class assignment, Poppy's enthusiasm for life and love may just save Casey's soul, but will she ever forgive Casey for using her to expose royal secrets? (978-1-63679-165-4)

Slow Burn by Missouri Vaun. A wounded wildland firefighter from California and a struggling artist find solace and love in a small southern town. (978-1-63679-098-5)

The Artist by Sheri Lewis Wohl. Detective Casey Wilson and reclusive artist Tula Crane are drawn together in a web of passion, intrigue, and art that might just hold the key to stopping a killer. (978-1-63679-150-0)

The Inconvenient Heiress by Jane Walsh. An unlikely heiress and a spinster evade the Marriage Mart only to discover true love together. (978-1-63679-173-9)

A Champion for Tinker Creek by D.C. Robeline. Lyle James has rescued his dad's auto repair business, but when city hall condemns his neighborhood, Lyle learns only trusting will save his life and help him find love. (978-1-63679-213-2)

Closed-Door Policy by Erin Zak. Going back to college is never easy, but Caroline Stevens is prepared to work hard and change her life for the better. What she's not prepared for is Dr. Atlanta Morris, her gorgeous new professor. (978-1-63679-181-4)

Homeworld by Gun Brooke. Headed by Captain Holly Crowe, the spaceship Velocity's crew journeys toward their alien ancestors' homeworld, and what they find is completely unexpected—and they're not safe. (978-1-63679-177-7)

Outland by Kristin Keppler & Allisa Bahney. Danielle Clark and Katelyn Turner can't seem to stay away from one another even as the war for the wastelands tests their loyalty to each other and to their people. (978-1-63679-154-8)

Secret Sanctuary by Nance Sparks. US Deputy Marshal Alex Trenton specializes in protecting those awaiting trial, but when danger threatens the woman she's falling for, Alex is in for the fight of her life. (978-1-63679-148-7)

Stranded Hearts by Kris Bryant, Amanda Radley, Emily Smith. In these novellas from award winning authors, fate intervenes on behalf of love when characters are unexpectedly stuck together. With too much time and an irresistible attraction, anything could happen. (978-1-63679-182-1)

The Last Lavender Sister by Melissa Brayden. Aster Lavender sells her gourmet doughnuts and keeps a low profile; she never plans on the town's temporary veterinarian swooping in and making her feel like anything but a wallflower. (978-1-63679-130-2)

The Probability of Love by Dena Blake. As Blair and Rachel keep ending up in the same place despite the odds, can a one-night stand turn into forever? Or will the bet Blair never intended to make ruin their happily ever after? (978-1-63679-188-3)

Worth a Fortune by Sam Ledel. After placing a want ad for a personal secretary, a New York heiress is surprised when the woman who got away is the one interested in the position. (978-1-63679-175-3)

A Fox in Shadow by Jane Fletcher. Cassie's mission is to add new territory to the Kavillian empire—murder, betrayal, war, and the clash of cultures ensue. (978-1-63679-142-5)

Embracing the Moon by Jeannie Levig. Just as Gwen and Taylor are exploring the new love they've found, the present and past collide, threatening the future they long to share. (978-1-63555-462-5)

Forever Comes in Threes by D. Jackson Leigh. Efficiency expert Perry Chandler's ordered life is upended when she inherits three busy terriers, and the woman she's referred to for help turns out to be her bitter podcast rival, the very sexy Dr. Ming Lee. (978-1-63679-169-2)

Heckin' Lewd: Trans and Nonbinary Erotica by Mx. Nillin Lore. If you want smutty, fearless, gender-diverse erotica written by affirming own-voices folks who get it, then this is the book you've been looking for! (978-1-63679-240-8)

Missed Conception by Joy Argento. Maggie Walsh wants a relationship with Cassidy, the daughter she's only just discovered she has due to an in vitro mix-up. Heat kindles between Maggie and Cassidy's mother in a way neither expects. (978-1-63679-146-3)

Private Equity by Elle Spencer. Cassidy Bennett spends an unexpected evening at a lesbian nightclub with her notoriously reserved and demanding boss, Julia. After seeing a different side of Julia, Cassidy can't seem to shake her desire to know more. (978-1-63679-180-7)

Racing the Dawn by Sandra Barret. After narrowly escaping a house fire, vampire Jade Murphy is unexpectedly intrigued by gorgeous firefighter Beth Jenssen, and her undead existence might just be perking up a bit. (978-1-63679-271-2)

Reclaiming Love by Amanda Radley. Sarah's tiny white lie means somehow convincing Pippa to pretend to be her girlfriend. Only the more time they spend faking it, the more real it feels. (978-1-63679-144-9)

Sol Cycle by Kimberly Cooper Griffin. An encounter in a park brings Ang and Krista together, but when Ang's attempts to help Krista go spectacularly wrong, their passion for each other might not be enough. (978-1-63679-137-1)

Trial and Error by Carsen Taite. Attorney Franco Rossi and Judge Nina Aguilar's reunion is fraught with courtroom conflict, undeniable chemistry, and danger. (978-1-63555-863-0)